I0744277

THE DETERMINER

DETERMINER SERIES

BOOK ONE

JEAN KNIGHT PACE

JACOB KENNEDY

Copyright © 2022 by Jean Knight Pace and Jacob Kennedy

All rights reserved.

No part of this book may be reproduced in any form or by any electronic or mechanical means, including information storage and retrieval systems, without written permission from the author, except for the use of brief quotations in a book review.

To my family, for the light your bring
JKP

To Cara, Cody, Ella, Sam, Peter, and especially Kipp, who
was Henry when I dreamed this all up.
JK

PROLOGUE

1772–1799

Territory of Columbia (modern-day Washington, D.C.)

David Burnes loped along the putrid creek, net trailing through the water. He hoped that today he would catch more than crawdads to feed his wife and young children.

A moment later, the line snagged, caught on something in the silt near the creek's edge. He stepped forward, forcing the net from the water, and tearing it.

Cursing, he looked into the shallow edge of the water for whatever creature had torn his net, only to stumble back. The crooked finger bones of a long-lost soul stabbed through the shallows, swaying among the weeds.

Burnes held his hands in the shape of a cross and

looked again. In what must have once been the palm of the hand, he saw a small, round stone. It was pale orange with streaks of white forming a faint square at the center. He moved the bones to the side, and picked up the stone. "Now, that would catch a lovely sum," he said, forgetting his torn net.

He intended to take a carriage into the large market at Georgetown as soon as he earned enough to pay a driver. In the meantime, he fastened the stone to a string around his neck for safekeeping.

His wife looked at it suspiciously. He had told her he had found in the river, but he hadn't told her anything about the dead hand holding it. Still she said, "Doesn't seem like something that would bring much good."

She was wrong.

The next day, walking to the small village market with a sack of seed potatoes to barter, Burnes had come across a rich old man just arrived from Scotland. The old man had been missing those particular varieties of potato from across the sea, and had paid a small fortune. Now Burnes had all he'd need to rent a carriage and pay a driver to go to Georgetown, but he hesitated to do so. Taking the stone off of his neck that night to look at it, the pale lines almost seemed to swarm with energy. When he held it in his hand or against his chest, he felt younger, stronger, more clever.

"Nothing good," his wife said when she saw him staring at it.

"Nonsense," he said. "If nothing else, it's brought me good luck today. We'll run a test. If it brings such luck the next week, I keep it. If not, I sell it. Either way, it means more money for us. Which feels a lot the same as luck."

She turned from him without a word, a gesture he took as consent.

The next week, he took bouquets of wildflowers and a number of pearlescent shells gathered from along Goose Creek to the market. The flowers sold within the first hour. And the shells fetched more of a sum than a full summer's crop normally would. All this as Continental troops in blue and gray coats were falling and dying up north.

He kept the stone.

And so it continued as the months wore on. Every business venture turned in his favor. His health and vigor improved. He bought more land, planted more crop, turned every penny he earned into triple the sum.

In time, even his wife was consigned to admit that the strange stone must be worth at least some good. Though she still didn't like to come near him when he wore it.

At first he would remove it when he desired to be near her, though gradually he found he preferred the constancy of the stone to the company of his wife.

The war ended, miraculously in the favor of the Continental Army. A few years after the war, George Washington began to proposition Burnes for his land. It would be, Washington said, the perfect location for the new capital.

Well, of course it would. Burnes had built it up, beautiful and prosperous from the swamp. It was worth much more than the paltry amounts of money the new president offered, and Burnes wasn't afraid to tell him so. Even when

Washington came for a personal visit, even when he threatened to take the land for the public good, even when the president insisted on calling Burnes 'obstinate.' If demanding a fair sum for such fair land was obstinate, so be it. The president could pressure him all he wanted. Burnes would not budge until Washington came to him with a decent offer.

Near year's end, just after a fat feast at winter's solstice, a strange woman came to their door—hungry, feet bleeding from walking many miles, eyes as gray as the winter sky.

His wife brought the woman soup and bread warmed in new cast-iron pots, while his daughter prepared a bed of straw for her to rest. Late the next afternoon, she seemed unnaturally stronger, and rose from her bed, thanking the couple for their kindness. "In exchange," she began. "I should like to do something for you. At certain times and seasons, the fates pull strong against my bones. Give me your hand, kind sir, and I will read to you your fortune."

"My fortune is naught but good, I can assure you," Burnes said, keeping his hand tucked close to his side. "On account of a stone I found several seasons ago."

His wife shot him a sharp look.

"Although," he said, pausing, "my wife is not yet convinced of its goodness, and if you could convince her I would be very much obliged."

He held the stone out to the old woman, and she stared at it, hesitant.

"I've been wearing it all these years," he replied. "It won't hurt you. However," he said, looking into her eyes. "Should you try to take it, *I* most certainly would."

"I would *never*, good sir," she said, holding out her hand to take the stone. Something in her tone gave him the slightest pause, not because he didn't believe her. But because he did.

Waiting to receive the stone, her hand trembled.

Dusk began to settle around them, the first stars breaking through the deep blues of twilight. As the stone touched her hand, a light burst from it, and the woman's eyes rolled into her head, her fist bound around the stone as light flooded through the creases of her fingers.

"Take it from her," Burnes' wife shouted. "'Tis from a devil or no one at all." She made the sign of the cross and began to pray.

But before Burnes could answer or take the stone from the old woman, the hag began to chant.

Power to save or destroy, destroy or redeem,
A force for evil and a compass for good.
Endless.

She stopped, sucking in a breath as though she was pulling light from the stars. Around them, the room seemed to dim.

He who speaks to Determine will have words revealed at his coming.
Power to silence the voice of the king.
For every world lost, a thousand worlds saved.
For every soul given, a thousand pieces returned.

She crumpled to the ground, a symbol flashing brighter

than the hottest fire at the center of the room. And then every candle went out and the room fell into black stillness, disturbed only by the gentle sobs of Burnes' wife.

In the morning, the gray-eyed woman was gone. The strange symbol was not. It smoldered, burnt, into the planks of the floor.

"Cover it," his wife demanded. "Cover it like a sin you wish to hide."

But it couldn't be hidden.

"Perhaps it is nothing more than an omen," Burnes said.

"An omen for evil," his wife said.

"No," he said staring at the symbol, knowing something from the strange curves and dips of the glyph that he didn't feel he should know. "An omen, I believe, of choice."

Yet there is only so much fate that can be chosen. Within a fortnight, his wife had fallen ill, followed soon after by his young son. "Yellow fever," the doctor said. "Make them comfortable, for they won't last much longer."

They didn't.

By week's end, his wife was resting in the ground, his son following her to the grave a few days later.

Two fresh mounds in a small cemetery that time and history and fate herself would forget.

Burnes penned a letter to Washington. If the general still wanted this land to build the new capital, he could have it, at whatever price.

Washington wrote back, offering more than he had in any previous offers.

Burnes touched the stone that hung round his neck. "It

is just as she said. *For every soul given, a thousand pieces returned.*"

The problem was that Burnes no longer cared for the pieces.

Tearing the stone from his neck, he crafted a heavy box and returned to the creek where the stone had first been found. He had expected the skeletal hand that had held it to be long washed away, but digging into the silt, he found the bones there, perfectly intact.

"You want it back?" Burnes asked the old hand. "Ah, but you can't return to me what has been taken." Lifting the heavy concrete box, he smashed it down on the skeleton, burying both box and bones in a shallow grave of silty mud.

In the distance, he could see the cornerstones being brought in for the president's house that would stand in the new capital. He turned from the progress, from the place he was sure would be blessed by the stone and cursed by it too. He returned to his adult daughter, sick now himself.

Months later, as she waited by his bed, praying for his health to come back when she knew it wouldn't, he told her of the two symbols he wanted carved into his tombstone. One was the strange marking on his floor that could not be sanded or whitewashed away. The other, an image of the stone he no longer carried, the stone he knew was connected to this land in ways he didn't understand.

His daughter nodded, and his breath grew thin.

When she came from his death room to face the small circle of waiting friends, one asked, "What did he say, Marcia?"

But Marcia did not wish to share. "He told me he'd made me the richest woman in Washington."

Within a year, she was married to John Peter Van Ness, her father buried next to his wife and son. Small square tombstones marked with small square letters. Names. Dates. And on one, two strange symbols.

————

When a man's luck begins and ends in flashes of light and darkness, there are those who take note.

A few months after Burnes' death, a crooked old man could be seen standing near the edge of the river.

Searching.

For what, it was never quite clear, since all who went to the river, preparing for the construction of the new President's Mansion, knew that there was nothing in the old creek but toads and mosquitoes and muck.

ONE

It started with tacos. Doesn't it always?

Henry almost never stayed after school. But today Lucy was begging. "Come on, Henry. Just this once."

"School's long enough already, Lu. You're supposed to hate middle school, not want to stay extra." The halls were emptying quickly, still thick with the scents of gym clothes and candy-flavored lip glosses. "Besides, I'm starving."

Lucy tossed a book in her locker and pulled another out. "Señora promised us food." She glanced at the book. "Your security picking you up?"

"Naw. Full-blown babysitting doesn't start till next week." He watched Lucy try to shimmy the extra book into her bag. "What kind of food?"

"Your favorite kind," she said, trying to close her bag. "You could text your mom and stay."

Henry's stomach rumbled. He shook it off. "Except that I don't want to go to Spanish club. I already speak Spanish."

"Right," she said, as several kids raced past them toward the exit. "That's why I need you there. Today."

"Because why?"

Lucy ducked her head into her locker, her voice muffled. "Some kid moved in. I just thought it'd be cool if you could help me talk to him."

Henry tried to give Lucy a hard stare, but she wouldn't look at him. Henry had seen the new kid in homeroom. He'd just moved from Chile. Thin, dark, interesting. Everything Henry wasn't.

"Come on," Lucy said, twisting her long, black hair into a clip, then turning to face him. "What's the use of having a language genius as your friend if he won't even help you talk to a guy?"

"So if I do this for you, what's the payoff? Because matching BFF necklaces definitely aren't going to cut it."

"I'd make yours extra sparkly," Lucy said. "Perfect for a potential presidential son." She glanced casually at the pearl ring she always wore. "Or you can just eat your weight in tacos."

Henry raised an eyebrow. "Tell me they're her great-grandmother's family recipe."

"They're from Taco Towne," Lucy replied.

"Even better," Henry said. "Okay, fine. I'll hang out with you and the new kid for a couple hours. You secure me as many tacos as possible."

"Done," Lucy said, and turned to walk off.

"What? No pinky promise?" Henry called after her.

She laughed and Henry turned back to his locker, the

smell of tacos wafting through the halls, cancelling out all the other scents.

———

Two hours and one full belly later, Henry sat on a bench outside the school. Full security detail started next week. That's how it went when your dad was governor of Michigan and the front-runner for president. Soon, he'd have his very own man in black to tail his every movement.

Just like a movie. A really lame movie where a kid goes to school and then home every day. And sometimes does his homework. And nothing else.

Henry's lack of personal awesomeness didn't stop his mom from worrying. She'd already hired a driver to tote him around in a bland black sedan.

Who never arrived late. Henry looked at his watch. Except today.

Henry pulled out his phone and texted his mom. No response. Everyone else had left and the September sun hovered heavy against the horizon. Henry slouched down on the bench, letting the tacos settle in his stomach.

Truthfully, Henry hadn't *hated* Spanish club. He liked languages. And tacos. Even the new kid hadn't been too bad, although when he found out Henry's dad was running for president, that was all he wanted to talk about. A day in the life of the kid of somebody important.

Lucy had managed to guide the conversation away from the election. Her father worked as the Secretary of Administration under Henry's dad, and she got sick of all the political talk, too.

Henry was glad. He'd spent the last several months trying not to think about his dad and the presidency. After all, his dad could lose. That would stink. But winning would be crazy too. He hated the thought of leaving Michigan and his friends behind. What would Lucy do without him to help her talk to her latest crush? Even more than that, he hated the thought of being important, but only because of his dad's title and talents.

Henry tapped on the back of his phone, then texted his brother, Chet. "How'd the world's best brother like to come take me home?"

"Walk," came Chet's prompt reply. Henry sighed. Chet thought the car and the security were all overkill. Henry agreed, but he still didn't want to walk home, especially with a stomach full of tacos. He hefted his backpack over his shoulder, grumbling.

The sun hadn't set yet, but it was definitely on its way. Orange and red streaked across the sky and the air smelled like football and sweaters. In two months they'd know if his father would be president. It seemed both impossibly short and ridiculously long.

Henry cut through a forested park lined with a few paved roads and walking trails. He pulled his backpack tighter, barely noticing the lengthening shadows, the dropping temperature, the silence. Until it broke.

The sound of a car door—common, harmless. Except

that something in the isolation of it wasn't. Henry turned, hoping to see a familiar car and driver. He didn't.

"Hey kid," a man in a black jumpsuit said. "Wanna ride?" The man stepped from the car while another man wearing dark sunglasses waited inside. Henry froze for just a moment before the man reached out a beefy, black-gloved hand.

Henry bolted. Which is hard to do when you've just put away five tacos and you weren't exactly built like The Flash in the first place. "Leave me alone," he shouted, hoping someone would hear him.

The man picked up his pace.

Henry ran harder. His mother had warned him about stuff like this. "Politicians have enemies," she'd warned. "Don't be alone. Don't talk to people you don't know." He'd thought her worry stupid, overprotective. He didn't anymore.

He could hear the man's strides, the strike of each footfall, fast, behind him.

Henry sprinted as hard as he could, wishing he could run like Chet, or even his parents. As it was, he was a short, stocky kid in a family of tall, athletic blonds. And now he was in trouble.

He tripped over a paving stone, slipping on the grass beside it. The man caught up to him quickly, reached out a thick hand. "Come on, kid," he said. "I don't want to hurt you."

Henry threw his backpack and the man stumbled over it.

Henry ran toward some bushes, sweat pricking up along his neck, his stomach full of acid and food.

The man lunged after him. His hand grazed Henry's back. Henry tried to pull out his phone to call somebody, but dropped it. As he did, the man lurched forward, crushing his phone with his foot and grabbing Henry's wrist.

"You know what, kid? For a chubby little nobody, you are worth a *lot* of money." The man wrapped his free hand around Henry's other wrist, jerking him forward.

"Hey," Henry screamed as loudly as he could. "Somebody help me!" But the air around him hung still, not even an echo to throw his words back at him.

The lights on the car blinked on and the engine revved almost soundlessly to life.

Henry struggled as the man's fingers pressed bruises into his skin.

"Stop it!" Henry screamed, feeling like his throat would split open.

The man laughed. "Nobody's around, kid. That's usually how this stuff goes down." He pulled Henry toward the car, and when Henry resisted, the man kicked his legs out from under him.

Henry stumbled, dragging his legs across the ground, letting all his weight pull against the strength of the kidnapper.

The man just looked at him and smiled. The smile was worse than the bruises and the scrapes, worse than the waiting car. In that smile, Henry saw that he was nothing but a couple of dollar signs. And people would do a lot of things for a couple of dollar signs.

Blood pounded into Henry's head—terror like icicles through his body. He pulled back harder than he had before, harder than he knew he could, all his weight bracing away from that man and his smile, all his everything focused on the one goal of escape.

As he did, something shifted around him. The colors no longer stabbed like flashes of light into his pounding head. Now the sky broke into a million points of a million different hues. Pinks and golds. Milky blues and dovetail grays.

Henry blinked, worried he was blacking out. Around him, the air slowed down. Leaves drifted lazily. Sounds deepened and distorted. He took a breath, trying to steady himself.

All at once he felt everything—the temperature of the air, the motion of the breeze, the slightest wisp of variation. He heard a bird call as it flew in front of him and when it did, he saw a thousand colors in its wings, felt the waves of air flowing beneath and around him.

The man still dragged Henry, snickering as though he hadn't felt the slowing, the shift.

Henry dug both of his heels into the ground, pulling his attacker to a sudden stop.

The man looked at him, his lips the slightest, slowest frown. Henry bent his weight into his knees, then sprang up. He wrenched his wrists away from the man's hands with barely any effort, heard a snap. One of the man's arms rested at an odd angle. He cradled it, crying out in pain.

Henry stood, and the man staggered forward, his body a clay figure, plodding.

Henry kicked his gut, then knee. The man stumbled, falling to the side and trying to catch himself on his good arm, then inching toward the car.

The engine cracked and rumbled, every touch of sound an explosion in Henry's ears. The car turned, a leaden, black slug. Brakes and gas punched back and forth, and Henry could hear each squeak, each press of air.

As the car came toward him, Henry anticipated each move, each sound it would make. With speed and more force then he should have had, Henry kicked out his leg, crushing the front right side of the car. He felt the metal bend under his foot like plastic, heard it like a thousand pieces of shattering glass. The sounds were music around him—swaying, breaking—crescendo and collapse.

The man on the ground screamed a curse, and scrabbled into the car.

Henry thought the car would come after him. He set both legs firmly on the ground, held his arms out as though to stop it. But instead, the wheels turned sharply, squealing away.

Everything that had been so slow, so soft, so melodious suddenly sped up and crashed around him. The car careened out of the park—a dark streak through the dusk.

Henry felt like he had fallen from the sky. His wrists hurt; his right shin was bleeding through his khaki pants.

Everything seemed dull now, colorless, blurry. His body felt heavy, yet empty.

Henry staggered to the bushes where his phone lay broken on the ground. He picked it up and began to walk. As he put one foot in front of the other, it seemed like the hardest work he had ever done.

When he finally got home, he walked past the security gate and into his room. He collapsed onto his bed, lying there for what seemed like hours, but couldn't have been. When he finally got up, it felt like he was coming back to Earth from a dream. Was he? He looked down at his arms. Finger-sized bruises bloomed over both wrists and dried blood stuck to both his skin and pants.

Adrenaline, he'd heard, could do some crazy things. But he was pretty sure that even adrenaline couldn't crush a car like it was a soda can. And although he had a few small injuries from the beginning of the attack, Henry felt no pain from anything he'd done after the world had slowed down. His muscles weren't even sore.

He flexed a bicep and looked at it. Even he had to admit that it wasn't particularly impressive.

His abs, he knew, were even worse. He glanced down and lifted up his shirt. Not only were they flabby, but his belly button was deformed—a normal belly button in the center with two smaller indents on either side. His mother said he'd been born that way and they hadn't had the money at the time to pay the out-of-pocket expense to have it fixed.

He yanked his shirt down over his stomach and picked up a thick notebook from his desk. He'd once seen a guy on a uVid tear one in half. He pressed and pulled against the papers, but couldn't even get the top tip of the page to tear.

He was already sweating, but the notebook made him mad. Looking forward, he pressed his back against the wall, then sprinted toward a chair, preparing to jump onto it. Unfortunately, he underestimated the height, or maybe he just didn't have the lift to make the leap. He bashed his shin against the wood.

"Oh man," he muttered, bending over to look at the fat welt that formed in a line along his shin. It hurt. But not just his shin. For a moment at the park, fighting for his life, he had become somebody, somebody who could do amazing things. And now he wasn't again.

Down the hall, he heard his mother tear through the front door, rushing toward his room. "Henry," she called, a small shard of panic in her voice.

"Hey, Mom," he called back, still nursing his shin.

She hurried into his room, her face flushed with worry, her hair falling out in wild wisps along her temples. "When did you get home?" she asked, then stopped, glancing at the crumpled blankets on his bed. "Have you been napping? I called over and over."

"Mom, I..." he began. He wanted to say he'd been jumped on the way home, wanted to show her the bruises on his wrists, wanted to tell her everything, but the words sat stuck in his throat. He cleared it. "Mom..."

He opened his mouth to speak, to say the words, to tell her how the world had slowed down and then sped up again, to describe how he'd beaten off an attacker.

But the words wouldn't come out, not because Henry was tired or scared or overwhelmed. Not because he was worried or terrified or proud. They simply wouldn't form, as though his vocal chords could not come together to create the sounds.

Finally, he held out his phone, grabbing onto the one small truth that his lips would release. "My phone got broken."

His mother looked at it, relief rushing across her face, softening the lines on her forehead and eyes. "You've got to be more responsible," she said, trying to sound stern. "But I'm glad you're okay. There was an...an issue with the car, and I was worried about you."

"Well," Henry said, the words still tangled in his throat. "I'm—" He paused, searching for a word he could speak. "I'm fine."

"I'm glad," his mother said, leaning over to kiss his head. She looked into his brown-orange eyes, ruffled his hair, and added, "You'd better grab a shower before dinner."

When he finally glanced in the mirror at his dirty face and brown hair crusty with sweat, he thought two things.

First, he didn't know what had happened to him—the pudgy, short kid who couldn't even do a pull-up well enough to avoid humiliation in gym.

Second, he could not tell anyone about it; and he didn't know why.

Two

In an office at the top of a skyscraper in Kansas City sat a man.

He was middle-aged, of average height and build, his hair and eyes a color that seemed to blend in with the large oak desk at which he worked.

The small office consisted of perfect angles—tight and sharp.

Carpet and walls melded together in shades of industrial blue that matched the sky when storms rolled in across the plains. No art hung from the walls, nor did the men and women who worked here adorn their workspace with pictures of spouses, children, or friends, for they had none.

The undersecretaries, as they were called by those who knew of their existence, got along impossibly well in their various roles, despite the small work space. No debate or consternation occurred among them, any more than debate or disagreement would exist between a person's own fingers and toes.

The man, now positioned at the command center, worked surrounded by dozens of monitors, recorders, and video clips. He had become used to the constant flow of information, had learned to ignore what was unimportant and focus on what was.

At this moment, the room was filled with the voices of presidents and queens, drug lords, drug ladies, the promises of rulers, the threats and bluffs and blackmails, the romantic advances of any number of government officials as well as various mafia leaders and lobbyists.

Any of the information on any of the screens would have made major news channels had it been available to anyone besides the undersecretaries to the Six.

But today, though large monitors flashed and occasionally sent alerts, the man fixed his eyes on only one monitor.

It did only one thing.

Constantly, for the last fifteen minutes, the screen had blinked on and off.

The man had not been surprised by the impeachment of Richard Nixon, the assassination attempt of Ronald Reagan, the declaration of war on Iraq, the many indiscretions of Bill Clinton, or the flooding in New Orleans.

He controlled satellites so powerful they could read even small words on business cards held at the right angle on Earth. He could hear pins drop in Bangkok, could watch any number of kings and presidents in places they did not believe they could be watched.

This man was not used to being surprised. But today, listening to the quiet beep of a single monitor, he was. Very much.

This monitor had been in this building for half a century. The tech had been updated regularly, so that it was the newest and the best. Always. Yet, in all those minutes in all those years, that monitor had never clicked on, never made a sound. Because it had never been able to find the one person they were looking for.

The man typed furiously now. The satellite connected to the monitor continued to flash, a simple light moving across the screen—up from Louisiana, over through Kentucky, beyond Ohio and Indiana, and into the Great Lakes region.

It stopped at Lansing, Michigan.

"You're kidding," the man muttered, tapping coordinates into another computer, sending six alerts to six people.

Just as the message sent, the beeping made a long, high-pitched sound, flat-lining. But that did not bother the man. The corners of his lips curled up to expose a faint line of white, straight teeth. A smile, or the nearest he had ever come to one.

"Gotcha," the man said, pressing a small tattoo at his wrist and listening for the communication that would come.

He felt the vibration and then the other man's response —his voice a silk string of a smile. "At last."

THREE

Four Months Later
January 20th

People lined the streets of Washington D.C. as the President-Elect and the soon-to-be first family rode in a limousine to the place where they would spend the next several years of their lives.

Henry could not believe the buzz.

People stood outside in the sub-freezing temperatures, filling the streets. Most were smiling, waving flags. But a few were holding signs, some even shouting. One sign said in bold, red letters, "GO BACK TO MICHIGAN, MILLER."

Henry looked over to see his mother biting her lower lip. "William Henry Harrison gave the longest inauguration address in history—over 8000 words," she said. "Shortly afterwards, he fell sick, and some say it was because of that long speech in the cold. He died a few months later. George Washington, on the other hand—he only spoke 135 words."

"A man after my own heart," Chet said, staring out the window. He had his thick winter coat shoved at his feet in a ball, and sat sullen despite all the excitement around him.

Henry cast a sideways glance at his brother. Chet had been sulking since November. He didn't want to be in Washington, D.C., a member of the new first family.

He wanted to be back in Lansing, hanging out with his friends and playing basketball for his senior year. Henry saw him steal a glance at his phone.

As they drove, a sound rose up, and both boys looked out the window to see a large group of girls gathered at the side, holding up signs. "Welcome to D.C., Chet Miller." Several of the signs were drawn with hearts, and one had a phone number written on it in dark, red smears that looked like lipstick. "CALL ME."

The president-elect raised an eyebrow, and Henry held up his phone to snap a picture. "Don't worry, Chet; I got that for you if you need it."

Chet tried not to smile. He didn't succeed. After that, he let his phone rest on the seat beside him, looking out the window at the herds of people lining the streets. "Where's your crew, little brother?" he asked.

Henry had been wondering the same thing. No throngs of girls had gathered together with signs begging him to call. Shocker.

He looked at his hands, at his legs that a few months ago

had put a solid dent in a large car. Since then, he'd tried over and over to replicate that power, that slowing, that strength. Nothing.

He was just the same thirteen-year-old kid—both heavier and shorter than Chet, winded any time he tried to go on a jog. His mother had told him once that to be remarkable, he just had to be who he was. But that wasn't what he wanted.

He wanted the other type of remarkable—one that could dent cars, one that could save people, one that could convince a girl or two to look at him. He pushed on his thigh. It squished under his finger. Maybe it had been some crazy spurt of adrenaline after all. He didn't know. He still couldn't find the words to tell anyone. And at this point, he wasn't sure if he even wanted to.

He wiggled out of his coat, feeling too hot.

"Seatbelt back on," his mother said.

"I got it, Mom," he replied, clicking it in, though it hardly seemed necessary. They were traveling at a whopping three and a half miles per hour, surrounded by Secret Service and a motorcade of black vehicles, some identical to the one they were in so that no one would be certain which car was actually carrying the president. Not to mention the dozen police and emergency vehicles that travelled with them, including an ambulance with a surgeon, surgery suite, and several units of blood matching his father's blood type.

City workers had shoveled the snow from the streets, where people stood in throngs. They wore hats and mittens, shivering and stamping, their breath misting as they talked and waved.

Inside the limo, you'd never know it was anything less than seventy-two degrees, warm air at their feet, cool drinks in the refrigerator. Chet leaned over their mother to grab one. Mrs. Miller took the opportunity to smooth down a patch of his hair. As he sat back up, he took the opportunity to mess it up again.

Mrs. Miller didn't react. Instead, she said, "You know, President Obama called this car *the Beast*."

Henry smiled. His mother did that when she got nervous—spouted off facts about whatever it was she'd been reading. And today, she was very nervous. She'd been talking like a presidential guidebook since they got in the car.

"The Beast," Chet said. "I like it."

"I was thinking we should call it Wally," Henry said.

"You would," Chet replied, jabbing him in the side. "It's the Beast. You can't change official White House names."

"Oh really," Henry said. "'Cause I'm gonna call it Wally."

Their dad shook his head and said, "You can call it Wallabeast."

"You could always just call it Cadillac One," their mother put in. "Cadillac has made vehicles for nine other presidents—starting with Woodrow Wilson."

"Then shouldn't we call it Cadillac Ten?" Henry teased.

She ignored him and continued, "The windows are six inches thick, bomb and bullet proof. They don't roll down, and the doors can absorb all kinds of projectile assault. The interior seals off in the event of a chemical attack and is equipped with oxygen tanks to provide breathable air for forty-eight hours. There are weapons accessible to the Secret Service in and around the vehicle." She paused. "Including rocket launchers. And in the case of an air attack, this car can produce a thick cloud of smoke to obscure it for up to five city blocks. The tires are bulletproof and can travel at high speeds even when deflated. Also," she added smiling, "we don't have to stop for red lights."

"Told you," Chet said. "Beast."

"Fine," Henry said. It *was* more of a Beast than a Wally. So was his brother with his constant sulking.

"Hey, Marie," Henry's dad said, taking her hand. "You don't need to be nervous."

"I'm not nervous," she said. "You know the inauguration is held on the twentieth of January at noon sharp because in the twentieth amendment—" She stopped. "Okay," she said, "I am really, *really* nervous."

Henry smiled and his dad laughed. "I know, sweetie; we all are." With that, the re-christened Beast pulled to a stop near the Capitol building, and a man in a suit stepped over and opened the door.

Henry's father stepped out first, waving, then his mother, Chet, and him. As Henry walked away from the car, he saw a woman in the crowd, staring at them. He wasn't sure how or why he noticed her, except that unlike most of the crowd who were watching his father and mother, and all the teenage girls, who were watching Chet, this woman was watching him.

Their eyes met and Henry cocked his head to the side. A few dark lines arched over the woman's wrist and Henry stepped forward, squinting. As he did, a Secret Service agent leaned toward him. "Everything okay?" he asked, scanning the crowd.

"Oh yeah," Henry said. "It's just, I don't know; some lady was staring at me. It was a little weird."

Henry felt like the Secret Service agent was trying not to smile, but he still muttered something into his mouthpiece. Two agents fanned out, eyes on the crowd, walking along as though nothing unusual was happening.

Henry tried to see past the black-suited figures that were his security detail. Catching glimpses of the crowd, he couldn't see the woman again anywhere. She had faded into the masses.

Chet nudged him as a man ushered the family onto a platform at the center of the Capitol building. Once there, they turned to face the biggest crowd Henry had ever seen stretching along the mall.

And that wasn't the half of it. In thousands of homes across the U.S., people were tuning in on phones, TVs, and the newly released uVisions. Henry thought of Lucy settling down with her parents, and felt a twinge of homesickness.

As his father stepped forward, Henry heard Chet mutter, "Remember, Dad, more George Washington, less William Henry Harrison. Long speeches kill people."

Henry shook off his worry and smiled. It was a big day. Big things were happening.

In front of him, and everyone else, his father, Douglas Howard Miller, placed his left hand on the Bible—the Bible that had once belonged to Abraham Lincoln, and raised his right hand.

I do solemnly swear that I will faithfully execute the Office of President of the United States, and will to the best of my ability, preserve, protect and defend the Constitution of the United States.

———

Henry heard a small ping just as his father finished. Before he realized what was happening, a Secret Service agent shoved him flat to the ground.

Four

A series of pings followed—like pops of glass shattering near the podium.

All around Henry, shouts erupted.

The agent who had shoved him down now helped him up, practically carrying him toward the Beast.

Henry watched as dozens of other Secret Service agents jumped into the crowd, all of them running toward one man who was also running toward them, charging, as though determined to break through a line of defense that was clearly unbreakable. The man was disheveled, tall, gaunt.

A ring of Secret Service members hustled the president and then the rest of Henry's family back into the Beast, as other agents drew guns on the man.

Watching, Henry felt like he should be terrified. Instead, he couldn't help but think of how fragile and pale the man looked—a moth caught in the sea of black birds that were quickly surrounding him.

Around him people screamed and moved as the man tried to raise his tattooed arms, only to be tackled from behind. He smacked into the ground, his face hitting the freezing concrete, and then for a moment, it seemed like he was gone, swallowed in an ocean of black.

When they jerked him up, he was handcuffed and bleeding. With the man's wrists forced together, Henry caught a glimpse of two rough, self-made tattoos that appeared to join into a shape. For a fraction of a second, the man's eyes connected with Henry's. Then the man looked down. Using his handcuffs, he began scratching at the tattoos. As he did, they seemed to fade.

Henry squinted against the bright light reflecting off the snow, but the man's wrists were now tight together and he couldn't see anything more.

"Man," Chet said, face pressed against the glass. "That was awesome!"

"Move your head back, son," his father said, his own face pale.

"But Mom said this thing was indestructible," Chet said.

"Move!" his mother shouted, and Chet moved back.

The shrieks of the panicked crowd settled into a whimper—police fanning out and trying to calm and corral them—as the man was shoved into a black armored car.

———

"Quite the start to your new presidency," the head of security said with a broken smile.

They sat around a large table for a debriefing. "You'll have the opportunity to greet the departing president and grab some pictures for the media in an hour or so, but for now we've pulled up several groups who may be responsible for today's special welcome." He glanced down at a small uVision in front of him and projected several profiles onto the table in front of them. "My guess is that it is connected to the group called The Ethereal."

Henry read the information scrolling in front of them, and noticed that of all the groups, The Ethereal had the least amount of information available. The group claimed responsibility for the deaths of several foreign dignitaries, and had supposedly killed a number of detectives and Secret Service in the U.S.

Henry's mother wrinkled her forehead. "I know that name."

"Yes," the head of security replied. "It is the same group thought to have kidnapped a number of politicians' teenage children several months ago." He pointed to a headline imaged across the table. "Several of the children's body-guards were injured or went missing."

"That's right," she replied. "But the children—all boys —were found two days later, unharmed, yet drugged and with no recollection of who had taken them or what had happened."

Henry stared at his mother. *Several months ago.* "What month?" Henry asked.

His mother shook her head.

"It's irrelevant," his father replied.

Henry opened his mouth to ask again, but the chief of security was already detailing a number of extra steps they would take at the inauguration ball and around the White House to provide added safety for the president and his family.

Henry realized he didn't really need an answer anyway. One look at his mother's taut profile and he knew.

The kidnappers had taken those children on the same night he'd been attacked. That's why his mother had been so freaked out. She'd known of the other abductions. But that was where it had ended. Henry had been unable to tell her what had happened to him, that someone had tried to take him as well. And she had assumed their family safe.

They hadn't been then. And they still weren't. The chief of security muttered into his phone, leaving detailed instructions to his people about increasing the perimeter of security around the White House and getting more snipers.

Chet looked like it was his birthday. The uVision projected a bird's-eye image of a map across the table, showing the different lines and types of security. It all looked like something from a movie.

"Mom," Henry began, his voice small.

His mother looked to him, worry lines digging around her eyes. "I know it's stressful," she said. "But the White House is the safest place on Earth."

"Yes, but," Henry continued, only to find that once again his voice cut off.

"You know, logistically," Chet interrupted, "some little

house in the middle of Nebraska is probably safer than the White House. I mean, who bombs Nebraska?"

"The corn bombers," his father answered without missing a beat or looking their direction.

Henry glanced up at his dad to see him solemn-faced, but with a twitch of a smile playing at the corners of his mouth. Henry started to relax. His dad had the most to worry about. If he wasn't that worried, well, then...

"The boring-stretch-of-road-on-the-way-to-skiing bombers," Chet added.

Henry couldn't help but snort out a laugh.

"This is very serious," Henry's mother said, glaring.

"It is," his father replied, looking at his wife, his tone getting a bit heavier. "But also inevitable. Marie, we knew things like this would happen."

The two of them exchanged a look.

"And they will keep us as safe as we could possibly be."

His mother nodded, but Henry had seen the look that flashed across her face. The look that said, *Will it be safe enough?*

———

A few minutes later, a large group of security escorted them to the second floor.

Doug Miller put an arm around his wife. "First sixty minutes on the job," he said, trying to make her laugh. "There are going to be crazies; we have to get used to that."

Marie Miller nodded, but she was still obviously shaken. "I'm a librarian, Doug. I only like to read about this stuff."

"Don't worry, Mom," Chet said, bumping his shoulder into his mother. "The scariest stuff is over. At least for you. For Henry, however, it's just beginning."

Henry shot his brother a look of concern, but then saw that he was laughing.

"That's right," Chet said. "I'm referring to the Inauguration Ball." He waved his hand in front of his face like a creepy magician. "An evening of horrors only a thirteen-year-old can possibly understand."

Their mother smiled. "Oh, it won't be that bad."

"That just goes to show how long it's been since you were thirteen," Chet said.

"Watch it," their mother warned.

"Not that you look a day over thirty," Chet concluded.

"Just tell me that's a spell that doesn't wear off at midnight," their mother said, cracking a smile.

"Of course not," their father replied, squeezing her shoulder. "And now you get to spend the night attending a gazillion balls decked out like a princess."

Henry burped. "Sorry, Mom."

His mother raised an eyebrow. "I guess after living with only boys for the last eighteen years, it might be kind of nice to be a princess for a night."

She looked over Henry and Chet. "Which means you two better start getting ready. After all, I can't be a princess without a proper entourage."

Five

Chet stood next to Henry. They were both dressed in tuxedos, and Henry didn't even mind. He felt like James Bond. Well, sort of. Standing next to his tall, muscular brother, he felt a little more like James Bond's short, pale sidekick, but that would have to do.

Chet, on the other hand, did not seem to appreciate his new spy wear. He squirmed and tugged on his bowtie. Henry was pretty sure Chet would rather get attacked by another potential assassin than spend the evening in anything other than his basketball shorts and a t-shirt.

They both turned as the band began to pound out a version of "Hail to the Chief."

"Do you think they'll get tired of that song?" Chet said, watching their parents. "I am, and it's only the first day."

"I don't know," Henry replied. "It's kind of catchy."

Chet rolled his eyes. "Mom looks buff."

"Buffer than you," Henry replied.

"Whatever," Chet said.

A spotlight fell across the room and people began to waltz.

By the second song, a girl had come over to Chet and asked him to dance. Which left Henry standing by the wall alone.

He might have felt sorry for himself except that every two minutes, a server came by with some new chocolate or pastry or drink. All of the servers knew his name and they always let him take as much as he wanted. Life could be worse.

A waiter came by, trailed by a blond boy in black pants and a white shirt. The boy looked a little younger than Henry, and he grinned as the waiter held out the drink. It was pink and frothy on the top, and as soon as Henry took it, the boy seemed to vanish. Which was a skill all the servers seemed to have.

Henry sighed. It would have been nice to have someone to hang out with while he was playing wallflower.

Henry was almost finished with the fizzy strawberry drink when Chet came over, grabbed it, and took a final swig. "I left the best floaties in the bottom for you," Henry said.

Chet ignored him. "Hey, check out that guy."

Henry looked across the room to see a tall man with black hair and white sideburns, dancing with a much younger woman. "He looks like Mr. Fantastic."

"Well, he isn't," Chet said. "That's Senator Masticor. He

campaigned hard against Dad. He's going to try to get in his way at every turn."

Henry knew the name. His father said nice things about most people, but he hadn't said very many nice things about Senator Masticor. "And who's that?" Henry asked, pointing to a girl about his age, who was standing nearby, watching Masticor dance.

"I'm guessing that's his daughter," Chet said. "She's not bad looking."

She wasn't. The girl had strawberry blond hair, which fell in soft waves over the purple evening gown that accentuated both her hair and her fair skin. She wore too much makeup and her chin was short for her face, but otherwise, she was really pretty. Except for the way she kept scowling at the Millers whenever they took a spin across the dance floor.

"I miss Lucy," Henry muttered under his breath just as Chet said, "You should go ask her to dance."

"What? Why?" Henry said.

"Because it would be hil-a-ri-ous," Chet said, drawing out the word. "And you haven't danced with anybody all night."

"Because I don't want to."

"Because you're scared to."

Sometimes Henry wished he could strangle his brother with his stupid silver bowtie. "Fine," he said, marching over to the girl.

She turned away as soon as she saw him approaching, and Henry immediately knew this was the worst idea ever, but he felt like a missile released from its launch. He couldn't stop.

"Hey," he said. He wasn't sure what to do next, so he held out his hand. "I'm Henry." His throat felt suddenly itchy, like he was getting a cold.

"Yeah, I know," she said, not shaking his hand, or even really looking at him.

"Do you want to—" Henry began.

But before he could finish she said, "No."

"Henry Miller," Senator Masticor said, coming over to his daughter. "I see you two are about to dance." He looked hard at his daughter.

She smiled with a smile so thin Henry wasn't sure he could ever see her as pretty again, even with her hair and that purple dress. "Of course. My name is Reylin." She finally looked Henry in the eye.

Senator Masticor pressed on his daughter's back, practically pushing her toward the dance floor.

Henry realized as they stood there that he didn't really know what to do. He'd gone to a school dance only once, and he and Lucy had just eaten cookies and told jokes until it was almost over. Then, someone had come and asked Lucy to dance.

Henry tried to imagine how she'd looked as he'd watched her dance. He remembered that Lucy's hands had gone up, which meant Henry's went down. He put his hands gingerly on Reylin's waist.

"So," he said, as she touched him like it was the last thing she wanted to do. "Have you been to a lot of these things?"

"No," she said, her voice just as clipped and thin as her lips had been when she smiled. "This is the first time Daddy's let me come."

Henry noticed that she had just the slightest southern accent. "Where are you from? Tennessee?"

"Yeah," she said, narrowing her eyes. "I was born there, but how'd you know? We've been in Texas since I was six."

"I can hear it in your accent," he said, stepping in an awkward circle.

"What accent? I talk just like everyone else in D.C." She sounded angry.

Henry tried to smile. "Not to me."

She glared.

"I mean, I'm good at hearing different accents, pitches in music, that sort of thing." Henry paused. Ever since he'd mastered his first foreign language at age five, his mother had been reminding him not to show off. But this was just an accent. It's not like he was launching into Mandarin or something. "My mom calls it a gift. She says I have a sound-o-graphic memory." He paused at Reylin's silence and cleared his itchy throat. "You know—like a photographic memory, only with sounds."

"Right," she said, and this time Henry felt like she distinctly let the accent drip in. "And with my little bitty accent you can even tell the difference between Tennessee and Texas. Nobody 'round here can do that."

"Uh, yeah," Henry replied. She'd let her accent go full force now, and somehow when she did, Henry felt like he'd just stepped in dog poo. Where was Chet when he needed him?

"Well, that's quite a gift," she said, smiling. It didn't sound thin and ugly anymore, but somehow it didn't seem quite pretty either.

The song ended, and Henry had never felt more thrilled in his life. He let his hands fall from Reylin's waist.

They stepped away from the floor and Masticor came over, his assistant trailing after him. The assistant was the most bland-looking man in the world. His suit literally matched his eyes, which matched his hair—all a pale brown. Henry was pretty sure if the man stood against a wooden wall you wouldn't even see him.

Henry's parents made their way over, holding hands, just as a Hispanic woman scuttled toward them with a tray of drinks.

"Well, congratulations, Mr. President," Masticor said, his voice as smooth as the wineglass he held in his hand. He smiled in the same pretty-ugly way Reylin had. He shook hands with Henry's parents. "I look forward to working with you."

The president began to reply, but Masticor cut him off. "And this is your son?"

"One of them," Mrs. Miller began, but Masticor ignored her.

"Quite the gentleman, I see." He patted Henry on the shoulder and looked down into his eyes.

Henry's throat felt thick. He used all his willpower not

to look away. Suddenly, Henry felt his nose twitch, and he sniffled.

Masticor stepped back slightly.

"Henry, have you been eating strawberries?" his mother asked. To Masticor she said, "He has a mild allergy."

Chet came over as Henry's mother pulled a tissue out of who knew where because she definitely didn't have any pockets in her evening gown.

"It was probably in that drink, Mom," Henry said. "I just figured it was strawberry flavored."

"Nothing in the White House is strawberry-*flavored,*" she said. "Unless you ask that it be so." She paused. "Which I will." She handed Henry another tissue.

"He guessed I was from Tennessee," he heard Reylin telling her dad. Henry blew his nose loudly.

"Really," Masticor asked, looking at Henry again, stepping closer and peering down through his designer glasses. "Well, that is remarkable. Or did you just read up on Reylin before coming here? She is quite the lovely young woman." The maid with the drinks came around again, but Masticor waved her away.

She stepped back like a statue, melting into the background.

"Uh, no," Henry said, a little too quickly. He had definitely not been internet-stalking Reylin. "I just have a good ear."

"Musical, really," his mother chimed in.

Masticor ignored her again, and she handed Henry another tissue.

"So do you play any instruments?" Masticor asked, stepping even closer. "I'm a bit of a music-lover myself."

Henry had the tissue up to his nose and he muttered something.

"What?" Masticor said, bending down and moving Henry's arm away from his mouth. "I couldn't hear you."

As he moved Henry's arm, the twitch in Henry's nose turned into a full-on sneeze, which hit Senator Masticor in the face as Henry desperately tried to bring the tissue to his mouth a moment too late. "Oh, sorry," Henry said, wiping his nose.

His mother's eyes nearly popped out of her head and she rushed at him with enough tissues to soak up Lake Superior.

Masticor had removed his glasses and was cleaning them with a satin handkerchief his assistant had handed him.

"I'm so sorry," the president said, glaring at Henry and motioning for Chet to get him away from them.

"Of course," the senator replied, a false smile frozen onto his face. "And *gesundheit*." He turned to Henry with a look that was neither a smile nor a frown, but a penetrating glasses-free stare.

"I'm really sorry," Henry said again.

"Of course," the senator replied again, replacing his glasses. "Of course you are."

Six

Henry trudged to a third floor guest room, where his mother had put his things until they chose a permanent room for him. He barely got out of his tux before the exhaustion hit. He expected to dream snow and sneezes and bleeding assassins and sleek black cars. But as the night dug into his subconscious, he found himself standing in an open field.

The sky was moonless with thick streaks of gray clouds that moved overhead, red wisps like static electricity sparking inside of them. Heavy, howling wind whipped against his body, blowing his clothes and hair. He became aware of a tree, large with a tall trunk and branches that reached into the clouds. The tree was cold, bare of leaves or fruit.

Henry felt the wind increase, cloth around him fanning out. He looked down and noticed he was wearing some kind of dark blue cloak. It was loose and moved freely around him, light when it needed to be light, heavy when it needed to be heavy.

He looked to his left and saw a figure standing near the tree, watching him. The man wore a cloak similar to his. Henry could not see the face or eyes, but he could make out features around the mouth, a scar reaching down into a crooked lip. Henry felt a light shudder, not fear, but something else, and the corner of the man's lip lifted into a small smile.

Then, instead of speaking, the man seemed to sing, his cloak billowing around him until the music stopped, and the cloak fell to the ground. The man was gone.

"Good morning, Henry," a voice said.

Henry bolted up like a piece of toast, and a man with a small scar above his lip stood beside his bed.

The man wore a dark blue suit, his curly hair combed flat. His skin was a pecan brown with deep wrinkles at the corners of his eyes and mouth. He spoke with a slight accent, and for once, Henry could not pick it out. Henry shook his head. He must have seen the man the day before. Dreams were weird.

"Your mother says it's time for you to be…I believe her words were 'up and at 'em.'"

Henry rubbed his eyes.

"My name is Mr. Taake Keikiki. I'm the chief usher, which means I oversee a lot of what goes on in the White House—from the food to the furniture. If you ever need anything, let me know."

"I will," Henry said, sitting up. "Thanks."

Henry was surprised to see a set of clothes laid out, perfectly pressed, on the dresser. He raised an eyebrow. "Do I have to wear that?"

"*That*," the chief usher said, "is not for me to say. Your mother had the clothes sent up."

"I thought I started school next week," Henry said.

"You do," the chief usher replied.

Henry didn't want to argue with this guy he barely knew, but he was thirteen and he was not going to have his clothes laid out like a baby doll every day. "Um, I'll probably just wear something else."

The man nodded, almost a bow. "I'll just hang these up then. You and your mother can discuss it whenever you'd like."

"Okay," Henry said, although he had no intention of discussing it with his mother or anyone else.

The man started bustling around the room. "We'll be moving you to the Lincoln Bedroom today."

"The Lincoln Bedroom?" Henry asked. He'd learned enough at the initial tour of the White House to know that it was usually reserved for dignitaries, cronies, and ghosts. None of those types of visitor appealed to Henry. "Why?"

"I believe," the older man said, smiling, "that your mother wants to keep you close. They'll be just down the hall."

Henry rolled his eyes.

"Don't be too upset," the usher said, still smiling. "The White House can be a shocking transition sometimes. And yesterday's events made it even more...memorable. But don't worry." He winked. "The staff and security do their best to make everything go as smoothly as possible. Now," he paused, "what would you like for breakfast?"

———

Seven blueberry pancakes, a banana, and a glass of milk later, Henry was too stuffed to move.

His dad came in holding a uVision, reading the morning news. "Morning, Henry," he said, glancing up and looking at Henry over his glasses. "Looks like you're off to a good start today."

"I'm not sure about starting," Henry said. "I think I'm just going to stay here forever."

His mother came in, but she didn't sit down. She looked at Henry's plate, then the blueberries and whipped cream, as well as the syrup. "You know, Chelsea Clinton preferred artificial syrup to the real maple the chef recommended, too."

"Sounds like I'm following a long line of good traditions," Henry said.

"Looks like you ate your weight in good traditions," his mother said, poking him and smiling.

"It had fruit," Henry said. "That makes it totally legit."

His mother ran a hand through his hair. "Just remember to be respectful to the staff," she said. "And grateful. These people devote their lives to caring for this house, maintaining it, and meeting the needs of the first family. Some of them stay for generations and then their children and grandchildren work here. There are over a hundred full-time workers here and they don't get paid much more than I made as a public librarian." She chewed on her bottom lip.

Henry knew it made her uncomfortable to be served by them.

"$60,000/year to care for six stories, 132 rooms, thirty-five bathrooms, three elevators, and eight staircases, a pool, bowling alley, basketball court, game rooms, a movie theater. All of that on the eighteen-acre plot of land," she continued.

"Mom, you should give the White House tours."

"I'd love to," she said, a little wistfully. "But today I'm meeting with an ambassador from Japan instead. Lucy's grandmother was kind enough to give me a few tips."

Henry smiled. Lucy's grandmother was about a million years old and lived on her own in Oahu. But she'd been born in Tokyo. Henry had met her a few times. She liked to give advice.

"And I will get to meet the head curator later, so that should be exciting."

Henry wasn't sure his mom quite understood the definition of exciting. "Just try not to encyclopedia it up too bad."

"Noted. And you stay away from the strawberries. Also, if you would refrain from sneezing on people, we'll be good."

"Deal," Henry said, surprised that that was all the reprimand he got for the night before.

"So," the president broke in. "Who wants to see Marine One?"

"Hello," Henry said, "count me in." He pushed back slowly from the table.

Henry's father gave his mother a quick kiss, then he and Henry walked downstairs, where they were instantly flanked by Secret Service and met by several staffers in the center hall on the ground floor.

"Good morning, Mr. President," several of the staff said, as the Secret Service fanned into a sort of V-formation along the sides. Henry had to resist the urge to make a joke about flying south as the Secret Service pushed them along so that they practically burst out the south entrance doors to the Portico and onto the manicured lawn. There, a huge white top helicopter stood ready to receive them, the door flanked by soldiers in full uniform.

"Now that's service," Henry mumbled to his dad.

"Want a ride?" his dad answered, grinning.

"I thought you had a meeting," Henry answered.

"I do," he replied. "But I also have a son. That deserves ten minutes of the president's day, don't you think?"

As they approached Marine One, two tall, clean-shaven men snapped into salutes.

The president smiled, returning the salute as the pilot came forward, verifying flight destination and going through several other details.

The president nodded before responding. "Excellent. But first, I'd like to take my son for a ride."

The pilot didn't bat an eye. "Yes, sir," he said, pointing to the sturdy steps that led to the door of the helicopter. "Welcome to Marine One."

A smile as wide as the Mackinac Bridge spread across Henry's face.

"We'll be back in a couple of minutes," the president said to his staffers while two Secret Service agents climbed aboard.

If it irritated any of them, Henry couldn't tell.

Inside there were two bucket seats near the front that faced one another. One had the seal of the president. Henry's father sat down. It was then that Henry finally felt it. His father was the president of the United States of America. The dances, the White House, even the oath of office and the gunman. It had all seemed like part of a play. But watching his father casually take a seat, the president's seat, on a presidential helicopter, it all sank in. "Dad, you're the president."

"That's what they tell me." His dad smiled, watching the Washington monument sail past. "It is a little surreal, isn't it?"

"A little," Henry mumbled, staring at the top of the Jefferson and then the Lincoln monuments. Great men who had shaped the country, the world. One had died before he was done. The face of the gunman from the inauguration popped into his mind and Henry felt sick. Presidents did not lead safe, friend-filled lives. He looked away from the window and back at his dad—his dad in the president's seat, smiling at the sights below them. Henry took a deep breath and forced himself to look back outside.

The pilot spoke to them through headset about the helicopter. "This fleet's been in use since the 1970s, but like all things presidential, it's been continuously updated with new technologies and maintained by the most qualified military professionals to meet standards for safety and function. It's one of the speediest forms of transportation available to the president and his guests."

"The '70s," Henry said, looking around. "They haven't replaced them since then? Why not?"

"Well," the pilot said, "efforts over the past decades to replace them have been stalled. The cost to build a brand new fleet, to meet all the specifications and everything, it's not cheap. But there are plans in place now for a new fleet. It should be ready in just a few months."

They were descending now. Henry could feel it in his ears, see the green expanse of lawn coming closer.

"Dad," he said quickly. "Have you ever had an experience where you felt super strong—like you could do anything, fight anything, get away from anything?" Henry was glad his throat didn't seal off when he asked the question.

"I suppose I felt a little bit that way the day I married your mother," his dad answered.

"Well, that's not really what I mean," Henry started.

"And the day each of you boys came along, I felt like I would do anything in this whole world to keep you safe," he continued. "I felt pretty super-charged then."

"Yeah," Henry said. "But, like, not like that. I mean, anything just out of the blue where you could...you could..."

"What?" his father said, looking into his eyes, deep into his eyes.

Henry's voice closed. He opened his mouth, shut it. "I

don't know," he grumbled, looking down at his regular hands, his regular legs.

"Don't worry, Henry," his father said, gazing out the window. "Give yourself a little time and you'll find your strength. And when you do, nothing will be able to stop you."

"Yeah," Henry said. "The thing is that once—"

He could say no more, not the month of the attack, not anything that happened.

"Once what?" his dad asked.

"Never mind," Henry said. "I just...I want... Be safe, Dad."

"I will," his father said, with a smile that almost seemed sad. "I promise I will."

Henry nodded as they hit the ground, the whir of the wind and helicopter blades drowning out any further conversation. Not that Henry could say what he wanted to anyway, not that he could *be* what he wanted to anyway: the kid from the park, the one who could protect himself and his family.

The kid who could be a safeguard for his dad, not a liability.

Several Secret Service members helped Henry out of the helicopter. "See you later, Dad," he called up.

His dad waved, but didn't reply. Maybe ten minutes really was all he was going to get of his father each day. Thinking of the assassination attempt from the day before, it didn't seem like nearly enough.

The head curator carried her briefcase up to the second floor, passing a lone maid with a feather duster. The curator walked quietly to Lincoln's bedroom.

She couldn't believe the new First Lady wanted to put her thirteen-year-old son there. It was embarrassing. Ever since Harry Truman, this room had been dedicated as the Lincoln Bedroom. It was a room for dignitaries and special guests, not a place to babysit one's child.

As a historian, the curator knew that it hadn't been Lincoln's actual bedroom, although Lincoln *had* used it as an office. It was a place with a deep history, and the room was filled with precious artifacts important to the sixteenth president of the United States. A signed copy of the Gettysburg Address sat on a small desk, along with two candlesticks owned by Mary Todd Lincoln, and supposedly used during the séances she often had after her son, Willie's, death. The room also contained several pieces of furniture used by Lincoln, as well as several presidents before him. She would have most of the furniture removed before the Miller boy moved in.

She huffed. Certain people had already messaged her, asking that she do all in her power to keep a child like Henry out of a room so filled with mementos of a man like Lincoln —a man who reminded people of all that was good, even in a world that had been racked with something as ugly as civil war.

The First Lady, however, could let her spoiled child stay

wherever she wished. Still, as curator, it was Madison Crossley's job to preserve the history of the house.

She opened up the briefcase and began wrapping pens, inkwells, pictures, and trinkets in the felt lining she'd brought. She took two prints of Willie Lincoln—one with the boy and his family gathered around a table, and one with him a little bit older, just before his death, standing beside a decorative curtain, hat in hand. She left the Gettysburg Address. She didn't want to, but she was worried the First Lady would fuss if it was removed from the room.

At the last minute, she also decided to leave the candlesticks—believed by many to carry a connection to other worlds—as well as a book she had personally selected from the White House library. *Haunted Washington: Ghost Sightings and Strange Happenings.*

She didn't know much about children, but she knew that most couldn't resist a good ghost story. And these were very good.

Maybe she couldn't persuade the First Lady to change her bedroom choices, but with any luck she could scare the boy enough that he'd beg to leave.

On top of the book, she left a small note. "So sorry there is no TV in the Lincoln Bedroom. If you head across the hall, you'll find a flat screen in the East Bedroom along with a new gaming system."

With a solid click, she shut her briefcase and walked back down the hall, just as soundlessly as she'd come.

Seven

The uVid had a hundred-a-day pushup challenge. Henry had gotten to twelve.

Now he sat on the floor in the small room connected to the Lincoln bedroom, watching the guy on the screen pump out eighty-eight more. Up, down. Each time, the man's muscles pulsed in streaks along his arms, cut like blades into his skin. Maybe this guy should have been the president's son. Henry smelled his armpits. He'd need a shower before school. First day. Midyear. Terrible combination.

He stood up, his muscles sore from the workouts. If you could even call them workouts. Each morning Henry had pulled up a challenge on his uVision. Squats, pushups, some kind of hanging leg raises. Each time he'd hoped for that surge of energy, that power he'd felt several months ago in an empty park in Michigan. That thing that had protected him, that could maybe even protect someone as important as the president. But each time he'd come up short. Not just a little short. But less than half the workout short. Usually less than a quarter. He grabbed a drink from a table and headed to the bathroom to take a shower.

When he came out, a uniform was laid out on his dresser. Sidwell Friends Middle School didn't have a dress code, so why was it there? Pants, light blue shirt, tie, and jacket. Add a cloak and he'd look like Harry freaking Potter. Henry sighed, staring at his reflection in the mirror. He'd started setting an alarm, so he didn't get awakened by some random usher or butler every morning. But, apparently, that didn't stop the staff from coming in and leaving wizarding outfits while he was taking a shower. As if the Lincoln Bedroom wasn't creepy enough.

He put on his slippers and sweatpants and wandered down the hall, looking for his mom and wondering if he should wear a t-shirt and jeans or give in and just wear the stupid outfit she had sent up. Before he could find his mother, however, he stumbled into the chief usher, Mr. Keikiki. He was no doubt coming to make sure Henry was awake.

"Do you know where my mom is?" Henry asked.

"Yes, I've just met with her. She'll be in a meeting by now. Can I help you with something?"

Henry scowled. The failed workout, the start of school, the stupid outfit—they'd put him in a bad mood. He wanted to say something snarky about being a White House orphan, but just mumbled, "No thanks," and went back to his room.

His mother knew this was his first day of school. Why had she scheduled a stupid meeting? Why had she sent up a stupid outfit? He threw on an old pair of jeans and a faded sweatshirt, taking a quick glance in the mirror—brown eyes so pale they were almost orange, messy hair. He looked scroungy and he knew it.

He wanted to say he didn't care and walk out the door, but he did care. Mostly because at Sidwell he didn't want to stick out. And this outfit would stick out just as much as his mother's Hogwarts costume. He found a clean pair of jeans and put on the blue shirt his mom had chosen, donning his dirty socks in a last ditch act of rebellion. His stomach was in knots, and for the first time since coming to the White House, he wasn't sure he'd be able to pack away a huge, starchy breakfast.

He pulled out his phone and vexted Lucy. "Here I go."

She must have known exactly what he meant because his phone pinged just a minute later. Her voice came through loud and clear. "You'll be great. Don't worry." Henry was glad that his parents had agreed to spring for new phones for him and Chet after his got broken. Vexting was so much cooler than just a plain text. And it made him feel a little less lonely to hear Lucy's actual voice. He hit the vext again and listened. "You'll be great. Don't worry."

Then he thought about what time it was. "I'm a jerk," he vexted. "School starts early here."

"I was up anyway," she replied. "And I'm glad for the distraction. Mom's got me doing extra bio homework for an entrance exam I'm taking."

"Sounds like some fun mother-daughter time," Henry vexted. He knew it made Lucy laugh when he joked about her family, though he was pretty sure Lucy's mom would have been less amused.

"Well, you know, I'm Hawaiian and Native American. So #superchill #ohwait #politicallyincorrect #hawkpride #dadsevenworse."

Henry laughed at the hashtags. They floated across the screen, but the vext also spoke them, just like he and Lucy would have. They liked to make up as many funny ones as they could. It was a thing they'd started doing back in fourth grade. Hashtags were a little retro, but they still got a kick out of it.

Lucy's were hilarious.

And it was true. Lucy's parents were both a little, well, uptight was putting it politely. One super-achieving mom, and a dad who'd spent his life trying to disprove negative stereotypes about Native Americans (and succeeding). Lucy had just enough of her Hawaiian grandpa in her blood to keep things light.

Henry sure wished he was going to see her face when he showed up for school today.

"Have fun," she vexted and a string of smiling emojis flew across his screen. "Seriously. You'll do great."

No, he wouldn't. He knew this. Lucy did too. He'd kill it in history and English and whatever other languages his mother had signed him up for. He was fluent in six languages, and had a working knowledge of at least ten more. That was probably the only reason he'd even been accepted into the school—well, that and his new presidential status, which wasn't supposed to count, but probably did. He'd drown in math and any sciences and all the rest.

"Got a surprise for you," Lucy vexted after a few more minutes.

"Hit me with it," he replied.

"Nope. Can't tell. Talk to you soon."

"That's not a surprise," he vexted back. "That's a secret."

But she didn't reply.

———

Two burly Secret Service agents sat on either side of Henry, making him feel like the insides of a sandwich. Henry felt too hot, even in the big car. He messed with his shirt, tugging at the collar, glad he'd only had an orange for breakfast, even if it had given Chet an excuse to bring up the time he'd puked on the school steps the first day of fifth grade.

His stomach felt a lot like that right now, which couldn't be good. Outside of the darkly tinted windows, Henry saw people staring at the sleek, black presidential vehicle.

They always gathered to gawk, and Henry wondered if he'd ever get used to it. Ahead, a boy just younger than him with blond, straw-like hair lifted a hand and waved. Henry thought he looked a little familiar—maybe the boy from the party. The boy seemed to be looking right into Henry's eyes, though of course that was impossible with the dark windows.

Another black vehicle drove behind them. "Is that

Chet?" Henry asked. His brother would be going to the high school.

The tallest Secret Service glanced out the window. "No, it's our escort."

"Escort?" Henry asked.

"Any time the first family travels anywhere, we have another vehicle to act as a decoy in case of an attack."

"But then wouldn't they get hurt? The escort?" Henry asked, slumping down in his seat.

"Not likely," the tall Secret Service agent said. "Those drivers are trained for this stuff."

Henry nodded. Trained to protect people too weak to protect themselves. "And if the attackers don't fall for the decoy?"

"Don't worry," the shorter Secret Service guy said. "This vehicle might look like just a comfy ride, but within minutes it turns into a tank. You see those panels?" He pointed to some brown panels along the interior.

Henry nodded.

"Those contain weapons, basically an arsenal of top secret military technology." He looked at his partner. "And, of course, if all else fails, we could eject you."

"He's just kidding," the tall one said. "We wouldn't really eject you."

The shorter one smiled at him, as though adding, *But we could.*

Henry was almost positive that he wouldn't—couldn't—be ejected from the vehicle, WWIII or not. But sometimes with the Secret Service, you couldn't quite be sure.

In just a few minutes, they arrived at Sidwell Friends School. The building sat blocky on a terraced lawn that spilled out in front of them. Several kids were walking towards the entrance, all of them unfamiliar. Except one.

Henry sank down in his seat, squinting through his window. The stiff shoulders, the long stride, the strawberry blond hair done up in a braid that was meant to look messy. It had to be her.

Reylin.

She went to this school. Could it get any worse?

When the driver came to open his door, Henry glanced at the sidewalk. All clear. He took a deep breath and stepped out.

The two agents followed.

Henry stopped. "You're coming with me?"

His mother hadn't prepared him for that. She'd been so busy with first lady stuff that she hadn't even thought to tell him he'd be at school with two security guys. Awesome. So the day *could* get worse.

"Sorry, Henry," the tall one said. He honestly looked like he felt bad to be trailing around a middle school with a kid who couldn't stop him.

"If it makes you feel any better," the shorter one whispered, "we don't want to be here any more than you want us here."

Henry wasn't sure whether it was meant to be snarky or funny, but he laughed. "At least you have cool sunglasses," he whispered back. "No one knows who you are."

"That's the idea," the agent responded.

Henry smiled, but his insides were boiling up again. As they approached the school, both of the Secret Service drifted back, blending in as well as two hulky guys in black suits possibly could.

The principal waited at the front entrance, wearing a sleek rose-colored suit and heels. Henry didn't know what he'd expected from his new principal, but it wasn't a tall, gorgeous blond who looked like she belonged on a red carpet. His snarky Secret Service agent suddenly looked a lot happier about his assignment. But Henry felt even more sick. He wiped his forehead with the back of his hand.

"Henry Miller," the woman said, as a Secret Service agent handed him a handkerchief. "I'm Ms. Smith. And I'm so thrilled to be welcoming you to Sidwell Friends School." She reached out to shake Henry's hand and Henry felt like all the blood from his body torpedoed into his forehead. He held out his own hand and when their palms met, his nausea increased.

Ms. Smith continued to speak and Henry made a conscious effort to look her in the eye, but he was having trouble focusing.

She was saying something about how many of the presidents and congressmen sent their children to Sidwell Friends School, and how honored they were to have him there. She squeezed his hand and Henry couldn't listen anymore.

His vision turned strange and blurry. The sky seemed to shift to a light shade of red. The air stilled and Henry could no longer see the school where it stood. Instead, it became a vast flat wasteland. No trees, no sustainable landscape, no people. The ground started to warm and harden, his feet blistering against it. When he walked, the earth felt hot and smooth like glass, like a different planet.

Suddenly, bizarrely, a strange feeling of power rushed over Henry. The air was filled with energy, the sky eerie, dark, and empty. Henry could no longer remember how it was supposed to look—before the red darkness. But that didn't matter now, as there was so much power, so much energy, so much rejoicing. The feeling lifted him up, carrying him. He wanted to hold that feeling, increase it. But even as the thought came to him, it started to fade, the sky growing lighter again, cooler.

"Henry Miller, the president's son," a voice was saying from far, far away.

Henry became aware of a white handkerchief in his hand. He swiped it over his forehead and the voice grew clearer. Ms. Smith had released his hand and was leading him through the building, introducing him to his homeroom teacher. He was standing here, at Sidwell Friends Middle School, blue sky outside the window, the principal holding the door for him, two men in black trailing behind.

Henry wiped his neck and shoved the handkerchief in his pocket. Everything from voices to colors felt hollow now, flat and empty, as though some kind of energy had dissipated, leaving the world a blank and weakened place.

He opened his mouth to say that he felt a little sick, but the words wouldn't come out.

EIGHT

After school, Henry dug up some uVids online about the kidnappings last September. He wondered if facing that fear might take away some of the stress that was obviously eating away at his brain. The official statements were easy to find. Anything else, not so much.

Nine kids. All taken the same night he was attacked. All returned two days later, drugged, no memories, but otherwise healthy and safe.

Their families—up-and-coming political families—had refused comment or interview about the incidents.

For whatever reason, Henry was kind of relieved. That, combined with the fact that all of the families had very different political leanings, assured him that it hadn't been some type of political plea for attention. The families seemed legitimately terrified and legitimately baffled. But their silences left the internet to go crazy with its own versions of the events.

Some were sincere attempts at understanding who had done the crimes and why. Many accused terrorists like ISIS and URWAN. Others blamed domestic groups they considered intent on derailing the country's current political system. Henry thought that made the most sense. It also explained the attack on his father on his first day in office.

But his favorite stories were the conspiracy theories and alien abduction hypotheses. They made everything seem less real and completely unlikely.

Two theorists even had images of a person they claimed to have seen that night—a tall black figure with a wispy cloak. The figure almost stood out from the pictures, like it had been badly photo-shopped in the 1960s.

A group from Kansas didn't have any images of the cloaked figure, but they did claim that the air traffic controls in their small airport had gone nuts just as the kidnappings were taking place. Of course. One had a picture of a completely black radar screen.

According to one blogger, this was evidence of an alien abduction. Henry tapped the uVid, powering it off. He knew there hadn't been a cloaked alien—just a driver and a dude in black wearing gloves.

The alien theorists had gotten the color right at least. Black. No red sky, no rusty wasteland. No connection to his first-day jitters. He tried to laugh at himself, but couldn't quite. Rubbing his temples, he rolled off of the couch in his room.

He should have had more than an orange for breakfast that morning. He figured his hunger had caused his weird blackout—well, red-out—at school. That, and a whole lot of stress. He needed to find a way to tell his mom about the attacks. Or maybe not. Maybe at this point, with security coming out their ears, it was best just to let it lie, and not give her one more thing to worry about.

He held up his phone. He'd been googling stress. It could cause all types of adverse reactions, including blackouts and, in some very extreme cases, seizures or hallucinations. Awesome.

Henry clicked his phone off and made his way down to the kitchen, thinking about that evening in Michigan—the two men, the dark car, the dollar signs in his attacker's eyes. *For a chubby little nobody, you're worth a lot of money.*

Who paid some thugs big money to abduct a few kids, only to return them a couple of days later? And why?

Great, Henry thought as he pushed open the door. *Now I'm thinking in conspiracy theories too.*

He wandered into the kitchen and wandered out with a fat piece of chocolate cake.

After his bout with the principal, the rest of the day had been pretty normal. Well, as normal as possible when you're the president's son at an expensive private school being trailed by security.

Henry passed the chief usher in the hall. The old man nodded toward Henry and didn't even bat an eye at the chunk of cake.

Henry took a huge bite as he walked. He kind of missed

having his mom around more often, and his first day at Sidwell had been a big stress party, but there were definitely perks to living here.

He banged into his room, kicked his shoes off like his mother always told him not to, then settled down into the pillows with his cake. He raised the cake to his mouth, not even bothering with the silver fork the kitchen staff had given him, when he noticed how quiet and cold the room felt—like a museum after visiting hours.

The long, thick gold curtains that adorned the windows seemed to sway. Across from the bed, a painting of an old woman wearing a flowery dress hung above the ornate fireplace. The woman's face tipped upward as though annoyed that Henry was interrupting her solitude.

Henry sat up and shuddered. Even Winston Churchill hadn't liked staying in the Lincoln bedroom. Henry had read that Churchill had emerged from a bath naked to see the ghost of Lincoln standing against the fireplace. Another time, an actor had woken to see Lincoln prostrate on the floor as if in prayer, wailing and digging his fingers into the carpet.

No thanks, Henry thought. He was going to tell his mom he just couldn't stay in this room. He cradled his cake against his chest, staring at the painting of the woman, when a voice jolted him. "That's Mary Todd Lincoln, the wife of the president."

Henry jerked around to see a small Hispanic woman in a maid uniform standing in his doorway.

He sighed in relief. "Oh...okay."

The woman stood in front of the door, holding an over-sized feather duster, and gazing at the picture of Mary Todd Lincoln. Henry took his cake and stepped toward the door when the woman said, "She was a wonderful person. Under-estimated and underappreciated by the nation. Overshad-owed by her husband. She deserves more credit."

The woman had turned her eyes on Henry as if waiting for a reply, but he had nothing to say. So he did the only thing he could think of, and took a bite of cake.

"You and your family are fortunate to live here, to come here now. Important things must happen." She paused. "It is not coincidence that you are here now, in this house, in this room." Her voice dipped, low and somber.

"That's great," Henry said. "But I have to—" He looked at the door she was blocking, wishing he could transport himself past her, just like Lincoln's ghost.

"The Civil War was an awful time. It was a war of guns and cannons and blood. But it was first a war of principles, of ideas." Her dark brown eyes fixed on his. "Some had to be sacrificed so others could live." She glanced at her wrist, sighed.

Henry nodded politely, easing his way toward the door, casting a quick glance at the sitting room that was attached to the Lincoln bedroom. Could he get out if he went through there?

"This room is special because when Mrs. Lincoln's son died, she held a séance to communicate with him." The maid nodded toward the candlesticks. "Did you know that after the death of his son, Lincoln went into his office and wept for an entire day? He would sit right at the desk and watch this very door, waiting for his son to come running through it."

Henry cleared his throat. "Oh, that's—"

"Typhoid," the maid said, not seeming to hear Henry. "He died because he lived and played and breathed on this land—designated so long ago as a place for presidents, but barely inhabitable until after Ulysses S. Grant drained the swamp." She looked around. "Now it's a place of opulence, of relative safety. But back then, a boy could come here and die from bad water. Back then, people could sleep in the lobby, waiting to petition the president. Back then a powerful man could go to a show with his wife and get shot in the back of the head by a disgruntled actor."

Henry stared at the woman, unsure of how to reply.

"Back then, they understood that some would die when you took a stand to protect others, that one was worth the rescue of a thousand."

Henry looked at the woman. Her tiny frame seemed to fill the entire width of the door, and she pointed at an old-fashioned desk at the side of the room. "The Gettysburg Address," she said. "Only five signed copies exist, and one is right here. With you. Why are you here, Henry? Why are you in Mr. Lincoln's office? What changes will you make for this universe we all live in?" The woman's voice was hushed, but sharp.

"My mom," Henry croaked. "She wanted me to be here. But I have to go." He shoved the last bit of cake into his mouth, hoping it would give him some courage, and then squeezed past the woman, out into the hall.

Maids walked through it with dusters, arranging flowers. Henry took a deep breath and then, against his mother's advice to be respectful, he put his plate and fork on one of the tables so that a maid would put it away and he wouldn't have to. He felt a little bad about that, but right now, he needed some fresh air.

———

Outside, he found Chet on the basketball court, slamming the ball through the hoop one shot after another even though it was freezing. Henry had probably never been more relieved to see his brother in his whole life.

Henry stood to the side for a few minutes, his breath coming out misty against the cold air. Henry didn't love playing with his brother, since it wasn't play so much as being demolished. But today being demolished by his brother in a nice normal game of basketball didn't sound so bad. Even if there were two Secret Service agents babysitting them on the sides of the court.

Suddenly, Chet turned and called, "Heads up," tossing the ball to Henry who caught it. Which was kind of a shock. There were a lot of reasons Chet was better at basketball than Henry. Age difference, height difference, weight difference. But the biggest difference of all was skill. Chet had a lot and Henry didn't.

"Take a shot," Chet said.

Henry jogged up for a layup and made it.

"Nice." Chet grabbed the ball, faked left, then jogged around Henry for another easy shot. "Come on, Henry. You didn't even try to block me."

"Was I supposed to?" Henry said.

"Well, if we're going to play, then yeah," Chet said, retrieving the ball and tossing it to Henry before successfully blocking, stealing the ball, and making another shot.

"Okay, so this is why blocking seemed a little pointless."

"Just try, Henry," Chet said.

Henry sighed. Maybe he wasn't any good, but losing at basketball was still preferable to blacking out at school, or reading conspiracy theories, or hanging out in haunted rooms with the Mary Todd fan club of one.

"So how was the high school?" Henry tried to grab the ball from his brother who finally missed a shot, slamming the ball so hard against the backboard that it shuddered.

"Alright." Chet grabbed the ball and tossed it to Henry.

"Alright's not bad," Henry said.

"It's not great either," Chet replied as Henry missed a layup.

Chet swiped the ball, turned, and dunked. "Too late to join the basketball team," he said. "But there are girls so that's good. Not sure they're as hot as Lansing girls, but then I'm biased."

Henry rolled his eyes and tried unsuccessfully to get the ball from his brother.

"I just miss my team." Chet tossed the ball to Henry, putting his hands on his hips and breathing hard. "They're headed to state. And it just burns to see it on uView and everywhere all the time and to not be a part of it."

Henry shot and missed, trotting after the ball.

"Lots of things burn," Henry said, tossing the ball back to his brother and feeling a little sorry for himself. "I guess that's what it means to be a son of the president." The lights on the grounds had come on and everything felt quiet and cold, kind of like when they were young and used to go camping with their dad in Ypsilanti—before he'd become governor. "But I have a feeling that no one's gonna feel too sorry for us either."

Chet's ball swished through the net, barely making a sound.

"I mean, maybe you should start your own basketball team or something. You're already eighteen—a bona fide adult." Henry grabbed the ball and threw it at Chet who caught it and paused—staring or glaring, Henry wasn't sure.

"My own team, huh? Comprised of a bunch of fat, rich congressman's kids. Or maybe the super athletic elite of Washington, D.C.?" Chet chucked the ball and walked off the court. "I miss Michigan," he said. "I miss our house and my friends and my crew. Even if I could make more friends, I don't really want them." He disappeared into the dark, his security guy following close behind.

"Got that right," Henry mumbled under his breath.

The remaining Secret Service agent walked out onto the court. Tonight it was a woman—tall and lean, bronze skin, black hair in a braided knot at her neck. She took off her shades and her gloves, tucking them into a pocket, and picked up the ball. "I'll rebound," she said, tossing the ball to Henry. He caught it, shot, missed.

"Bend your knees, keep your elbow in, and follow through on the shot." She showed him. "Try again."

Henry did. The ball swished through the hoop so smoothly Henry almost wasn't sure he'd made it. He tried it several more times from several different positions on the court, making it almost every time. "Hey, thanks," Henry said.

"No problem," she answered. "I played a few years of college ball before coming here. Spent some time coaching kids, too." She paused. "And you were right what you told your brother. There're kids in this world—a lot of kids—who don't even dare to dream what you guys wake up to every day." She stepped off the court and put her sunglasses back on, even though it was pretty dark.

"I don't know," Henry said, aiming toward the hoop. "Sometimes it feels kind of dangerous—being here."

"And it kind of is," she replied, gesturing to his arm, to remind him to hold his elbow in. "So thanks for my job. But compared to so many other countries, compared to neighborhoods a couple miles from here, this is no kind of danger. And, not to preach or anything, but as scary as your first day here might have been, the sound of gunshot is something a lot of kids grow up knowing. And most of those kids don't have a bulletproof car or a bulletproof life to stop it."

Henry smiled in the darkness. "You want a mic to drop?"

"I really should start carrying one," she answered. "Who needs a gun?"

"Yeah, well, a gun is cool too," Henry said. "But don't go dropping it."

"Yes, sir," she replied, grabbing the rebound and sinking the ball from the side of the court without even glancing at the basket.

NINE

The First Lady rode in the Beast with her secretary, going through several hand-selected pieces of mail. She read accounts of blue alien tunnels to the sky, promises to the president if he would grant certain favors, warnings about the end of days, and plenty of crude threats to the first family.

Under normal circumstances, she never would have seen this mail, letters the staff and Secret Service would have sifted through and sorted out, leaving her with only the sweetest, fluffiest invitations and thank you notes. But with the attack from The Ethereal on her husband's first day in office, and with Henry's interest in the attacks from September, she had requested to see other pieces.

Mail was a strange thing in this day and age—used only by the most desperate or most polite. She now, unfortunately, had more interest in one of those groups than the other.

She set the stack of mail aside. Small white envelopes, lumpy manila folders, a few thin cardboard boxes the Secret Service had already checked for dangerous items. She wasn't sure what she had thought that she—a middle-aged librarian from Michigan—might find that the Secret Service or FBI had missed.

Her secretary handed her another bundle of mail. "If you're ready for a break from alien conspiracies," he said. "I've got some more usual mail for you—invitations you should respond to as well as a few personal notes."

She took the much smaller stack from her secretary, smiling in thanks. "The word *ethereal*," she said. "It means delicate, immaterial, unearthly, other-worldly. Its root is from the word *ether*." She slipped a letter opener into the first envelope and asked, "Do you know much about ether?"

"I'm afraid not, Mrs. Miller."

Marie Miller nodded, opening the letter, then setting it down without reading it. "Ether is a pleasant-smelling, colorless liquid that is highly flammable. It can be vaporized and used as an antiseptic to cause numbness. But it can also be used in the industrial sector to dissolve other compounds. Incredibly volatile. Incredibly dangerous. Incredibly useful. Of course, in literature, it just means the air."

She looked up to see her secretary staring at her like her sons often did when she went off on a fact spree. She put her glasses on the tip of her nose and examined the note in her hand. "We've got a lot to do before the state dinner in two days."

Her secretary nodded.

She peeled through several more dull pieces of mail before coming upon a small, perfectly square card written with unusual typeface. It was sealed with a square of blue wax that looked like a miniature map of the earth divided into four quadrants. The first lady paused, running a finger over the soft blue lines of the wax, as though remembering something.

"What's this?" Marie Miller asked her secretary.

The older gentleman looked up and took the card from the first lady. "I'm so sorry, Mrs. Miller. This, I'm afraid, should have been with the other pile."

"Is it dangerous?" Mrs. Miller asked, still staring at the blue seal.

"I dare say it isn't," her secretary replied, holding it up to the light. "We've been getting these for years. They're harmless, so don't worry. They're just perfectly useless."

The first lady took the card back from her secretary. It was a solicitation from the Flat Earth Society—begging the president for an interview so that they could discuss the "pressing matter" of the enormous "scientific conspiracy" that claimed the earth to be round when they had solid proof that it, indeed, was flat.

"Fascinating," she said. "I read something about this group once. They believe space programs and satellites to be a government lie." She paused, looking at the envelope. "And you don't believe there could be any connection to The Ethereal?"

"The Ethereal," her secretary said, "are not a segment or break off or any part of the Flat Earth Society."

"I don't suppose they are," Mrs. Miller replied, pressing her hand against the wax seal, as though trying to imprint it there. "Nothing, it seems, is connected to The Ethereal." She sat quietly for several minutes before murmuring, "That is, after all, practically its definition."

"Excuse me, Mrs. Miller," her secretary replied.

"Whatever else it is, The Ethereal is expert at being *dis*-connected."

Her secretary shifted.

The first lady sighed. "But if not part of any of these crazy groups, then who, who *are* The Ethereal?"

Her secretary stacked the letters beside him. "There are a whole lot of people right now trying to figure that out. All we know is that they don't seem to favor any party lines or world leaders. They are people unhappy with government, people who are calling for what they term the Refining." He nodded to the card in the first lady's hand. "But they are not part of the Flat Earth Society. Those letters have been coming to the White House for decades. The staff just sticks them in the slush pile with the messages about alien sightings and black-hole-about-to-destroy-Earth notifications."

He looked down and cleared his throat. "Truthfully, the staff gets a kick out of these particular cards. We, uh, well I don't have any proof, but it wouldn't surprise me at all if some of the staff even rescued them from the paper shredder and took them home as souvenirs." He cleared his throat again. "No proof, of course. Just a guess. There's that interesting seal. And they come with little poems."

"I see," Mrs. Miller said, a touch of a frown at the corners of her mouth.

Four corners fold a page together,
Smaller now, but still no heavier.
Earth a blank evasive expanse
Given now a final chance.

Her secretary reached out to take the card from her, but she held tight. "I think that the First Lady will hold onto this one as her own little keepsake, if you don't mind."

"I never saw a thing," he said.

TEN

For the first time since the inauguration two weeks ago, all four Millers sat down like a regular family to eat. The meal involved duck and cheesy stuffed spinach as well as some white asparagus that Henry was scowling at.

His parents were both distracted, his mother pushing food around, as though thinking. Finally she looked up at the stalks left on Henry's plate.

"Eat that," his mother said, picking up one of her own asparagus and taking a bite. "The asparagus is from the White House garden, and it's delicious. Do you know that the first White House vegetable gardens were established by John and Abigail Adams, with fruit trees added by Jefferson? During World War II, Eleanor Roosevelt established a Victory Garden at the White House, and then, of course, Michelle Obama instigated the creation of the largest-scale White House garden yet."

"Awesome, Mom." Chet snapped off an asparagus head. "Now Henry will eat them for sure."

"Boys," their dad said, a little distracted, "Please be polite." He chewed slowly, as Henry poked his asparagus with his fork.

Mrs. Miller cleared her throat in her husband's direction.

His father lifted an eyebrow, then set his napkin on the table. "I've got a surprise for you two," he said. "Especially you, Henry."

"Of course," Chet grumbled.

"Surprise?" Henry hoped it was a really tall carrot cake with his favorite cream cheese frosting.

"It's not food," his mother said, seeing his face. "And you need to eat all your asparagus if you want dessert."

"Mom," Henry said.

"Just eat," his dad said, then took a breath. "The big news is that my pick for secretary of state has been approved."

"Dad." Henry set down his albino asparagus. "You seriously need to work on your surprises."

"And the new secretary of state is..." His dad paused like there was a drumroll. "Martin Hawk."

It took Henry a moment before it sank in. Lucy's dad. The new secretary of state.

"They'll be moving here?" Henry asked, his asparagus forgotten.

"Yup," his dad said. "Masticor and his cronies wanted to block it, but it was clear to the rest of the Senate that Mr. Hawk was the best man for the job." He smiled. "It's actually been all over the news, but I figured you wouldn't be following my cabinet selections too closely, so I kept it a secret. I didn't want you to be disappointed if it didn't work out."

"Mr. Hawk will be the first Native American secretary of state in our nation's history," Henry's mom said. "There will be a huge press release first thing in the morning."

Henry didn't even know what to say. The butlers brought out cherry cobbler, Chet's favorite dessert. Henry could barely eat it, even though he'd choked down three whole asparagus for the privilege.

After dinner, Henry vexted Lucy. "Secret's out."

"Isn't it awesome?" she replied immediately.

"Yup," Henry vexted. "But where will you be going to school?"

"Passed my entrance exam," Lucy vexted. "Sidwell Friends Middle School."

Henry pumped a fist into the air even though no one could see, then vexted, "When do you get here?"

Lucy didn't respond for a minute. Then she sent about 700 emojis. "You'll see in the morning."

For the first time since arriving in the Lincoln bedroom, Henry slept a deep, perfect sleep—no dreams, no ghosts, no assassins, no wastelands. Maybe this place could feel like home after all.

ELEVEN

enry and Chet stood on the Truman balcony. Adjacent to them, in the yellow oval room, their parents and a few French dignitaries munched on hors d'oeuvres and mingled before heading down to the formal event in the stateroom on the first floor.

Henry listened to the military band play on the north lawn beneath them. He felt the music drift skyward, almost like he could reach over and grab a piece of it.

Below, partygoers gathered in clusters. Everything on the north lawn seemed to glow—like the night sky had turned upside down—the stars in a dark basin below them. He stared down at tiny candles, blinking lights, and champagne glasses filled with sparkling liquids.

A butler came out to the balcony with a tray of drinks and tiny rolled meats. "At least the French like good food," Chet said, popping an hors d'oeuvre into his mouth. "I'm starving."

Henry had drunk enough soda to not feel hungry exactly, though he sure didn't feel full either.

"Hey, check it out," Chet said, gesturing to a group of teen celebrities who had just arrived below. "Maybe the night won't be a total wash after all."

Henry squinted to get a better look at one of his favorite singers when another butler came out to the balcony. "Henry, you have a guest."

Through the door walked a petite black-haired girl, wearing a dark dress, satin slippers, and a thin necklace made of turquoise and pearl.

"Henry," Lucy squealed in a voice so happy, even Chet smiled. "You're in a tux."

"Yeah," Henry said as Lucy hugged him. "Mom wouldn't let me wear my 'Got French' t-shirt, so I had to settle for this." He smiled at Lucy. He'd seen her for just a minute at the press conference, but they hadn't had a chance to talk before Lucy was whisked away for pictures and a million other things.

"Everything is so exciting here," Lucy gushed. "You can touch things famous people have touched. And, I mean, look at the view." She leaned on the balcony, looking at the brilliantly lit Washington Monument.

Henry laughed. "Crazy, huh? The view is even better when you consider that just over our heads on the roof is a small army of snipers, ready to shoot someone."

Lucy gasped, twisting around to try to see the ledge above them.

Just then, an usher came out. "Time to make your

entrance," he said with a smile, leading them back to their parents. "Hail to the Chief" began to play as Henry made his way down the grand staircase and over to the stateroom floor with his family.

The large, shining room was full of people, music, flowers, and food.

Henry walked behind his parents and the French president, who was whispering to her husband rapidly in French.

Henry followed every word as she smiled at the crowd, but complained to her husband. "I have a blister on my toe, and do not want to stay long at this party. My stomach hurts and the Americans are such bland conversationalists." She sighed. "I don't want to sit here bored all night while they talk about American basketball." She looked at Henry and Chet and smiled sweetly.

Chet leaned over to Henry and whispered, "What are they saying?"

Henry looked thoughtful and murmured, "She says you look interesting and that she hopes someone will talk to her about basketball, because she's a big fan."

Chet nodded, as though making a mental note.

The two presidents and their spouses stood while the press took pictures. Looking at them, Henry realized it was hard to tell the difference between the politicians and the celebrities. Nobody looked like the lanky, solemn Lincoln, much less the morbidly obese Taft. Some of the politicians were older; some were younger. But they were all beautiful.

Standing in the reception line, Henry felt suddenly squirmy in his suit, standing next to his brother who could have been modeling the tux. Movie stars were coming through the line and he felt for the millionth time like a goose in a flock of swans.

He got a hard shove in his ribs. "There's Masticor," Chet hissed. "Quick, eat some strawberries so you can sneeze in his face again."

"Maybe I'll save it for Reylin this time," Henry said. She was there behind her father, her blondish-red hair braided and wrapped, held in place with rhinestone hairpins.

But Chet wasn't paying attention to Reylin. Suddenly quiet, he was staring past Masticor, down the line.

Henry followed Chet's gaze and then shook his head. There, behind Masticor and his daughter, was Marxma Frey.

"Is that?" Henry started.

"Shhh," Chet hissed, as she approached. He held out his hand for the actor to take. "Hello," he said. "Pleased to meet you."

"Pleasure's all mine," the tall, nineteen-year-old starlet replied with a slight drawl. "I'm Marxma Frey."

"I know," Chet said, smiling in a way that made Henry want to gag. "I'm kind of a fan."

"Oh," Marxma said. "Well, I'm flattered."

"Yeah," Chet said. "I've seen all your movies. I even watched *Monster Vice* twice."

Marxma raised a dark, perfect eyebrow. Henry wasn't sure that Marxma found it impressive in the way Chet meant for it to be impressive.

"I'm Henry," he cut in. "Henry Miller."

"Oh, I know," she said, smiling at him in a way that suddenly made Henry understand why Chet wanted to impress her. Her eyes looked like pieces of solid topaz, her hair a deep curly brown, chocolate silk skin, full lips. All of a sudden Henry had nothing to say. He looked around a little desperately for Lucy, spotting her and waving her over. "And this is Lucy," Henry added. "She's the daughter of the new secretary of state."

"Pleased to meet you," Marxma said. "And I just love your hair. Half the people I know would kill for it." And just like that everyone but Marxma was too star struck to say anything, so Marxma added, "I'm here with the Masticors— staying at their estate. Our families go way back."

That broke the spell. "Oh," Chet said. He'd been holding on to her hand and now released it so that she could move through the line.

When she was out of earshot, Lucy said, "I read on the *Teen Scene* app that Marxma is now single. Just broke up with some musician."

"You're my new favorite person, Lucy," Chet said. "Because that is just what I wanted to hear."

The guests moved along. Four hundred people. The state dining room was full and the north lawn buzzed with guests being served in lavish heated tents. Henry noticed that, even with all those people, Chet kept glancing at Marxma as she talked and laughed. He also noticed that Marxma stayed within Chet's view.

Lucy must have noticed too. "I'm going to invite her to our table," she said.

Henry raised an eyebrow and Chet said, "If you ever want to become my sister, there's an opening."

"What if you have to invite Reylin too?" Henry asked. The two girls were chatting, sodas in hand, heads close together.

"Then I'll invite her too," Lucy said.

"Great," Henry mumbled.

"She can't be that bad," Lucy said.

"Can," Henry countered. "And is."

"Still worth it," Chet cut in.

The first course consisted of slivers of broccolini from the White House garden along with Virginia-grown truffles served in a creamy white sauce. Chet had squeezed himself between Reylin and Marxma and was peppering the star with questions about her films while Lucy somehow managed to carry on polite banter with Reylin, talking about the orchestra, the gowns, and the pink rosebuds that were the French president's favorite. Reylin was surprisingly polite in return, and soon they were chatting away about school.

It didn't take Henry too long to realize that he was the only one not talking to anyone, or being talked to. He tore into the food.

"So," Lucy was asking, "how do you two know each other?"

"Well," Marxma answered, "before Reylin's dad was a senator, he worked with my dad at a law firm in Nashville. They were partners, and our families did all sorts of things together. Then my dad changed jobs and moved to L.A. That's where I got into show business."

Henry wanted to be annoyed, to dislike her, but she really was incredibly nice, smiling at him just as much as she smiled at everybody else.

Reylin jumped in. She didn't even glance at Henry. "That's when we moved to Texas."

"Where Reylin became a computer whiz," Marxma said. "She's been doing summer courses at Texas A&M since she was seven."

Reylin laughed, and it didn't even sound fake when it was for Marxma. "We stayed friends all of these years," Reylin said. "Marxma is like my sister."

Henry expected Marxma to look embarrassed or annoyed, but instead she smiled warmly at Reylin.

"You guys must be old pros at these state dinners then," Chet said.

"Marxma's been to several," Reylin said. "But this is the first time we've had friends in *the family*."

Henry thought she emphasized those words a little too much.

"Maybe you can show us around sometime?" Reylin said.

Henry looked around desperately for some strawberries, so he could sneeze in someone's face, but Marxma jumped in. "Oh, that would be amazing. I've never been upstairs." She looked at Chet with her topaz-blue eyes and Henry knew that no number of sneezes was going to get him out of giving them a tour.

Just as dessert was served, Masticor walked up to his daughter. "This looks like a fun table." He smiled, then gestured to the man standing next to him. The man was tall and thin with a beard that smoothed out a rough face. "I'd like you all to meet Ambassador Fournier," Masticor said. Then to the ambassador, "My daughter's been learning a little French herself."

Reylin smiled, and said, "*Bonjour, monsieur. J'espére que vous vous aspergez.*" Only her accent was really heavy and instead of telling the ambassador she hoped he was enjoying himself, she'd accidentally said she hoped he was spraying himself.

The ambassador still smiled politely, and responded slowly in French, "Very well. *Merci.*" He looked around at the teens seated at the table. "And it's nice to meet all of you," the ambassador said in clipped, careful English.

Masticor leaned over and whispered something. The ambassador smiled and spoke to the group for a minute in quick French about Paris and the sights and attractions he enjoyed in D.C. He said his allergies had been horrific with the smog and that more people should ride bicycles. He talked about the French Embassy, only a few miles away on Embassy Row. He told Marxma she could visit any time day or night, which Henry thought was a little inappropriate.

Reylin looked like she might die. Henry was pretty sure she had no idea what the ambassador had said. With her fake smile plastered to her face and a hot blush rising from her neck, Henry almost felt sorry for her.

Anyone else speak French?" Masticor asked.

"Not me," Chet stated proudly.

"I wish," Marxma said.

Henry was shaking his head when Lucy blurted out, "Henry does. Also Spanish, Russian, Mandarin."

Henry shook his head harder. "A little, not good. I mean, just a few words in each."

"Ah, don't be shy," Marxma coaxed.

"Or humble," Lucy said, giving him a weird look. "He's really good."

"Wow, really?" Reylin said, staring icicles at her father.

Henry hesitated. His mother had reminded him before the dinner not to show off. But for the first time that night everyone at his table was looking at him—Reylin with an annoyed frown, Marxma with her beautiful smile, Lucy with a simple pride, even Chet with some expectation. Carefully, he started speaking—telling the French ambassador that he would like to go to Paris, that he would come visit the embassy sometime, and would love to swim in the pool. The ambassador nodded and laughed.

"He speaks perfectly," the ambassador said. "Like he was born and raised in Lourdes."

Everyone smiled. "Wow, that was amazing," Marxma said.

"You really can speak French," Reylin said. "I'm impressed."

"Do another," Lucy added.

Henry paused, glancing at his mother across the room, before switching to Russian. A few other ambassadors stopped and looked their direction.

The French ambassador waved them over and one began to speak with Henry. Henry went off about how his brother always hogged the bathroom and how it was nice to live in a place with so much extra plumbing for a change. A small cluster of dignitaries surrounded the group now.

Henry launched into Spanish. A Spanish ambassador stepped near and a few of the butlers stopped to watch. Soon Henry was chatting with both dignitaries and staff like they were old friends. A small, Hispanic maid wound her way over to them, but Henry barely glanced in her direction.

For the first time the whole night, Henry felt like he was the center of attention, like he was somebody that mattered. As he reached the peak of his performance, he caught the gaze of Masticor. Their eyes met and there was something in Masticor's look that was strangely...*satisfied*.

Henry stopped what he was doing almost as abruptly as he'd begun.

Masticor turned to the group of different ambassadors, jovial and animated. "Quite a bright future we've got at this table, don't you think?"

"*Oui*," the French ambassador replied, waving good-bye to the teens as the group of dignitaries dispersed, laughing and talking.

"That was amazing," Marxma said. "I've been to all those countries and can't speak a lick."

"It *was* amazing." Lucy smiled.

Henry wanted to smile back, but he felt odd. "I shouldn't have shown off."

"Whatever," Lucy replied. "Everyone enjoyed it."

Even Reylin nodded in agreement.

The teens went back to their dessert and Henry tried to shake off the slight unrest he felt. After all, he'd probably just imagined it—that look in Masticor's eyes, like he was a card shark who'd just seen you play your best hand.

———

Later that night as the East Room of the White House erupted with the music of V-Set Hover and then filled with the ballads of Dalia Lamb, the crowd of people danced, laughed, ate, and drank.

Chet was rocking out with Marxma while everyone else danced around them. Henry just shuffled. "I'm going to get a soda," he said to Lucy.

"Don't stress," she replied. "About the language thing. Everyone shows off. Look around. You've just got a really cool skill."

Henry took a deep breath. "Yeah, it just felt weird. Masticor was staring. And Mom's always telling me to try not to make a spectacle of my 'gift' at big parties like this." Henry held up his fingers in air quotes.

"Put the air quotes away," Lucy said. "It is a gift. And why does she want you to hide it? It's awesome."

"Who knows," Henry said. "She worries about everything. She's always fussing over privilege and that's the reason she gives for me not showing off. But sometimes I wonder if it's bigger than that. Did you know a few months ago, a bunch of politicians' kids got kidnapped? Then returned. It was really weird."

"Yeah actually, I did know that. I heard my parents whispering about it one night," Lucy said. "But when I asked they wouldn't tell me anything."

"My mom wouldn't even tell me the boys' names," Henry said.

"They're all boys?" Lucy asked.

"Yeah," Henry said. "And the names are hard to find online because they're minors and all, so you have to dig up info about the families and then look them up."

"Sounds like you've been digging," Lucy said.

Henry shrugged, trying to look casual. "It's a slow process. But I've found several of the names."

A waiter walked past them, carrying some type of crisps with meat in them. They smelled just like tacos.

"You know it was that night..." Henry began.

"What night?" Lucy said, her eyebrows dipping together.

Henry couldn't finish though, couldn't tell her what he wanted to. "The kidnappings happened that night I stayed after school with you for Spanish club."

"You're kidding," Lucy said. Then she laughed. "So I basically saved you from being kidnapped by a crazy extremist."

Henry opened his mouth, but the right words wouldn't come out. "Crazy *alien* extremist if you ask the internet."

"Even better," Lucy said. "And after this conversation, I definitely intend to ask the internet."

"You won't find much. Just a bunch of conspiracy theories."

"Sounds fun. Hey, remember that guy I liked?" Lucy said, still laughing. "He's got some other girlfriend now. So I'm glad to know it did *some* good to make you stay with me."

"Well…" Henry said, trying to shake off the panic that rose every time he tried to talk about that night, trying to untie his tongue. He couldn't. "…You learned Spanish too," he finished instead.

"Kind of, sort of," Lucy said. "Nothing like you."

"And we're back to me showing off," Henry said. "When all Mom wants me to do is lie low."

"Look, I get it with your mom, and it makes sense for her to be a little nervous with, well, everything that's happened, and could happen, to your family. But face it. You've got a really amazing talent. Sooner or later, people are going to notice."

Henry squirmed under her smile, thought about Masticor's face. "Hey, do you want a soda or something?"

"I'd rather have a dance," Lucy said, as the music shifted to a slow ballad. "Come on. Let's have some fun."

Henry took a deep breath and shook off the tension that had started crawling from his shoulders to his neck. "Do we get to hang out by the punch and eat cookies afterwards?"

Lucy snorted. "Of course. Wouldn't be much of a party if we didn't. Now come on."

Henry laughed and followed Lucy onto the floor. The

music was great. The food was excellent. Everything was beautiful.

The first Miller state dinner was a success.

———

Across the room, as Henry walked to the dance floor, a pair of eyes watched him. He wasn't much to look at. Nothing like expected. But the time had come, after hundreds of years of waiting. They could finally make a difference at the event.

The piercing eyes suddenly broke their stare, any dark thoughts masked by a quick turn and a slight shuffle.

Twelve

enry walked alongside Chet down the hall to their rooms, both of them on their phones, a habit their mother solidly hated.

Henry was trying to find the last few names from the night of the attack and Chet was texting someone.

It wasn't hard to guess who, especially since Chet wasn't vexting the message. He didn't want Henry to hear it. As Chet walked and texted, he also bounced a basketball.

"Mom's gonna freak if she sees you doing that," Henry said, his face in his phone.

"She's not gonna freak 'cause she's not gonna see it and no one's gonna tell her," Chet answered. "Right?"

"I'm not going to rat you out," Henry said. "But you never know where she'll pop out from. She has a gift, you know."

"It's all those years as a librarian," Chet said. "But I'm safe because she's in meetings all afternoon." Chet hit a button on his phone like he'd finally decided to send the message. "I think she's meeting with the curator right now."

"Lucky her."

But Chet was ignoring him, checking his phone every few seconds. Henry buried his own face back in his phone, scrolling through an article about a senator's kid from Mississippi as they walked near a long line of vases, each one on its own pedestal with a little plaque on it.

"Yes!" Chet said suddenly. "She said 'yes'!" He jumped up and slammed his basketball down like he was dunking it through an imaginary hoop.

Unfortunately, there was no hoop, no backboard, nothing except a row of antique vases.

Both boys watched like it was a slow motion horror show as the ball bounced up and hit one of the vases. The vase crashed from its stand, shattering into hundreds of pieces against the wall behind it, before falling to the floor in a cascade of crystalline tears.

Henry and Chet stood in complete silence, the basketball rolling the rest of the length of the hall, like it didn't have a care in the world. It stopped at a plush throw rug under a painting of Washington.

They heard the clamor from the staircase, Secret Service first, rushing into the second floor hall like a plague of locusts, and then the bright dress of their mother, followed closely by the drab brown of the curator.

"See you on the other side, man," Henry muttered to Chet as the curator's voice rose into a scream that rose into a wail that rose into the most impressive string of curses

Henry had ever heard. After that, the curator burst into a series of blubbering sobs.

Their mother wasn't too happy either.

The first lady marched both of them to her office, asking one of the Secret Service to contact the head usher for an impromptu meeting.

Henry sat to the left of Chet, who was positioned directly in front of their mother.

Behind them, the curator still cursed and cried, pacing back and forth in their mother's office.

The silver lining was that at this rate Henry wouldn't even need to mention the D+ he'd gotten on his last Bio test. In fact, at the rate the curator was going, Henry might not have to mention a single science grade for the rest of the year.

"Ms. Crossley," their mother said. "Can I get you something? A glass of water? Or...anything else?"

"No," the curator said, grinding her teeth so hard that Henry could hear the grit.

"Then please," their mother said, "have a seat." She gestured to the spot beside Chet. The curator remained standing, her face purple, beads of sweat melting into little rivulets down her temples.

Henry thought she might combust.

Until the head usher came in, calm as ever. He carried a drink of some sort in one hand and a small white pill in the other. "Madison, I'm so sorry," he said, pushing both things into the curator's hands, then taking the handkerchief from his pocket and handing it to her. "Let's get you a chair."

Henry rolled his eyes, which earned him a look from his mother that could have soured ice cream.

The chief usher helped the curator into a soft chair as far from Chet as possible.

"Okay," Henry's mother said. "Let's figure this out."

"Figure this out!" the curator shrieked. "Mrs. Miller, that was a 200-year-old vase. Such a thing can never be *figured out.* A vase like that can never be replaced. There is no amount of money, no favor to call in. It is simply gone."

"It is a terrible tragedy," their mother replied, and Henry could see in the wrinkled frown lines that shot down from her mouth that she really thought it was. "The White House is home to some of our country's most valuable artifacts." She glared at Chet. "But you are correct. We cannot bring it back, so it's up to us to figure out how to proceed from here. I would like you to remove any breakable items from any location on the second floor where we live." Under her breath she muttered, "Jackie Kennedy is probably rolling over in her grave."

"Including the Lincoln Bedroom?" Ms. Crossley asked, sniffling like that might actually be the bright side, looking first to Mrs. Miller and then to the chief usher.

"What is left in that room?" Mrs. Miller asked.

"The writing desk with a *signed* copy of the Gettysburg Address, and some of the larger furniture."

Henry's mother paused. "I hate to have it *all* removed from the Lincoln Bedroom," she said softly, then looked at

Henry. "I trust you not to abuse these pieces. Don't even touch them if you don't have to. Do you understand?"

Henry nodded. "I could change rooms—" he began, but his mother held up her hand.

The curator glared.

"Thank you Ms. Crossley," Mrs. Miller said, standing. "We appreciate all your efforts." she opened the door and politely escorted the curator from the room.

As soon as the door clicked shut, Mrs. Miller leaned her head against it, letting out a long sigh.

Henry couldn't help but notice how much more comfortable she was around the chief usher than the head curator.

Mrs. Miller straightened, returning to her desk. "Honestly, I was almost hoping she would resign."

Chet tried to smile and his mother cut it off. "Her behavior," she said, her voice rising slightly, "is no excuse for you. What were you thinking, bouncing a basketball down the hall?"

It was not a rhetorical question. Chet cleared his throat. "I was just distracted." He paused. "Sorry, Mom."

"Distracted?" Mrs. Miller said. "By what?"

Henry had a pretty good idea. And if his mother thought about it for four seconds, she would too. Chet had been vexting Marxma every ten minutes since the state dinner on Saturday. Even Mr. Keikiki must have noticed because he gave their mother a brief look.

She paused for a moment and then sighed. "Chet, I'm glad you, uh, enjoyed the state dinner so much. I know this transition has been hard. I know you miss Michigan and your friends and your team. I know it stinks to spend half your senior year in a totally new school. And it's great that you're finally meeting some new people. But a basketball through a row of freshly placed flowers? That's not okay. It hasn't been okay since you were three. You don't have to act like the president, but you don't get to act like a child, either."

She sank down into the seat at her desk and put her fingers to her temples. "It just so happens that I can't think of an appropriate punishment for breaking a centuries-old artifact. So I'm going to leave that to you. I expect an outline of your plan for restitution on my desk by Monday. Think Eagle Scout project. But bigger."

Chet sighed. "I *am* sorry, Mom. It was an accident."

"I know," his mother replied. "But you are still old enough to know that accidents are more likely to happen when you do dumb stuff. Now, go on. I need to talk to Henry."

Henry's head snapped up. He had assumed he was just here on a witness-only basis, and maybe so his mother wouldn't have to give the protect-the-White-House speech twice.

The door closed and his mother said, "Your principal, Ms. Smith, called me this morning about your biology test..."

Henry shrank down in his seat.

"I thought you said you and Lucy were studying for that test on Tuesday," his mother said.

Henry tried to shrink lower. They *had* studied. It's just that first he'd shown her the second floor and the Lincoln Bedroom, then the ghost book, which she'd refused to read. And of course, he'd had to show her the theater room, where they'd watched a movie, and the game room where Chet had been hanging out. All three of them had previewed the newest Monster Vice video game.

It had felt good to finally relax in the White House together. He and Chet had even started making some plans for turning the Solarium into an appropriately awesome man cave.

"All afternoon Tuesday," his mother was saying.

"Yeah, we didn't study quite the whole afternoon," Henry replied.

"But you did play the pre-release of Marxma Frey's new game, I see."

Henry gave his mother a look that he hoped seemed innocent.

"That's right, kiddo. The buck, as Harry Truman said, stops here." She pointed to herself. "All these people who bring you drinks and snacks and clean up your messes—they work, for the next four years, for me and your father. And I hope," she said, looking at the chief usher, "that they feel that we are doing our best to work for them." She turned back to Henry. "But you guys just get doted on and served. That's fine. Until I get a test with a D+ on it when I know you can do better."

Mr. Keikiki tried to give an encouraging smile, but when Henry looked at his mother, it didn't really look like encouragement was her main goal. "Do you know how many people apply to the Sidwell Friends School?" she asked.

"No, ma'am."

"10,562 every semester. And do you know how many kids get accepted?"

"No," Henry said.

"Only a handful each year. Sometimes there's not a spot at all. But you got a spot, didn't you?"

"Yes, ma'am," Henry said, looking down at his hands. "Do you need my punishment plan on your desk by Monday as well?"

For the first time since entering the office, his mother smiled. "Nope. I've got one for you."

Henry groaned inside. He hoped there were no White House frogs to dissect.

"You have a gift with languages, Henry. One you occasionally even show off." She paused. "Mr. Keikiki is from an island in the South Pacific. He speaks a challenging language only a small group of people know. He's going to teach it to you. And it won't be easy."

Mr. Keikiki smiled again—his broad white teeth like an empty canvas on his face. Henry realized he'd been smiling the whole time, and it annoyed him.

"What language?" Henry asked.

"It is called kee-dah-boos," he replied, "spelled K-i-r-i-b-a-t-i."

That was unusual, but probably no worse than Russian or Mandarin.

"I do not expect it would be something you would use

much, but I think you would enjoy having the ability to speak such a beautiful language. And I would be honored to teach you the language of my fathers." Mr. Keikiki leaned forward. Henry leaned back.

"Do you know," Mr. Keikiki said, "that only about 70,000 people in the world speak Kiribati, and you cannot learn it anywhere, except on the islands in the South Pacific?"

Henry opened his mouth to argue about the point of learning a useless language and wasting the chief usher's time. Then he glanced at his mother. In her eyes, he saw the look of a woman ready and willing to revoke dessert privileges for the entirety of his years at the White House. "Um, yes," Henry said. "Well, thank you. Do you think that, um…" Henry looked again at his mother. "Do you think that maybe Lucy could join me?"

"She is not my child and doesn't need to be included in your punishment. I doubt she brought home a D+ on her Biology test either."

Henry doubted it too. "I'm not sure she'd consider it a punishment."

He hoped so anyway. With a bunch of his afternoons and Saturday mornings now taken learning a barely-spoken language, Henry hoped Lucy would want to join in, at least to hang out.

Mr. Keikiki cut in, for the first time without a smile. "I am not sure it is the best idea. The language is very difficult and she would struggle."

"She's really smart," Henry said, pressing. "And with two of us, we could practice it together."

"Like biology?" his mother said.

"No," Henry replied quickly. "It'd be cool. A language we could speak to each other." It was way better than BFF necklaces.

Henry caught his mother giving a questioning look to the chief usher. Something about the look was strange. Like they'd been planning this, like it wasn't a spontaneous punishment after all.

Mr. Keikiki frowned and said, "She will have significant difficulty. The lessons might grow boring for her and I doubt she will stick with it." He paused, looking at Henry. "But if it will make it more pleasant and interesting for you, then I suppose she can try it for a while if she wants."

"Okay, we start next week," Henry's mother said. "The Solarium."

"But Chet wanted to make the Solarium into a man cave," Henry complained.

"Chet just broke a priceless artifact," his mother said. "I think the man cave will have to wait." Seeing Henry's face, she softened just a bit. "We'll see how fast you can learn this language *and* how quickly Chet can complete his own punishment. When you're both done, you two can man cave it up, however you like. I'll give the instructions to the chief usher myself."

Mr. Keikiki winked at Henry. When he did, the dagger-like scar on his lip moved down, as though slicing into his face.

Henry looked away, back to his mother. "Deal," he said, rolling his shoulders to release the tension he didn't realize he'd been holding.

He didn't know about Chet, but he was pretty sure the man cave could be his in two weeks or less. Languages were fun. Maybe his mother was hoping she could find a language hard enough or obscure enough to teach him a lesson, but the truth was that if she wanted to punish him, she should have made him dissect a frog.

Thirteen

Richard Masticor set the phone down, loosened his tie, and slipped off his shoes.

So far, President Miller had managed to overturn at least three of his party's bills and was in the process of making huge changes to the healthcare plan and budget, as well as expanding the space program in a futile attempt to search for resources on other planets.

Masticor could not care less.

What he needed from the president was so much bigger, so much further-reaching, so much more comprehensive than most of the American people could ever imagine. Which was good. He didn't want them imagining it—even if it would serve the greater good, even if it would save numberless concourses of people, even if it would supply energy for billions.

It certainly wouldn't hurt his lifestyle either.

He hung up his suit jacket and rested a hand on the neatly folded swimsuit and towel.

He needed the Americans bickering over penalties for lack of insurance. He needed the news articles about the pros and cons of programs at risk of being cut from the budget. He needed groups like The Ethereal threatening the political world.

He needed conspiracy theories, the Illuminati, Area 51, and every irritating and asinine comment on the internet.

The higher they escalated the crazy meter, the less obvious his sleight of hand became.

Masticor slid into his swim trunks and put on a robe. He'd have a glass of brandy sent down after Mannivera arrived to discuss their plans.

His source had gone to inspect Marine One. Everything was in tip-top shape. That was just what he needed—not a wire out of place, not a gauge loose, not a scratch to the paint.

He had his aides positioned where he needed them, his daughter and Marxma busy with their social lives, and his plans coded and ready.

Life couldn't have been better.

Masticor walked into the warm poolroom—the air sweet with chlorine and fresh flowers. He slipped out of his robe, stretched his arms, and dove in.

———

Henry ducked out of the Lincoln bedroom in his flannel pajamas and slippers.

He did not know why any dignitary or friend to the president would ever want to stay in the Lincoln Bedroom.

If you asked him, it was where the president should put his enemies. Not that anyone ever asked him anything. Except to learn a super obscure language for no apparent reason.

Well, if Henry was going to have to pay that price for his man cave in the Solarium, he was going to pay it quickly, and then make the most of his reward.

Tonight instead of just playing video games, he was going to map out some plans for the Solarium. They'd need a huge TV or two—maybe a screen along one wall, a couple of gaming systems, a sweet uVoice activation set up. And, most importantly, a couch that could be converted to a bed for him to sleep on. That way, he'd kill two birds with one stone: cool entertainment room on the one hand; non-creepy sleeping quarters on the other.

Henry tucked his alarm clock and a notepad under one arm and carried a bag of chips in the other. He left his phone in his room so if anyone checked his location, it would look like he was there, sleeping soundly.

Walking down the hall, he cast a glance back at his dark bedroom. The Lincoln Bedroom was begging to be ghost central. From the antique couches to the crown canopied bed to the dark wood of the vanity to the thick, golden drapes—tassels and all. He shuddered and opened his bag of chips, scooping out handfuls, eating as he walked.

Why didn't his mom just tell him to sleep at the cemetery? It would be less spooky. But, nope, she wanted him *close*. At least at night. During the day, she was too busy in meetings or throwing tea parties for important people to worry about his room accommodations.

Which is why the man cave would be perfect. They would do it sleek and modern, the opposite of the Lincoln Bedroom. He would even put a sparse metal bookshelf in. That would make his mom happy.

Henry paused on the thought, still standing in the hallway. For a moment, his mind flew back to Michigan—before the governor's mansion, before the presidential race, before the attack at the park, before life felt complicated.

He used to walk from his elementary school to the library where his mom had worked. He'd hang out there for a few hours, eating snacks, looking at picture books, and lounging around in the back room with stacks of books that needed to be shelved or repaired or logged into the computer.

Henry shook more chips into his hand, remembering his mother's desk at the library. He hadn't thought about it for ages.

It was there he'd found the stack of pictures—tucked under a pile of ancient overdue notices. He'd never talked to his mother about it, the dozens of pictures—nameless, dateless—bound together with an old rubber band. But he'd never forgotten them. And he never would.

A series of ultrasounds, followed by the saddest shots Henry had ever seen. A newborn baby—swaddled and blue-capped. Curled tight against his mother's white hospital gown.

In the first image, the baby had had blue fingernails, in the next, blue fingers, then gray arms and face. The color draining from the baby in each progressive image. His father holding the child, not even trying to smile for the camera, but gazing—love torn and grief stricken—at the faded baby.

It wasn't Chet. And it wasn't him. They had pictures galore in albums that sat like fat, brown sentinels on the shelves in the den. A wall of leather-bound protection against this thing his mother had hidden.

Henry crinkled up the top half of his chip bag, suddenly exhausted.

He remembered that when he'd reached the end of the stack of photographs, there had been no coffin, no funeral. The pictures had just ended. Gray child. Grief-bleached parents. Ghosts, all of them.

Henry looked back down the quiet hall. He was pretty sure the baby had been born somewhere between him and Chet—a blank space in the life his mother must have expected.

Henry didn't know much about babies. But he knew something about expectation. It was no wonder his mother wanted to keep Henry as close as possible with all the dangers that lurked around their family now. No wonder she still stared at children, falling into their bright, round eyes. No wonder she stressed over his health—worrying over what he ate, obsessing over him tripping and breaking a bone. No wonder she poured information into him. No wonder when he sucked that information up and tried to spout it out, she quieted him, as though to say, "Let's not be too brilliant. Brilliant things sometimes wash away."

Henry slipped into the East Bedroom with the huge TV and gaming system—the one the curator had told him about. He tried to shake off those pictures, that memory of the day in his mother's office.

He measured the TV and made a short list of games he'd like to add to the collection. He wandered to the couch and picked up the controller for the uPlay11.

His mother had asked the staff to hang a huge family picture above the couch. Looking at it now, Henry saw the empty spot between him and Chet—the hollow place that his mother covered with a huge smile. A smile like she'd never cried a day in her life.

Henry found that he suddenly wanted to take the picture down, but he couldn't. He couldn't remove the heavy frame bolted to the wall, couldn't remove the blank space between him and Chet, couldn't remove his mother's too-big smile, or the feeling that maybe he was a sad misfit consolation prize after the baby she'd wanted had died.

Henry flopped onto the couch. Didn't the White House have enough ghosts without him adding his own to the mix?

He checked his watch. It was almost midnight. And he had school tomorrow. He'd planned to play video games until he fell asleep. Lately, it had become his favorite routine, but tonight he stood up, went back into the hall, and unfolded the bag of chips, digging to the bottom for a handful.

Maybe when he was honest with himself, the reason the Lincoln Bedroom scared him so much was *because* his mother wanted him close.

There were just so many things to worry about here. So many things that had scared him since that first attack back in September: the impossible way he'd escaped, the fact that he hadn't managed that strength since then, the silences all around him—from his own sealed lips to his mother withholding information about the boys who were attacked, to the silence that surrounded the threat of The Ethereal, to the maids and ushers who padded through the house in the careful hush that framed presidential life.

The hall stretched quiet in front of him and it seemed darker than usual. Henry stopped shoving fistfuls of chips in his mouth. A draft blew through the hallway.

Case in point. Henry shivered and walked faster.

Tonight he'd head to the third floor to check out the Solarium, maybe measure the walls before heading back to bed, see if the staff had sent up both the Monster Vice games —the ones that had inspired two of Marxma's movies. Chet said she'd be working on the third one this summer.

Across the long hallway, Henry noticed something move behind a chair. He stopped and watched for a second. A dark shadow wiggled in the corner, black tail flicking out. "What the..." Henry muttered.

Then he heard a long "Meeeooooowwww."

He sighed in relief. A cat. It shouldn't have been here. Chet was allergic, but a cat was better than a rat. "Here, kitty kitty," he said, bending down and setting his bag of chips on the carpet. He made kissy noises at the dark figure crouched under the chair.

The cat stayed there, motionless, its eyes almost glowing in the dim light. Henry scowled. His mom had probably told the ushers to set the lights on low to save taxpayer dollars or something. Now, he could barely see.

Henry got up and walked slowly toward the cat, holding out a hand. The cat raised its hackles and when it did, it seemed to grow bigger.

Henry jerked his hand back, scooting away. The cat hissed. Its eyes glowed brighter, almost reddish. The cat looked the size of a dog, and Henry swore the lights around him dimmed further.

The cat slunk out from under the chair, toward him, baring its teeth, which looked old and yellow.

Henry looked to his right. There lay a long pole, used to help the maids dust the high ceilings. He grabbed it as the lights dimmed to near blackness and the cat's eyes glowed redder.

Henry lifted the pole and turned to the cat. It leapt at him. He swung at it, and the pole seemed to drift through empty air. Henry lost his balance, stumbling and landing on his back, just as the lights came back on.

The cat was gone.

His mother and father came up the stairs, laughing. They stopped when they saw Henry on his back, a crushed bag of chips peeking out from beneath him.

"Henry, what are you doing?" his mother asked.

"Um," he said, standing up. "I was going to check out some video games—"

"At this time of night," his mother cut in.

"Mom, listen," he said. "I saw a cat in the hall. A mean one. And Chet's allergic."

His dad glanced down the hall. "Well, it's gone now," he said.

"You sure you didn't imagine it in the shadows?" his mother asked.

"No, it was huge," Henry said. "With red eyes."

His parents exchanged a quick look.

"And speaking of shadows," Henry said. "Why'd you change the lights to be so dim here at night?"

"We didn..." his father began, but his mother cut him short.

"If there's a cat that got in somehow, we'd better find it. The last thing Chet needs is an allergy attack to make him hate this place more."

His dad sent a text. "Okay, they'll send someone up tomorrow to look around."

"Now back to bed," Henry's mother said, scooting him down the hall as his father followed.

"I need a glass of water," Henry croaked, dreading a night in the Lincoln Bedroom even more now.

"Someone will bring up a glass," his mother said. "Brush your teeth and get some rest. Looks like you've been staying up way too late."

"You don't believe me?" Henry asked suddenly. "About the cat?"

Another look between his parents.

"I believe you need to go to bed," his mother said. "We'll search for the cat in the morning." She gave him a big hug. "I'll get you a glass of water myself," she said. "Now, bed."

Henry climbed into the large canopy bed, trying to rationalize away the vanishing cat.

Just like he'd rationalized away the blackout at school. Just like he'd rationalized away the super-human strength he couldn't get back. But in that dark room, encased by bedposts and golden draperies, his reasonable explanations about lighting and adrenaline and stress weren't doing the trick.

Something wasn't right.

FOURTEEN

The president sat at the English oak Resolute desk in front of the large windows, between the American flag and the presidential flag. The Oval Office. It was where diplomats and dignitaries met with the president. Where Nixon had telephoned Apollo 11. Where John F. Kennedy had announced the Cuban Missile Crisis. A place for jubilation and disappointment, for announcements and secrets.

Today, the president sat, thumbing through a book featuring a garish cover of a clearly photo-shopped image. *Unveiled: The Paranormal White House*. Next to it sat two similar books. *White House Ghosts, Then and Now*; and the most recent edition of *Aliens and Apparitions: Secrets of the U.S. Capital*. The president flipped through, looking for references to White House cats, unusual ones.

Across from him sat another man, watching quietly, as though waiting was the one thing he'd been trained to do his entire life. His shoes and suit were impeccably neat, hair combed in one straight line to the side.

"They all say the same things," the president said. "National disasters, assassinations. The stock market crash in 1929. The shootings of Abraham Lincoln and JFK. All after the sighting of a cat. A black cat who grows in size." He looked to the man in front of him. "Have you seen it?"

"No," the dark man with a scar on his lip answered. "But then I have never been one whom disaster follows."

"You forgot the end of that sentence," the president said.

The other man raised his eyebrows.

"Until now," the president concluded. "You have never been one whom disaster follows *until now*."

"Yes, well," Mr. Keikiki said, a smile breaking across the dagger of his scar. "I'm honored to begin."

———

Henry caught up to his mom and Lucy as they were walking up to the Solarium. They were easy to find since his mom's voice was running on overdrive. "The third floor was not originally part of the White House. William Howard Taft had it built to create a sleeping porch—a cool place to spend hot nights. Truman added a kitchenette. The Kennedys held a small kindergarten class in the Solarium. Lucy Johnson hung out with her friends, and they had a soda fountain installed."

"Cool," Lucy said.

"But it's not all fun. Ronald Reagan recuperated in the

Solarium after he was shot. It's been used for many purposes over the years, as diverse as those living in the Residence."

Henry paused on the stairs, listening. His mom usually only went off on a facts spree when she was nervous. He knew Lucy wasn't making her nervous. What was? She rambled on about all the first children who'd snuck up to the roof from the Solarium—from Alice Roosevelt with her cigarettes to the Bush daughters and their boyfriends.

"You nervous about something, Mom?" Henry asked. "Or are you just trying to give Lucy ideas?" He swore Lucy almost blushed, but his mom just paused, then smiled. "Every inch of this house is fascinating. I guess I just get carried away."

True enough. Still, everything felt off. He wished he could talk to Lucy about it, but his mother was pushing them up to the Solarium where Mr. Keikiki waited, beaming as usual. Something about that frustrated Henry too—like the man was just a portrait and not a real person. A fact he seemed almost intent on proving.

The chief usher clicked his laptop shut and put an expensive pen into its case, which he then carefully placed in a small drawer. He had created a miniature office for himself in the sunny room: small table, several books standing upright, each spine flush with the other, held in by decorative, black bookends. He'd brought no knickknacks, souvenirs, or pictures; and good luck finding a speck of dust on any of his things.

For the first time, Henry looked at Mr. Keikiki closely. Suit starched and pressed to perfection, shoes that could have just come out of the box, and a blue square of handker-chief positioned in his lapel pocket as though glued in place. To look around was to think that Mr. Keikiki had never existed anywhere outside of the White House. In fact, if he didn't have the hum of an accent, the dark hair, or the white scar that bent into brown lips, Henry wouldn't have believed that he'd ever been more than a fixture in this place—his own brand of carefully preserved antique.

"Hello, children," Mr. Keikiki said, as they settled into the sunny room.

The windows allowed a nearly panoramic view of the grounds. Mr. Keikiki had set up a whiteboard in front of them. But that wasn't all. At the corner of every window in the room sat a small iron statue, and they were all connected to each other with a delicate iron chain. Some looked like tribal soldiers; others like princes; one wore a suit of ring armor, although the links appeared to be an assortment of stones and gems. It was the only statue that displayed any color and at its feet was an old woman, crouched in a bow.

Most of the statues depicted men, but among them, Henry noticed a pregnant queen, a slender cloaked figure who struck Henry as feminine, and—right next to the exit— a large figurine of a young girl looking down at an hourglass.

"I am delighted you would take the time to learn the language of my fathers," Mr. Keikiki said in that clip of an accent.

Lucy looked to Henry, then back at their new tutor and said, "We are too. Thank you for teaching us."

Henry sat, thinking about cats. He didn't say anything.

His mother cleared her throat and he looked up, then nodded at his new teacher. Behind him, he heard his mother sigh.

Mr. Keikiki just smiled and reached out a hand to Lucy. "Ms. Hawk, it is a pleasure to meet you."

Lucy beamed and Mr. Keikiki gestured for her to take a seat.

Henry twisted toward her, relieved the formalities were over, and the poofy leather chair squeaked. Lucy glanced at him, obviously trying not to laugh, and Henry couldn't help but smile back at her.

"Henry," Mr. Keikiki said. "I'm glad you're here. I think you'll be challenged by the language, and find it very interesting."

Henry wasn't so sure. They'd already been here for fifteen minutes and all they'd accomplished were a bunch of stuffy introductions in plain old English. *Welcome to the White House*, Henry thought. Important stuff going on all over the place and all everyone spent their time on was saying hello for as long as possible.

He must have been frowning or something because Lucy kicked his shin.

"Ow," Henry said, looking at her.

"Pardon," Mr. Keikiki said.

"Nothing," Henry mumbled.

Mr. Keikiki cleared his throat, and wrote letters on the board in black marker. "K-I-R-I-B-A-T-I. Pronounced kee-dah-boos. This is a language, not of sound so much as one of patterns. We must appreciate the patterns in the sounds, not the sounds themselves, which makes it more difficult." He paused. "From this point on, we will refer to it simply as The Language."

Beside him, Henry heard Lucy scratching in her notebook. It was going to be a long few weeks.

"I will begin our lesson," Mr. Keikiki said, "with a story of an ancient King. This king had a great treasure, and throughout the known world, his military might was unparalleled. One day some men from a nearby nation, not large enough to rival his own, came to admire the king. They heaped upon him great praise, gifts, and honor for his glory.

"The king, in his conceit, allowed these men into his treasure rooms, his armory, his hidden chambers, and counting rooms. They were thrilled by what they saw, and made great homage to the king. However, within a few years, the other nation—now grown stronger—returned. This time, having seen the might of the king, they decided to steal what he had shown them in his immodesty. They destroyed the king's armies, stole his treasure, and enslaved his children. The king, had he not put his greatness on display before his enemies, would have preserved his treasure, and his posterity." Mr. Keikiki tapped one of the statues—an old king who looked to the ground, his once-fine clothes shaped to look loose and ragged.

Lucy was writing feverishly. Henry pulled out his own notebook, and in letters small enough that Mr. Keikiki wouldn't see them, but big enough that Lucy could, he wrote, "Saw a black cat on the second floor last night. Something was off about it."

"Henry, Lucy," Mr. Keikiki said, looking at both of them in turn. "I would always encourage modesty, and with this language, you must realize this."

Henry tried to angle his notebook so Lucy would notice, but instead he felt like both Mr. Keikiki and his mother were staring at him. He looked up.

"There is something unique about the language," Mr. Keikiki continued. "Through its patterns and pulses you will be bound to a people, a very unique place, unlike those you have seen so far."

Henry pushed his notebook toward Lucy, but she ignored him.

Mr. Keikiki continued. "Listen as I give you a salutation."

Another salutation. Awesome. He really wanted to talk to Lucy, or head to his room and do some research about the missing politicians' sons, or alien abductions, or maybe mysterious monster cat sightings, but he was stuck here learning to say "Howdy" in a dying language.

And then Mr. Keikiki made a sound unlike anything Henry had ever heard. It was melodic with a series of noises that seemed to push into his skin. A beautiful sound, but also a confusing one. Henry had studied all sorts of languages from various cultures, and when he heard them, his mind had wrapped around them easily, unraveling the patterns. But this felt different.

Everything was quiet. Henry looked at Lucy, who was smiling like she had just heard a strange and wonderful symphony. In truth—the few words Mr. Keikiki had spoken did seem to hang in the air—tones that still quivered, drifting and diminishing like steam released from a pot.

Henry opened his mouth, trying to form something similar to that sound, but no noise came out. He couldn't even understand how his teacher had formed those sounds with his teeth and tongue.

Mr. Keikiki stood motionless. "Henry, are you ready to learn?"

"Yes," Henry said, looking at his teacher for real for the first time that day. "I am."

"Very good," Mr. Keikiki said. "All language gives us power to communicate. Some languages give us more than that."

FIFTEEN

enry fell into bed. He'd been practicing the new language almost all week and still could barely make a few basic sounds. His subconscious, however, must have been picking up on things because he'd begun dreaming it incessantly. So much that he wanted nothing more than to fall into a blank, soundless sleep.

Beside him, his clock ticked, the digital minutes flipping. 11:22. 11:23. 11:24. Henry sighed and rolled over. He propped himself up on his elbow. February 20th. He closed his eyes, hoping that when he opened them, it would be February 21st and the sun would be shining. Instead, a sharp ping hit the window.

Henry's eyes snapped open. 11:28. 11:29. He was about to settle back into his pillows when the clock flipped again. 5:00. Henry squinted, then reached over and shook the clock. It didn't change.

A small light came from the adjoining sitting room.

Sometimes he hated the automatic, timed lights in this place. Henry rubbed his eyes and threw his legs over the bed. He took a few steps toward the connecting room and stopped. Mary Todd glared down from her painting. Henry shuddered, groping along the wall, searching for a light switch in his own room when he heard...singing. The hum of a tune Henry had never heard before.

Henry froze. The voice was quiet, young. Tentatively, he stepped toward the room. Sitting on the floor was a boy, a little younger than Henry, hunched over some marbles. "Um," Henry said, relieved, but still weirded out. "What are you doing here?" The boy looked familiar and Henry tried to place his face. He was pretty sure he'd seen him around the White House before.

"I come to this room a lot," the boy replied.

"You haven't come here since I've been here, or I'm pretty sure I would have noticed," Henry replied.

The boy just shrugged and shot a marble. "Want to play?" he asked.

Henry yawned. "It's really late."

The boy shot another marble, and Henry paused, wondering if he should let security know about some kid. Henry took a step closer.

On the table next to the boy sat a small lamp that somehow managed to light up the entire room. Next to the lamp lay a bouquet of flowers. That was nothing unusual for the White House, but these flowers had a very particular smell—pleasant and strong.

Henry couldn't help but take a big whiff. The boy

looked up from his marbles. "Mignonette flowers. Nice, aren't they?"

"Sure," Henry said. "But—"

"The mignonette has such a persistent odor that even when cut, it's often used to cover up other unpleasant smells," the boy interrupted. "Although, of course, there is nothing in the President's Mansion that stinks." He gathered his marbles into a bag and stood up.

"Who are you?" Henry asked. "The florist's son or something?"

"Me?" The boy laughed as though he thought it was a stupid question. "I'm Will."

"Okay, Will," Henry said curtly. "Let me put it this way: What are you doing in my room?"

Will cocked his head to the side. "I spend a lot of time in the House. Because of my dad's job."

"Do you have security clearance?" Henry asked.

The boy looked at him like he was an idiot. "Of course."

Henry sighed. Will was short and thin. He wore dark slacks, a button-down white shirt, and black shoes with a buckle. Henry shook his head. There was so much staff at the White House, and everyone wanted to see the Lincoln bedroom.

Will walked into Henry's room without being invited, and stared at the Gettysburg Address. He touched it for a moment, then turned away. "You know what you're missing around here? Animals."

Henry tugged on his pajamas, making sure he was awake.

"Animals?" he asked, remembering the cat, the way his parents had acted.

"Yes, animals," Will said loudly.

With his malfunctioning clock, Henry wasn't sure what time it was, but outside it was dark and still. "You should be a little more quiet. Your dad could get in a lot of trouble if they know you were up here on the second floor at this time of night."

Will made a face that seemed to say *I doubt it*. But he lowered his voice. "Anyway, animals. Are there any around here? I mean, besides the rats. We've always had a problem with rats. Once, during Benjamin Harrison's presidency, they got ferrets to chase out the pests. Funny, huh?"

"Hilarious," Henry said.

"And Truman smelled something awful for days before crews had to smash in a wall and remove a dead rat that had snagged a hambone from the kitchen."

"Gross," Henry said.

"You have no idea," Will replied. "Once Barbara Bush was swimming in the pool, wearing a scuba mask, and a rat swam right up to her. George H.W. had to drown it. And then there was the time Barack Obama made a speech in the Rose Garden and a large rat was caught on camera, scampering past his feet."

Henry held up a hand. Will was definitely the eleven-year-old, male version of his mother, which was comforting in a weird kind of way, though Henry couldn't get a word in.

Will didn't seem to notice. "Most of the first families have had pets. The Obamas had Bo—a Portuguese Waterdog that was hypoallergenic. George H.W. Bush had a springer spaniel and his son George W. had one of the puppies. Amy Carter had a cat named Misty Malarky Ying Yang. President Johnson had beagles. But my favorite was Macaroni, a pony that Caroline Kennedy used to ride all over the southern lawn."

"Will," Henry cut in. "Have you ever seen a black cat around here?"

Will stopped abruptly. "No."

"A huge one?"

Will looked down, fingering the silver candlesticks next to the Gettysburg Address, then picking up the ghost book Henry had left there. "My mother says animals notice things people don't, that they can tell you things."

"Yeah, I guess they're more in tune with their instincts than we are."

"True," Will said, "but that's not really what I meant." He dog-eared a page in the book.

Henry opened his mouth to ask what he'd meant when the lights in the other room flickered.

"Well, I guess it's getting late; I'd better go."

"*Getting* late," Henry said.

Will nodded, not catching the sarcasm. "But I'll come back sometime. I know basically everything about the President's House."

"Yeah, I noticed." Henry smiled.

"Next time I'll show you some things."

Henry nodded, and Will set the ghost book down, walking back to the other room. "Good night, Henry."

"Night," Henry replied. "And would you hit that light on your way out?"

Will didn't reply, though he'd started to sing again. This time Henry recognized the tune, "Ring Around the Rosie," though Will had changed the words. *"Riding through the ether."* Then another phrase.

"Wait, what?" Henry said. But the light flipped off, leaving the room in perfect silence and perfect darkness just as the minute hand flipped over on Henry's alarm clock.

11:31.

Sixteen

Henry jerked awake, sun streaking through his room in offensively bright lines.

The song the boy had sung still pulsed through his mind to the melody of "Ring Around the Rosie." *Riding through the ether...* The boy had pronounced 'ether' with a short 'e,' not a long one as was usual.

And there was another part, another phrase—something he couldn't quite grab from his memory.

Henry rubbed his head, glancing at his clock. The time matched his phone.

"That was a dream, right?" he mumbled to himself, sliding into his slippers and making his way into the adjoining room.

The flowers were gone, or, well, were never there. But the dream must have been a vivid one because Henry felt like the scent of them lingered in the room.

Riding through the ether. Through the ether. The ether. Then what?

Stumbling back into his room past Mary Todd, he stopped at the desk to stand one of the candlesticks upright —the curator would pitch a fit if anything was out of place. And there, right by the desk, was a dark blue marble, swirling like the ocean.

Henry bent to pick it up, rubbed it between his fingertips. It grew warm from the friction, and he dropped it on the desk.

Riding through the ether. What a weird word. It meant the air.

A translation from the language he'd been learning tapped against his head, but he couldn't get the tones to line up.

He plunked onto his bed and opened his laptop, thinking about the boy from the dream. In that weird way of dreams, Henry was pretty sure the boy was someone he'd seen before in real life, here at the White House, though Henry couldn't place when or where.

Riding through the ether. Ether. Ethereal. Henry typed in the word as he'd done a million times before. "Wispy, floating, unstable."

He hummed the melody. *Riding through the ether. Da dada da da-da.* Something that rhymed with 'ether'—the boy's short pronunciation of ether. Feather, weather, leather, pressure, tether. Tether.

Henry stopped. He clicked open the window of the article he'd been reading the night before. The same type of article he'd been researching for the last month as he dug through information about the families of the kidnapped kids, looking for the names. The names of the boys.

Riding through the ether...

Nine boys kidnapped in September. Nine boys captured. *Tethered.*

Riding through the ether. The melody lilted against his brain, the words banging against his skull.

Nine boys in a tether.

Henry stopped. That was it.

Riding through the ether. Nine boys in a tether. Nine boys in a tether. Nine boys in a tether.

Nine boys kidnapped. Nine boys returned unharmed.

Nine. Not ten. One not taken. Him. Empowered, then de-voiced.

———

Henry pulled up the names of the nine other boys. None with a memory of what had happened. Everything swallowed up in a big, black hole.

A terrible thought crept in as Henry typed the names into his computer one by one. *Joe Jones. Benjamin Hamilton, Bishop Wiles.* What if he hadn't really fought back that night?

What if he had been taken, drugged, his memory altered? But what if it had affected him differently? What if, instead of forgetting, he had hallucinated, created a false reality for himself?

What if the power he'd thought he'd had had only been some trippy dream? *Harold Smith-Esparanza. Eli Coltraine, Matt Moore.*

Maybe it had made him a difficult kidnappee, and they'd dumped him back out of the car, not willing to take a risk with a kid who wasn't reacting right to the drug? Then he'd come to, gone home, been too confused to express himself, too altered to find the right words? *Hunter Sammons, Jonathan Patel, Gerome Owens.*

Henry paused on the last boy's name, something familiar to it.

He needed to talk to one of the other boys, needed to hear how it had felt for them. But none of the victims' families had made more than a formal statement. None of the boys themselves had said a word and all had deleted their social media accounts.

Gerome Owens. At the bottom of the search page, another man came up with the same name—a scientist studying unusual types of matter—gasses, dust from meteorites, strange substances that had come to Earth from space. He had a blog about it that he'd begun only last September, and a few pages into Henry's search, he noticed something else—a bit of a family feud. This man's sister wanted him to shut the blog down. Santana Owens. A senator from Virginia.

The light bulb clicked on. Gerome Owens. The kid in biology who had outscored Lucy.

A kidnapped kid who went to Sidwell Friends School.

SEVENTEEN

Henry flew through the doors of his school, determined to find Gerome before the first bell went off, when a woman's voice called after him, "Mr. Miller, may I see you for a moment in my office."

Henry felt like his feet hardened into blocks of ice. He mumbled a response, turning into the principal's office as Ms. Smith held the door for him. His security waited on a chair outside the office window.

Henry started to sweat. The last time he'd seen Ms. Smith up close, he had nearly blacked out, and it seemed like he was on track for a repeat performance. She laid a paper face down on her desk in front of him. He stared at it, unwilling to look into her face.

"Mr. Miller, please sit down," she said, straightening her suit and sitting at her desk.

He tumbled into the seat in front of her.

She pushed the paper toward him, lifting it. He felt his

breath thinning. "Well, Henry—" Her voice sounded far away. "—you had me kind of nervous when you first arrived. But..." She turned the paper over. "You're really starting to shine."

It took him a minute to process the words she had said. *Shine.* Henry looked down at the fat 'A' at the top of his latest biology test. He wasn't in trouble. His mother wouldn't have to sign him up for another impossible, obscure language class with a bizarre White House employee. He wouldn't be racked with even more strange dreams. His breath steadied.

"Thank you for working so hard to improve," Ms. Smith said.

Henry nodded.

She opened a file with several more papers. "I've also spoken to a few of your language teachers—both English and Japanese."

Henry waited, trying to peek into her folder.

"They are, to put it simply, blown away by your performance. Truly, you have a gift." She pulled out several papers and pulled up a uNote on her computer. "I'd like to recommend you for a summer linguistics program connected to Georgetown University. It would be an accelerated course of several different languages from several different regions of the world, ancient as well as modern. I've sent your parents the necessary paperwork, but wanted to inform you as well."

Henry didn't know what to say.

Ms. Smith smiled. "Every once in a while a student comes along with the potential to truly change the world. I like to give them all the opportunities possible to fulfill their potential."

"Thank you," Henry finally stuttered. "That would be really cool." He wasn't quite sure he wanted to do an accelerated college study. I mean, how much time over the summer would it take? But to be asked, to be recognized, it felt pretty amazing.

Ms. Smith shut the folder. "Henry, I'm curious. When did you know you were good at languages? When did it first manifest?"

Henry shrugged. "I don't remember. According to my mom, she bought one of those phonics programs when I was young, maybe two years old. I started reading within weeks."

"English?" she asked.

"Yes. But once I started reading, some of the picture books had Spanish words in them. And Mom says I started reading them too. Accent and all. She figured I didn't know what they meant, but I did. I could figure it out somehow."

"I see," Ms. Smith replied. "And your brother? Is he also good with languages?"

Henry smiled. "Truthfully, he's better at basketball. And a lot of other things. But no. It's kind of a standing joke that when Mom realized how good I was with the phonics that she tried it with Chet, too. But, um, it didn't work for him."

"And do you remember," Ms. Smith asked, her manicured fingers tented over her desk, "how you felt when those early languages came to you? I also am quick with languages, and I love cultures and history. But, to be honest, my skill level is not even close to yours."

Henry thought about it for a minute. "I don't really remember. I could just tell the words were different, and somehow they made sense to me. I kind of remember later when I was learning German. It was like a blanket moved off of a side of my brain, and the words were there waiting."

Ms. Smith smiled. "Well, your brother and I might have more in common then. It has definitely not been that way for me. More like hours of study, hours of practice, sometimes a special teacher." She touched the folder. "Have any languages ever given you a challenge, been more difficult to conquer?"

Henry paused for a moment, thinking of Kiribati. "There's an island one I've just started on with a tutor. It's tougher than most."

"Is it?" Ms. Smith said. "And can I ask which language?"

"Kiribati is what it's called. I'd honestly never heard of it."

"Nor have I actually," she said, smiling. "I'll have to look it up. Can you say something in it, let me hear it?"

Henry cleared his throat. "Actually, I'm still mastering the tones."

"Tones?" she said. "An island language with its own set of tones. Fascinating."

As she said it, Henry noticed something he hadn't before—the slightest touch of an accent—one Henry couldn't identify. He smiled to himself. Maybe Ms. Smith was better at languages than she let on.

"And where are you from?" he asked.

"Indianapolis," she said.

"Oh," Henry replied. "But I meant, where are you from originally?"

For the smallest moment she seemed to hold her breath, a slight crease forming on her forehead. "No one has ever asked me that before."

Henry cleared his throat. It didn't seem like she wanted to answer the question. "I'm sorry, I wasn't trying to snoop. It just kind of sounded like—"

Her slim fingers brushed the papers back into her folder, and the crease in her forehead went away. "Ah, but you are gifted. If you must know, I am from a place with many troubles." She looked up from the folder, her smile returning. "You are lucky to be where you are, Henry, and who you are. Luckier than you can know."

Henry blinked awkwardly; people kept saying that. He looked around the room, wondering how he could change the subject, when he noticed a large painting. "The Battle of Stalingrad," Henry said.

"Yes." Ms. Smith nodded. "European studies is where I began my education. And this battle is a fascinating event in European history." She opened her mouth, as though to go on, but Henry interrupted.

"Thousands of lives were lost," Henry said, unable to resist showing off just a bit.

Ms. Smith raised an eyebrow, obviously impressed that Henry was familiar with the battle. "Yes," she said, "but that battle turned the war. Because of it, generations were saved.

The Holocaust stopped. Children and families reunited. Allies made from countries that had been enemies."

Henry nodded. It was true. "But everything Stalin did seemed wrong—letting his people starve to encourage his troops to fight harder, forbidding the citizens to leave the city, executing any soldiers who lost ground."

"Stalin was definitely not Santa Claus," she replied. "War is a dirty business. The price was thousands of lives. But the prize, millions. One life for one thousand. In my mind, that's a pretty good trade."

One for one thousand. Something about that phrase sounded familiar to Henry, although he couldn't remember who had said it. He also couldn't really argue with the logic. But for some reason he found that he wanted to. "I just feel like there could have been a better way."

"Well, perhaps you can put that genius mind of yours to the task of solving some of these problems in the future. I did not realize that you were also so well-versed in history."

She stood, signaling the end of their conversation. "I look forward to seeing the great things you do in the future, Henry. It is one of the amazing privileges of someone in my position."

Henry found himself almost giddy from the compliment. His parents had always been positive, encouraging, kind. The first time he had come to his mother speaking German she had actually cried, pulling him close and murmuring, "Oh, Henry, you are something special." Although in the next breath, she had told him, "Hold your gift close; use it well. Remember it's not just a party trick, not something to show off."

Henry knew he wasn't learning all these things just to impress ambassadors at a party, but he also wondered why they didn't want him to have a little bit of public credit for the things he could do. In fact, it seemed that rather than gushing over his abilities like Ms. Smith just had, they purposefully avoided bringing any attention to them. Sometimes it seemed they would have preferred it if Henry had just gone *un*-noticed.

Henry floated out of the office, the words from dozens of languages tumbling happily and neatly through his mind.

Then Gerome Owens walked through the cafeteria door.

The words stopped.

Nine boys in a tether.

Henry pushed himself forward.

———

"Gerome, right?" Henry said, sitting down beside the boy at one of the tables in the commons area. His security settled nearby, and Henry noticed that Gerome also had a security guard a table over. "I'm Henry."

Gerome looked up, a little surprised, and nodded. "Yeah, I know. The president's son."

"Yup," Henry said. "And you're the whiz in my biology class."

"Yeah, science kind of runs in my family." He tipped his head toward Lucy, who was helping another girl with her homework a few tables over. "I think your friend kind of hates me for it though."

"Lucy?" Henry asked. "Naw."

Gerome kept staring at Lucy.

"I mean, don't get me wrong," Henry said. "She definitely wants to knock you down so she can rise up as science queen, but that's a lot different than hate."

"How different?" Gerome asked, looking at Henry with a bit of a smile. "She's pretty hot."

"Lucy?" Henry asked again, as though he'd never thought about it.

"Seriously, dude, you're not blind and I don't think you're gay, so you've probably noticed. Anyway, is she dating anybody?"

This was not going the right direction. "Um, no," Henry said.

"Do you want to date her?" he asked.

"Lucy, no. We're just friends."

"Okay," Gerome said. "I think you're nuts, but whatever, I'll take it."

"Hey, um," Henry said, trying to steer the conversation back to, well, anywhere but where it had gone. "Listen, I was googling some stuff online and I saw this crazy thing."

Gerome got quiet and looked away from Lucy, straight at Henry. "I'm not really online much, dude."

"Yeah," Henry said. "I *know*."

Gerome sighed and Henry lowered his voice. "Listen, I'm just... Well, I just... My dad got shot at on his first day in office and they think it might be the same group and...can I just..."

"Yeah, man, I get it. Ask away. But don't expect me to be able to answer much. It's all a weird blur—not even a blur actually, just a big black spot in my brain."

"So they drugged you? Whoever it was."

"That's what they tell me, us."

Henry tipped his head to the side. "What do you mean?"

"I mean," Gerome said, "that everyone told us we must have been drugged. But when they took us to the hospital and tested us, nothing showed up in our systems—any of us. They think it was some type of experimental drug that vanishes from your system almost immediately."

"Whoa," Henry said.

The boy nodded, then looked away.

"But you don't think that?"

"I don't think anything. My mind was completely wiped. The last thing I remember was a dude in black, pulling me into a car. Tinted windows. Black. Everywhere. In my memory it feels like even the air went black, billowing beside me, in front of me. Just clouds of darkness."

"A cloud?" Henry asked.

Gerome squinted, remembering. "A cloud of darkness, like the form of a person in a dark cloak. I guess that was the drug speaking, maybe even the drug itself if it was a gas. Who knows? Not me. Because the next thing I remember is waking up in the park with the other guys, our wrists and ankles wrapped in duct tape."

"I'm sorry," Henry said. "That sucks."

"I guess," Gerome said. "Truth is, it could have been a whole lot worse."

"Got that right," Henry said. They both paused for a moment. "And you didn't have any hallucinations, any after effects?"

Gerome tapped a stylus on his uNote. "Believe me when I say, it gave me absolutely nothing. It's like I fell asleep and woke up a minute later. But two whole days had passed. And, no, I haven't had any effects since." He stopped talking.

"But you don't think it was a drug? What else could it have been?"

"I guess that's the golden question," Gerome said. "And it doesn't have an answer. Which means it was a drug. An experimental drug that vanishes very quickly. The problem is that there's no drug that can do that, not a single substance or combination of substances found on this planet."

Henry stared at him. That last phrase. The blogger studying strange elements. Science in the family. "You think it came from something not found on Earth?"

"I didn't say that; it'd sound crazy," Gerome said. "And it is most imperative that I not sound crazy."

Henry cocked an eyebrow at him. "Your uncle?"

Gerome looked at him. "Did your homework, huh?"

"You have the same name," Henry said.

"The thing is, if it's not from an element or combination of substances found on Earth, then what could it have been? Science is wide. Politics isn't."

"Got that right," Henry said again.

"So you got drugged by some, uh, space dust," Henry said.

Gerome gave him a look.

"No judgment," Henry said. "Science is wide. But then, why? Why all the trouble and why'd they let you go?"

"Another golden question," Gerome said.

"And?" Henry prodded.

Gerome leaned in. "You want to know what I think? I think they got the wrong guys. Whatever they did, they did it wrong, had to abandon ship, maybe hatch a new plot."

He stopped for a minute, took a breath. "You know what else, I'm happy they doped us up on their crazy space juice because it meant when the time came, they could give us back. No harm. No foul. Whatever they want, it's something specific. And I'm glad I wasn't it."

Eighteen

When Henry got home, he went straight to his mother's office. She had known about the kidnappings. How much had she known? How much would she tell him?

Lately, it felt like not much. Maybe that was part of being the president's wife, but Henry didn't like it.

He barreled into the office, but his mother wasn't there. Soft music played and he padded over to her desk and plunked down in her chair.

She definitely wasn't Mr. Keikiki. She had a thousand little succulents along her desk and windowsill, some of them yellow and withered—looking as neglected as Henry felt. Papers splayed across her desk in messy piles of various sizes, her glasses sitting on top of a square envelope with a blue wax seal.

But right at the center she'd cleared a little space, and in that space sat the letter from Ms. Smith, along with a polite decline printed on letterhead paper.

The doorknob turned just as Henry picked it up.

His mother jumped when she opened the door. "Henry," she said, startled. "I thought I'd locked that door. How was school?"

Henry shook his head, unable to answer the question. He held up the paper she had typed. "Why?"

She shut the door softly and Henry heard the click of the lock. Walking toward the desk, she took the paper from him and scanned the first few lines, her face creasing. "Because I won't have you losing your childhood to overly competitive pursuits."

"It'd look great on my resume."

"As will a million other things that you can do when you're a little bit older." She sat down in the chair opposite him—the chair he usually sat in when he was in trouble.

"What things?" Henry asked, waving the paper. "Because it kind of feels like any time I get an opportunity to do something great with my languages, you stop me."

His mother flinched. "You'll do more great things than you can even imagine. My job is to give you a childhood."

"And a future," Henry said.

"The future is for you to give, Henry," she said, gazing at him with those blue, blue eyes. "Or not. I give you a past to draw from, a present to hold onto. For just a little longer."

Henry hadn't really wanted to do the summer program, but now it felt like the most important thing in the world. "I want to do it," he said.

"Maybe next summer," she said, sitting up straighter, as though she was remembering she was the parent.

Henry crumpled the paper and held it in his fist. "That's not even really what I came to talk to you about, but come on, Mom. You can't keep me young forever. You can't keep me here forever. Look, I know you want to protect me and hold me close and everything. I know you've—" Henry stopped, stumbling for the right words. "—I know you've lost things, but at some point, you've got to let me spread my wings a little."

A sad smile cracked her lips. "At some point, they'll burst open no matter what I do. That's why I hold you. Henry, I know you think you know things, but—" She leaned forward, not breaking their gaze.

Henry stared at her in a challenge. "But what? Who kidnapped those kids? Who shot at us? What are they after?"

"What are they after, Henry?" Her voice hung deep, still. "Everything. They're after everything. And so I hold it close. As close as I can. For a few more years. My everything. Our everything."

———

Henry flopped onto the couch in the Lincoln bedroom. He hadn't been able to get anything more out of his mom and had stomped out of her office, slamming the door behind him. Maybe not his best choice ever.

Just as he burrowed into the couch for a nap, Chet barged in.

Henry didn't even turn to look at him.

"Hey," his brother said. "You look…"

"Shut up," Henry snapped. "And I'm not going to that stupid party tonight." Chet had been trying to talk him into it all week. So clearly if his mother wanted to keep Henry from potentially dangerous influences, she should start with her oldest son, not some nerd camp in Georgetown.

"Whoa. What's up with you?"

"Mom." It was all he said.

"Really, bro. She lets you get away with just about everything most of the time. I mean, what'd she do?"

"It's what she won't do."

"So, chocolate cake. Did she take dessert away?"

Henry didn't reply.

"Hey, hey. Sorry, bro, just trying to lighten it up. What was it you wanted to do that she so cruelly ripped from your grasp?"

"It's not just what she won't let me *do*," Henry said. "Although that's annoying too. It's that when I have questions about stuff, she just won't…"

Chet picked up the crumpled paper from Ms. Smith about the language camp and started scanning it. "Wait, let me get this straight," Chet said. "You are sulking on the couch because our mother told you you *couldn't* go to school all summer."

"I mean, that's part of it, but it's way more complicated than that," Henry muttered into the couch.

"Okaaaayyy."

Henry sat up. "Look, I didn't expect you to understand. Any of it."

"And I don't. Because Mom *is* willing to let you go to the party of the year tonight and you've told me all week you won't. Tons of celebrities, musicians—"

"—Reylin," Henry cut in, trying to end the conversation. "Do I really look like I'm in the mood for Reylin tonight?"

"Right. Because you're bummed over some dork camp. Still trying to wrap my brain around that. But Reylin is just one of the many, many girls who will be at this party."

"She's still enough to make me not want to go."

"Dude," Chet said. "Just come."

"Why do you even care?" Henry snapped. "I just want to stay and relax and not think about anything and watch *Monster Vice* in the theater room with Lucy."

Chet ran a hand through his hair. "Just bring Lucy." Then she can hang with the actual star of *Monster Vice*."

"I don't want to," Henry said again. "I want to stay here. And watch a movie with Lucy. And unlimited popcorn. And most importantly—no Reylin. I'm not going." Henry folded his arms over his chest.

Chet looked him straight in the eyes. "Come on. Reylin's not so bad. She's not nearly as skeezy as her dad. She doesn't even like him; you can tell by those looks she's always giving him. You two just got off to a rocky start."

Henry stared at him, not speaking.

Chet sighed. "Okay, what can I give you to get you to come?" He pulled out his wallet.

"Seriously?" Henry said. Then squinted at his brother. "And why? Why are you willing to pay me instead of just going on your own?"

Chet sighed. "Because Marxma wants a picture with the *first brothers* and I told her I'd bring you."

Henry sat up on the Lincoln couch. "You're kidding?" He was surprised that Marxma had bothered to notice him at all, especially with Chet around. "Marxma. As in Marxma Frey, movie star of the universe, wants me to come. Not just you."

"I mean, she definitely wants me to come."

"Right. Too. But Marxma wants me to come just as much as she wants you to come."

"Don't know that I'd say *that*," Chet said.

"Well, maybe you should," Henry said, finally smiling. "It might convince me to go."

Chet looked at the ceiling. "She does want you to come a lot," he began. "She seriously will *not* let it drop."

"Keep talking," Henry said.

"She called you 'adorable,'" Chet continued, the slightest hint of a grin tugging at his mouth.

Henry shrugged. "Adorable and dashingly hot are pretty much the same thing to girls, right?"

"Riiiight," Chet said.

"So I go to this party, hang with you and Marxma, model for a few pictures, give Mom a full report of the goings on once we get home." Henry said, enjoying the look on Chet's face. "Why didn't you just say so? That's better than what money can buy anyway. Might even be better than dork camp."

"So you're coming?" Chet asked.

"Sure," Henry said. "I can't wait to follow you and Marxma around, squeeze between you on the couch, ask you to bring me drinks. And cookies. Some things are priceless."

Chet shook his head and started to put away his wallet.

"Well, almost priceless." Henry held out his hand. "We'll call it even at $50."

"You're an extortionist," Chet said, plunking the cash into Henry's palm.

"You haven't even heard my terms and conditions."

Chet folded his arms. "I'm starting to think it might be a better choice to invite Marxma over for tea with Mom."

"Probably," Henry said. "But Marxma won't want to miss the Masticors' party."

"True," Chet said.

"So, terms," Henry continued. "You get me whatever food I want when I want it. You position me as far away from Reylin as possible or I'm telling Mom you ditched me to go make out with Marxma."

Chet raised an eyebrow.

"And," Henry continued. "You introduce me to as many hot girls as possible, and say awesome things about me."

"Aren't you bringing Lucy?" Chet asked.

"Yeah, why?" Henry said.

"No reason," Chet said, leaning back.

"What?" Henry said. "She's just a friend."

Chet shrugged. "Okay, whatever."

"You can introduce Lucy to hot guys too, if it makes you feel better," Henry said.

"It's not *my* feelings I'm worried about," Chet said, tucking his phone, wallet, and a pack of gum into his pocket.

"Whatever," Henry said. "Maybe I should just stay home." He turned to go out of the room.

"Alright, alright," Chet said. "I'm sorry. Lots of cookies. No Reylin. And hot girls. I agree to your terms. Now change your shirt, vext Lucy, and let's go."

Chet threw on a jacket and grabbed the bag with his swim gear.

"What's wrong with my shirt?" Henry asked.

"Did Mom buy it for school?" Chet asked.

"Fine," Henry mumbled. "I'll change."

Nineteen

Henry, Chet, and Lucy showed up at the Masticor's mansion in the Beast. When it drove away, two Secret Service agents stayed behind, but Henry couldn't help but feel a little naked without it.

He'd never been to the Masticor mansion and it was huge, Victorian, and terrifying.

Masticor and Reylin stood near the entrance, greeting people as they came in, though even Henry noticed that there seemed to be a little tension between the two of them. Neither would look at the other. They just stood by the door with their trademark plastic smiles, talking to guests as though the other person wasn't there.

Behind Masticor, Henry noticed a tall, blond woman dressed in an airy white dress. "Ms. Smith," Henry whispered under his breath to Lucy.

"Interesting," Lucy murmured back. "Do you think our principal and Masticor are, like, an item or something?"

Before Henry could reply, a shrill voice rang out. "Henry! Lucy!" Reylin stepped forward, taking their hands in each of hers. "I'm so glad you came."

"Thank you," Lucy said as Henry pulled his hand back.

"Pool's down the hall and to the left," Masticor added. "You kids have fun."

They walked down the hall, their Secret Service agents trailing at a respectful distance behind them.

"Chet!" Marxma's voice lilted through the gray-tiled entrance. She walked up to him in a cut-out swim top with a short sarong wrapped around her waist. Her legs were long and brown, her hair wet. Henry felt like his tongue was stuck to the top of his mouth. No wonder Chet had been willing to pay him to come. This was going to be the best babysitting gig ever.

"Come on through here," Marxma said, her Tennessee drawl just as mesmerizing as her legs.

Chet took Marxma's hand as Henry and Lucy fell in behind them. "You look great," Chet said, leaning closer.

"Thanks," she whispered back. It was so normal Henry found himself staring again.

"She's really nice," Lucy whispered. "Also, you're blushing."

"No, I'm not," Henry replied. "It's just so hot in here."

"It's not," she said, smiling.

When they got to the indoor pool area, people had crammed themselves into every corner. Chet was right. A lot of them were famous. A group of kids from the Pixie

Channel sat in the hot tub, while two singers from Street Beebees talked near the food table, wearing only bikinis.

"That's Marxma's ex," Lucy whispered, pointing to a guy in the corner.

"The plot thickens," Henry replied.

"Not really," Lucy said. "She doesn't even seem to notice him. Or, at least, she's no different with him than anyone else. She's not even being extra clingy with Chet, not that he would mind. Anyway, if she was, I'd think she was trying to make her ex jealous. But she's not. It's cool."

Henry shrugged.

"You're blushing again," Lucy said. "Bummer—all those fair-skinned, European genes. They make it so I can read you like a book."

"You can't read me like a book," Henry said, starting to feel sweaty and itchy and annoyed.

"Right," Lucy said. "I can read you like a boy. Even easier."

Henry wanted to argue, but there were a lot of girls in swimsuits standing around. And his face did feel really hot. He tore off his shirt and stuffed it into his bag. "Let's dive in."

At that moment, Masticor came up and put a hand on Henry's bare shoulder. He said something, but Henry didn't hear it. For a second, he saw a flash—the red sky, the flat dry earth. No mansion, no water. Just dust. Dust like electrons, carrying so much energy, so much power...

Henry pulled away. "I'm sorry," he said. "I feel a little lightheaded. Is there...could I get a drink?" Did something happen when he got overheated? Did his blood pressure shoot up, giving him these weird mini-hallucinations? The same thing had happened the first day of school. Some type of waking dream.

Lucy was staring at him, her eyebrows bent together in concern, but when Henry looked at Masticor, the senator was smiling. He motioned to a butler, who brought an iced glass with pineapple floating on top. "I'll adjust the temperature," Masticor said. "The pool room can get a little hot."

All around him kids were laughing and someone got thrown, squealing, into the pool. The sounds floated to Henry as he toweled off his face.

"Thanks," Henry said, handing the towel to the butler. "I'm fine now." He got up and went to the buffet table, Lucy trailing after.

"Henry," Lucy said. "Are you okay?" She handed him a cool cloth that she'd dipped into the pool.

"Yeah, I'm fine. I just got really overheated. You know—hot girls in a hot room. Read me like a book."

Lucy's face seemed to thin out and she looked down. "Henry, I'm sorry. It was just a joke."

"I know," Henry said, grabbing another drink. "And I'm being a jerk." He looked at Lucy's face and softened. "I'm sorry. That guy just creeps me out. And lately when I get really hot or uncomfortable, I just get these weird—" Henry waved his arm. "—spells."

Lucy nodded. On the other side of the room, Masticor was talking with some of the teens near Reylin.

"He did try to help, though," Lucy said.

Henry shrugged, wiping his forehead with the wet cloth.

They watched Masticor, who was now talking with Reylin, their voices tight. A few kids had stopped to stare.

"Maybe we should get in the water," Lucy said.

Masticor's face was angry now, and Reylin looked like she was almost in tears. All at once she spun on her heels, stomping out of the room, swiping at her eyes.

Masticor whispered something to a DJ, who turned the music up.

Kids bent their heads together, whispering. Henry scanned the room for Chet and Marxma. But they were gone. "I lost them," Henry said as they made their way to the pool.

"Who?" Lucy asked, sticking her toe in the water.

"Chet and Marxma."

Lucy shrugged. "You weren't really going to follow them around all night, were you?" She waded down the steps into the pool.

Henry smiled. "Yeah, kinda." He sat by the side, dangling his legs in the water.

"You're the worst," Lucy said, and splashed Henry in the face. He jumped in the water and dunked her. She came up laughing.

"I'm the worst, am I?" Henry said, acting like he'd dunk her again. "I think that award needs to go to Reylin. What do you think they were arguing about anyway? She probably got the gold bonds cut out of her weekly allowance."

"Oh, come on, Henry, she's not that bad."

"Of course she is."

Lucy rolled her eyes and pulled herself up on the side of the pool. "She really isn't. We got paired together for our computer science project, and the truth is that she's been really nice. She's kind of a genius with code." Lucy glanced away for a second. "She's even helped me a couple of times with my part of the assignment when I got stuck. Which is more than I can say for most of the group project partners I've had."

Henry held his breath and let himself sink into the water. He didn't want to talk about Reylin. He shouldn't have brought it up.

When he came up, Lucy said, "Look, I know you don't like her and there's a lot of bad blood between your dads. Let's just agree that sometimes she can be okay-ish, and at least she's not her dad."

Henry let himself sink again, which was his way of saying fine, whatever. Lucy must have gotten it. They spent the next hour playing, eating, and talking. They met two of the stars from "Dragons and Divas" and the lead guitarist from Metal XT. They drank so many slushed drinks that Lucy started to shiver.

"There's a sauna down the hall, babe," one of the Divas stars said. "Go warm up."

Ms. Smith entered the pool area as they grabbed towels. "Heading out?" she asked.

"Trying to find the sauna," Lucy replied, looking to the hallway, which branched both left and right. "Do you know which way it is?"

"I believe it's that way, dear," Ms. Smith said, pointing

left. "Although this place is so huge. I'll send someone to look for you if you don't come back." She winked and turned to her phone, typing a quick message.

Henry and Lucy thanked her and headed down the long corridor, shadowed by Henry's security detail.

Lucy's hair fell straight down her back in a sheet of black, even more impressive than Marxma's.

"Your hair is so long, Lucy," Henry said, reaching out to touch it.

"Yup," Lucy said, a little distracted. "Do you think we're going the right way? I don't see anybody else."

Henry looked up. He hadn't really noticed, but it was true. "Maybe not," he said, turning around to look. His security guy was a ways behind them, walking slowly and looking bored. Henry and Lucy walked a few steps farther when they heard a small sound.

"Someone's crying," Lucy said.

Down the hall, they saw a person, sitting in the corner, head bent down, sniffling.

Henry was about to take Lucy's arm to lead her away, but she was already walking toward the person. "Hey, are you okay?"

Henry trotted after her.

The girl looked up and when she did, Henry stopped. Makeup smudged, hair a mess.

It was Reylin.

Lucy seemed a little surprised too. She took a small step back. "Oh, hey. Are you okay?"

Reylin didn't look okay. She stared at the two of them like she was haunted and then started crying again.

"I mean, we can go," Henry said, grabbing Lucy's wrist.

"No," Reylin mumbled. "Stay...I..." She started to cry again and then looked around the hall.

Henry looked nervously down the hall at his security guy who hung back, giving them their space and leaning against the wall.

This crying stuff was not his territory, and Henry didn't even like Reylin. He was way out of his league.

"My dad's just—" Reylin started again, and then lowered her voice. "—I don't know. He got himself tangled up with some things."

She sniffled and Lucy put a hand on her shoulder, looking to Henry like she was asking for help.

He shrugged.

"Earlier I was on his computer..." Reylin started blubbering again, "which he told me never to do. But..."

"But what?" Lucy asked.

"This is crazy," Reylin said. "But I...I found something."

"Um," Lucy said. "Do you want to tell us what? Or is it, like, personal?"

Henry looked at them. Clearly, Reylin had found some scandal about her dad.

"It's not personal," Reylin whispered. She took a deep breath, glancing down the hall. "It's about Henry's dad."

He narrowed his eyes. "What? What did you find?"

"Look, don't freak out. I mean, maybe I misunderstood or something. But I just...on my dad's computer—"

"Your dad?!?" Henry growled. "What did he do?"

Reylin glared at him. "Listen, he's not involved. But this group, they have some information on my dad. I was trying to dig into that—I'm really good with computers, so I was tracking their internet activity—and I found something else. Something worse."

"About my dad?" Henry asked.

"Not *about* him," Reylin said. "Well, not exactly."

"What do you mean?" Lucy asked. "And did you hack into someone's computer system?"

"I'm *good* with computers."

"At hacking?!?" Lucy said, her voice rising.

"Look. I just...found something, something that's off."

"Off?" Henry asked.

"Well, wrong," Reylin said.

"Wrong?" Lucy said. "If President Miller is in danger, you've got to report it, no matter how you found it. You—"

"No," Reylin said, her voice turning to a sharp whisper. "That's part of the problem. They...If they know someone knows, they'll change the plan. But if—" She stopped again and wiped her nose on her towel.

"Plan?" Henry asked. "What plan?"

"Just listen," Reylin said. "There's this plan. Against the president."

"You've got to report it," Lucy said, turning in the direction of Henry's security.

"No, don't." Reylin grabbed her arm. "Listen. If someone outside of their circle finds out and reports it, The Ethereal will just change the plan."

The sentences jumbled in Henry's head, leaving only one word dangling in front of him. *Ethereal.* This was a plan of The Ethereal.

Lucy practically pushed Henry to the side. "What did you read?" she asked Reylin.

Reylin took a deep breath, looking down the hall, and spoke quietly. "Well, you know Marine One?"

They both nodded.

"The whole fleet needs updates, and Congress is funding a new fleet of helicopters that will be ready this summer, but for now they're vulnerable."

"Vulnerable to what?" Henry asked. His dad flew in that helicopter all the time.

"Something called EMP."

"What's that?" Henry asked.

"Electromagnetic pulse," Lucy answered before Reylin could.

"Which means?" Henry said.

"It's created by an electromagnetic burst in the proximity of the device," Lucy said, spinning her pearl ring around and around like she did when she was thinking. "The burst changes the electric and magnetic fields, causing damaging current and voltage surges."

Henry and Reylin both stared. "Which means?" Henry said.

"Which means if a helicopter is in the air when an EMP happens, all its controls will be disabled, and it will crash."

"Yes," Reylin said. "That's what they were talking about —crashing Marine One."

Henry looked like he was about to punch something. "But how would we even find an EMP device?" Henry asked. "What would it even look like?"

"I don't know exactly," Reylin said. "But maybe I can find out more. I really am good with computers."

Henry opened his mouth to say he didn't want her help, but Lucy cut him off. "That'd be great, Reylin," she said.

Henry glared. "We don't need help later. We need to know what to do right now, where to start, where to look."

"Well," Reylin said, leaning in, then taking a deep breath. "I found a name, and I think it's a clue."

"The name of one of the people plotting this?" Lucy asked.

"No," Reylin said, her lips a straight, pale line. "The name of somebody who's already dead."

TWENTY

here are no portraits of Mr. Burnes.

Henry read the sentence over and over again. They were in the Solarium looking for a guy who'd been dead for over 200 years.

He was sure he'd heard the name Mr. Burnes before, but he couldn't remember where. Now he and Lucy sat side by side scrolling through their laptops, scanning articles and ebooks.

"He was one of the original landowners for what now makes up a big chunk of Washington D.C.," Lucy said.

"Especially here—these grounds," Henry added, chewing his lip. It didn't explain where he'd heard the guy's name. He sure hadn't spent a bunch of time researching real estate in post-colonial America.

"It seems that history can't quite agree whether he was really 'Obstinate Mr. Burnes,' as George Washington called him, or he just wanted a fair price for his land," Lucy said, skimming an article.

"Probably both," Henry said, yawning. He scrolled through the blog post he was reading and then stopped. He stared at a small whitewashed house—tall chimney, ancient windows, bowed roof. He knew that picture. The house used to stand on White House grounds and several times in the centuries that followed his death, the owner's voice had been heard in the Oval Office.

Henry set his laptop aside and got up to take his ghost book off the desk. "I'm Mr. Burnes," Henry said, flipping through the pages.

Lucy looked up at him, like he'd finally cracked.

"That's the voice people heard—FDR's valet, a White House guard, a reporter during the Truman administration. Each time near the Oval Office, and each time all the voice said was, "I'm Mr. Burnes.""

"Well, that's not creepy," Lucy said. "Remind me not to hang out near the Oval Office."

"Don't worry," Henry said. "He hasn't been heard since the Truman administration. Although he *is* the oldest ghost to haunt the White House."

"Ghost *voice*," Lucy said, fidgeting with her ring. Thoughtfully, she added, "Reduced to only words. An introduction repeated over and over again."

"Sounds like a bad White House party," Henry said.

Lucy shut her laptop, then stood up and stretched. She was wearing her outfit from school—plum-colored skinny jeans and a black t-shirt that said 'Part Wolf.' "Ghosts creep me out. Other stuff—vampires, zombies. I know they're not real. But spirits are different. If we carry on after this life, and I guess I kind of believe we do, then it makes sense that some of those spirits might stay here." She paused and sat down again, crossing her legs. "Native Americans are big on spirits. They're not afraid either. But those spirits," she said, pointing to Henry's book. "They're different. Trapped souls. People who won't, or can't, leave. I guess it makes sense that they might come back to their old haunts." She paused. "Pun intended."

"Yeah, you're ready for that comedy career," Henry said.

Lucy looked away, tapping her chin. "So was his house, was it where the White House now is?"

"No," Henry said. "I don't think so. Part of the agreement with the sale of his land was that his house would stay. They built paths and things around it."

"That's right," Lucy said, opening her laptop again and tapping the screen. "I read that. Then after his death, his daughter actually moved the homestead house to her property when she got married. It stayed there for about a hundred years until it was torn down in 1896."

"Wait," Henry said. "Do you think that if we find the location of the original house we might find the place they're planning to plant the EMP? That's why they mentioned Burnes."

Lucy was already googling maps.

They spent the next half hour searching, but none of the old maps had any kind of exact location. Finally, Lucy looked up from her laptop. "We could explore his property, look for...well, something."

"He owned 650 acres," Henry said, a little gloomily.

"Then we'll walk them all," Lucy said.

"And we don't even know how much time we have. We know the attack will have to happen before May when the fleet gets replaced, but it could happen any time before then —a week, a month, whatever. Reylin's looking into it, but for now, she has no idea."

"Then we'll run, not walk." Lucy poked Henry in the gut. "We'll tell them you're trying to work off all that White House cake."

Henry glanced at his watch and sighed. Mr. Keikiki would be arriving any minute to try to teach them more Kiribati. Henry and Lucy shut their computers. Mr. Keikiki didn't permit any electronics when he taught them, even for Lucy's notes.

They looked at each other as the door opened behind them.

"Good afternoon, children," Mr. Keikiki said, walking to his makeshift desk, and touching a statue of a prince like it was an old friend. "I hope everyone came ready to concentrate because we'll continue our work on introductions."

Inside Henry groaned. They were like old Mr. Burnes. Doomed to say the same few words over and over again for all of eternity.

Lucy was trying to smile, but she looked about as excited as Henry felt.

Today learning an almost impossible tonal language

spoken by less than one percent of the world's population wasn't scoring very high on the "deserves concentration" list.

Not when his father's life was at stake, along with anyone else on board Marine One when the EMP was set to go off.

His mom came into the back of the room to observe the lesson. Henry didn't dare turn around to look at her. He wanted to tell her, stop the flight, and not worry about finding the EMP, but more than that, he wanted to keep his family safe. And if he told, the risk would rise.

Henry hunched over his desk, and Lucy took out her notebook.

Twenty-One

Chet stood with a whistle in hand, surrounded by fifteen underprivileged seventh graders. This was it—the punishment he'd assigned himself. Eagle Scout, but bigger. He squirmed.

He was wearing a sleek black hoodie and the shiny, blue warm-ups he'd requested for Christmas last year. The boys had been chosen for two factors: potential and need. *Need.* Being denied the newest gaming system for Christmas because your mom wanted you to read more books was not need.

Looking at these kids, that was easy to see. Most of their clothes were nondescript—cheap, new clothes chosen to blend in and work for playing ball with the president's son— off-brand tank tops and shorts. But some stood out, and in all the wrong ways.

One kid was wearing a pair of really nice shoes, which Chet could tell were two sizes too big. Another had a pair of name-brand sweats so old and pilled they looked almost fuzzy.

"Alright boys," Chet said, blowing his whistle. "Let's start by forming a straight line. The boys shuffled around, but their new line wasn't any straighter than their old line. One of the Secret Service agents on the court raised an eyebrow.

In the distance, Chet could see a familiar figure walking toward them, and a few of the kids turned to watch as well. When she got a little closer, the whispers started and one boy even whistled low.

"Hi guys," Marxma said, standing in front of them in an appropriately subdued outfit—simple gray leggings with a long t-shirt and jacket.

"This," Chet began, "is Marxma Frey. She'll be helping with a lot of the drills. I'll be coaching the basketball skills, but Marxma will be working agility drills with you. She is trained in both gymnastics and martial arts, which she uses in her, uh, movies." Chet turned to see the Secret Service agent rolling her eyes.

"I thought that was you," one of the slouchier kids said to Marxma. "You be looking fine in them *Monster Vice* movies."

"Hey, we gonna get to be in one of your movies?" another piped up.

"I got the video game," another said. "Show us some moves."

Chet took a breath. Maybe this had been a colossally bad idea. He knew Marxma valued her privacy and he was worried the boys would be too star-struck to get any work done.

Marxma smiled. "Of course. But first we'll be running sprints down the court. Fastest one gets a signed Monster Vice t-shirt. So does the one who Coach Miller decides is working the hardest." She looked at the clump of boys. "For now, you better form up."

Chet watched in awe as the boys straightened, focused, and magically fell into a perfect line.

———

Henry opened the *Haunted Washington* book, thumbing through for more information on David Burnes. There wasn't much, and nothing even resembling a map. Henry flipped through absently, stopping on a page about something called the demon cat.

The page had been dog-eared and there was a blurry black and white photograph, obviously taken a long time ago. In the fuzzy picture, the cat appeared as a large black mass, blank eyes, eerie.

Henry went to turn the page when a sentence caught his eye. "The creature referred to as the demon cat has been seen many times at the White House—often before a huge national disaster. The animal always starts small and seems to grow, its eyes glowing and red."

Henry held the book, frozen to the page. Was that what he had seen? A ghost cat that appeared before national disasters?

He pictured his dad going up in a helicopter, coming down in an explosive crash. He slammed the book shut, goose bumps rising along his arms. He had to figure out who was trying to kill his father. He had to do it quickly.

He turned to leave the Lincoln Bedroom, and there she was—the maid with the feather duster. She wasn't staring at Mary Todd this time, but at Henry—like she was looking straight through him. "You've seen it," she said. "The cat. You've *seen*." On the last word she started to tremble.

"No," Henry said, trying to walk past, still thinking about his dad and not really following what she had said. "Now, excuse me." He was ready to push her aside if he had to, but she dropped to the floor at his feet.

"Please," she begged. "You've seen it and you can stop it. Communicate with your father, gain his help. Please. So much destruction already."

Henry stopped. "What did you say?"

She didn't answer. Instead, she put her head on Henry's shoes.

"What did you say?" he said again, his voice rising. "What do you know?"

"So many people," she said, starting to cry. "Thousands of my people that you could save."

Henry's head started to pound. What was she talking about? Probably people in some war-torn country. She was sobbing now.

He tried to tug away from her, almost tripping. "Listen," Henry said. "I don't know what you're talking about. I can't save your people." He pulled away from the maid, and she seemed to crumple on the floor.

Henry turned to the door as she slowly began to pick herself up. On her wrist, peeking out of her sleeve, he noticed several faint curved lines he hadn't seen before.

She was on her knees now, but upright. "You say you can't help when I know you can. If you cannot help, then I will."

She broke her feather duster open, a glint in her hand. Something went off in Henry's head as she pulled the thin, straight knife from the hollow tube of the feather duster.

The world slowed down. Henry stepped away, feeling each bend and twist.

"Our way is not their way," she said, drawing the dagger back, "but in the end, it will be done." She threw the knife with more strength than it seemed the small woman should have.

Henry bent his body to the left, his head moving as the blade soared past his throat. He felt the rush of wind, heard the high-pitched whine of metal through air, and then he moved a hand, as though following the sound, and caught the blade by its handle.

For a moment, he just stared. He could barely catch a basketball when Chet threw it to him.

The woman seemed to wither. "They said you could not be convinced. Or killed," she sobbed. "But I had to try."

Standing there, holding a knife that had been meant to stab him, Henry didn't feel like he should pity the woman— for all he knew she was an agent of The Ethereal. But somehow he still felt sorry for her. She was obviously very troubled; maybe she had family in a corrupt or impoverished country.

Moving in that way that felt slow, though Henry knew it was impossibly fast, Henry bent down and whispered, "I'm sorry." Then, lifting his index finger, he tapped her on the temple. To him, it felt like a gentle knock on a wooden door —soft and unobtrusive. But the woman sank to the ground, unconscious. Henry looked at his hand, then the knife. All at once, the world sped up.

"Mom, Mom!" Henry screamed as he ran down the hall —his voice a shriek, his legs like lead. "Dad. Mom!"

A thunder of feet joined his own footsteps. Black suits swarmed the hall.

When they arrived, Henry found that he could barely speak.

He pointed to the Lincoln Bedroom, then bent over his knees, breathing hard. "Here," he said finally, holding out the knife. "She threw it at me."

Twenty-Two

M s. Smith gathered up a cluster of papers. Reckless that the school still used so much when they had more environmental options available to them. Had Americans learned nothing from other cultures and peoples?

She opened the file labeled 'Henry Miller' and sat down, her perfectly manicured hands slipping down the page.

She wasn't supposed to know about the events at the White House. But she had too many connections to people in and near the White House to know nothing; and since her work had brought her closer to Richard Masticor, she knew even more.

The boy had drawn notice, and he'd been attacked.

She set the paper to the side, her eyes resting on the remainder of Henry's record. Perfect attendance. Only the vaccinations required for the schools he'd attended. No hospitalizations, no surgeries, no broken bones. Ever.

Exceptionally high marks in English and history in both school and standardized tests. Lower than average scores in both science and math.

Normally, she would consider that a nearly fatal flaw in today's competitive world. But with his language fluency— Spanish, French, Portuguese, Russian, Mandarin, German, and soon Japanese—she doubted he would need it.

Henry, it was easy to see, was a bit of a word genius. No wonder he had drawn attention to himself.

It was a wonder he hadn't been noticed sooner by those from foreign places seeking a very specific type of relief they wanted him to help them gain.

———

Against all reason, Henry's mother had insisted he stay in the Lincoln bedroom.

"First of all," she'd said the day after the attack. "This would have happened no matter what room you'd been in. Secondly, I cannot permit you to be ruled by terror. I know this is a mature concept for you, Henry"—she'd put her hand in his hair and held him there—"but terror doesn't leave when you run from it. It must be faced." She'd taken her hand off his head. "And thirdly, it gives you this great view."

She'd gone off about fountains and the Kennedys and sheep, but Henry had struggled to concentrate.

Maybe his mother dealt with terror by hurling random

historical facts at it, but Henry was working through his with a fantastic series of nightmares involving helicopters, bombs, knives, and tiny women with feather dusters.

It wasn't the best coping strategy.

Neither was trying to replicate the surge of power he'd felt when she attacked him. That morning, he'd created a mini obstacle course for himself on the south lawn—things to hurdle, grab, and catch.

He'd tripped, fumbled, and missed. Now his body just hurt, not to mention his pride. Whatever power he had, it couldn't be replicated. In fact, it seemed to come on when danger headed his way.

Henry didn't know whether he should be comforted or terrified by that fact. If it was a fact at all. He couldn't seem to test it, short of finding potential kidnappers and assassins and throwing himself in their paths.

And he was pretty sure that's not what his mother had meant by facing his fears.

To be fair, in addition to telling him to face his terror, his mother now had a new security guard posted by his room at all times. And every member of the staff was being questioned and getting a fresh background check.

Alone in his room, Henry stood by the window staring at the fountain Jackie Kennedy had used as a pool, at the basketball court Barack Obama had had built, and at the long stretch of grass that sheep had been grazed on in 1919 to save federal monies.

Somewhere out there was a secret place where a device

would be hidden—set to destroy his father's life and presidency. He had to find it. If his mother wanted him to face terror, then that was how he would do it.

It really might mean bumping into some potential assassins—members of The Ethereal who were against his father and maybe even his whole family. Desperate people.

He pictured the look on the maid's face—sad, but deranged. Still, finding the EMP meant a chance to do something important, to help his father in a way that he never could if he reported the plan.

Henry paused, chewing his cheek. But if he had to—if he couldn't figure it out by himself—he would let someone know about the plot before his father and other innocent people got on a helicopter destined to go down.

Henry pushed his fists into his temples and tried to take a deep breath just as someone tapped on the door. Henry jumped and then turned to see a boy—Will—standing there.

Henry blinked. "You're real," he said.

"Of course, I'm real," Will answered, glancing down at himself.

"I guess I just thought I was dreaming that night," Henry grumbled.

"We talked about animals," Will said.

"Yeah, and you sang some song," Henry said.

"What song?" Will asked.

"Well, maybe that part was a dream," Henry said. "It was kind of a strange song anyway."

"Lots of songs are strange," Will replied matter-of-factly.

Henry glanced at the door, surprised that the guard hadn't escorted Will in, although looking at him, Henry realized Will was probably the least threatening kid alive.

He just had that kind of face—naïve, but a little mischievous. In fact, after the stress of the last few days, Henry found that he was kind of happy there was another kid hanging around the White House.

"Looks like you've created quite a stir," Will said.

"You think?" Henry replied, sinking down on a couch.

"Yes, I do," Will said.

Henry shook his head. "Come on in."

Will looked fresh and polished—white shirt and slacks, shiny pair of brown dress shoes, and some kind of fitness tracker Henry hadn't noticed before. It was the only part of his outfit that looked mildly cool—the leather band holding a pale orange circular stone that Henry couldn't help but notice.

Will wandered to the desk with the Gettysburg Address and opened a drawer. Henry detected that sweet smell again—musky flowers.

"Wanna explore?" Will asked.

"Not really," Henry said, leaning his head back against the couch.

"My father says that's when you need it most because it's the best distraction. Makes it easier to sort through things that are on your mind."

Henry just closed his eyes.

"Come on," Will said. "You'll feel better."

Henry heaved himself up off the couch. "Fine," he said. "As long as we get to end up in the kitchen."

"Oh, look, my old marble." Will flicked the bright blue marble at Henry and Henry caught it using both his hands.

"I used to play with that when I was little. It was my favorite one," Will said.

"Yeah, I think you left it the other night." Henry looked down at the bright blue orb.

"You can keep it," Will said cheerfully.

Henry wasn't sure what he would do with a marble, but he shoved it into his pocket anyway.

"Okay, let's go," Will said.

They slunk past the curator's office, where she seemed to be reaming her assistant on the phone, and then they scampered down the hall across plush red carpet, under vaulted ceilings and through a large passageway.

Will stopped at the North Hall and said, "Look at this."

Henry looked up. At the edge of the stone, along the doorway, were burn marks. Right on the stone. "What is it?" Henry asked, reaching up to touch the scarred entryway— surprised to see a flaw in the otherwise pristine building.

"They keep this here, unrepaired, as a reminder of history," Will replied. He continued to look at the stone, as if he were remembering something. "There was a great fire here, in the Executive Mansion. This place was built in 1792, but was burned to the ground when the British invaded the Capital, during the War of 1812. Dolley Madison was able to save some things, but most of it was lost."

Henry frowned. "What got saved?"

"Paintings and some other things," Will replied in a way that seemed evasive, considering the way he liked to spew out facts. "The curator would know."

"Yeah, well, I don't want to know that badly," Henry said.

Will shrugged. "Let's go to the basement."

They walked past the White House chocolate shop. "Detour!" Henry said, turning in. The aroma wrapped around him like all the good things in the world had combined into a singular scent—cooked, cooled, and molded. Henry was pretty sure that smell would lift you to heaven.

"Hello, Henry dear," a sweet voice called from the kitchen. "Come for a snack?" Miss Ruby walked from the confectionary to the front of the shop.

"Nope," Henry replied. "Just stopped in to talk to the most beautiful member of the staff."

"Got that right," the plump, older woman replied, patting her hair. "Now, what'll you have? I just turned out some caramel truffles for a luncheon this week." She grabbed some tongs and a piece of wax paper to serve him.

"Not only are you beautiful," Henry said. "But you also know how to hold a riveting conversation."

"Ah, you. I think you're the one serving up sweets, not me." Miss Ruby handed him a truffle, then paused and got another. "This, for that pretty little friend of yours."

Henry tipped his head to the side and made a face at Will, who was standing near the back of the shop.

Will just shrugged.

"Now what's that girl's name?" Miss Ruby said.

"Girl?" Henry asked, shooting Will another look.

"Well, of course," Miss Ruby responded. "Lily? Laurie?"

"Oh," Henry said, pausing. "Lucy."

"Yes, that's it," Miss Ruby said, and then leaned in and whispered, "Cute little thing. Maybe not quite as sugared as you, but still sweet." She smiled. "And I know sweet."

"Well, thank you, Miss Ruby," Henry said, holding up the chocolates. "A pleasure as always."

"Ah, go on now," Miss Ruby said. "And come back soon."

"Yes, ma'am." Henry touched his fingers to an imaginary hat as he turned to leave.

As soon as they were out the door, Henry handed Will the extra chocolate and collapsed into laughter. "Oh man. I can't even eat," he said, bending over and holding his side. "I don't know if she thought you were Lucy or just didn't notice you. But I could barely hold it together in there with darling, nearsighted Miss Ruby talking about that 'cute girl.'"

Henry stood up and Will gave him a hard stare.

"Though now, of course, I can totally see the resemblance. Oh wait," he said. "I can't." Henry started laughing again.

"Who's Lucy?" Will asked.

"Just a girl," Henry said, standing upright to catch his breath. He sighed, popping the truffle into his mouth. "Wow," he said, mouth full. "Who needs good vision when you can create stuff like this? It's a good thing Lucy won't know what she's missing. She'd never forgive me for not saving this for her. Consider yourself lucky, Will—you were in the right place at the right time."

"I always am," Will replied.

Henry smiled. He never could have teased Lucy like that. Hanging out with Will wasn't half bad, kind of like having a little brother.

Will shook his head, savoring his own chocolate as he led Henry past the carpenter shop toward the bowling alley.

"Up for a game?" Henry asked.

"Sure," Will said. "You know, Truman and Nixon both loved bowling."

"I didn't know that, but somehow it doesn't surprise me that you do."

Three games later, they plunked down. "I'm starving," Henry said.

Will cocked his head to the side and replied, "That seems unlikely."

Henry laughed and picked up a phone to ask that two trays of food be sent down.

"Will Chet or Lucy be joining you?" the polite voice on the other line asked.

"No, my friend Will is here, and I think he's pretty hungry," Henry said.

In no time at all, a butler arrived with two trays of steaming food. Just the way Henry liked it: scrambled eggs, crispy bacon, slightly burned toast, raspberry jam, and a cup of chocolate pudding.

The butler set both trays down in front of Henry, as

though he was some kind of prince. It made Henry uncomfortable. He scooted Will's tray over so he could grab it.

"Would you like anything else?" the butler asked before leaving.

"Um, no thank you," Henry said, as Will began to chow down, starting with the pudding.

They both ate silently until the clock in the room hit 10:00 with a decisive click.

"It's time," Will said, shoving the last of his toast in his mouth.

"Time for what?" Henry followed Will up the stairs to the west end of the state floor.

Will nodded to the door in front of them.

"Henry," a Secret Service agent said as he started to open the door. "There's a tour starting right now and we'd prefer you stay away from public areas."

Will's face fell.

Henry felt bad for him. Will had raced up here; it was obvious he loved this sort of stuff.

"Um," Henry said. "Are you sure you can't let me in? I was really hoping to see a tour in action."

The agent sighed, then pulled out his phone to make a call.

Finally, the agent opened the door and the boys stepped from the center hall into the visitor's foyer in the East Wing. The Secret Service agent in the room stepped quickly toward Henry, and a bubble of space seemed to form around him. A rush of excitement rippled through the room, along with a lot of whispers and pointing.

"You know," Will said. "This House was always meant to be the 'people's house.' Anyone could come and personally lodge a complaint with the president until after the Civil War. In recent years, security has gotten much tighter. Now it's rare to even catch a glimpse of a member of the first family."

"Will," Henry said, shushing him. "The tour's starting. The official one—not your jabbering." Will was definitely like a little brother. But Henry understood why Will was rambling. It was unnerving to have everyone staring at them.

"Well, this is a treat," the guide chirped, gesturing at Henry. "It looks like we'll be honored to have Henry Miller joining us today."

Henry cleared his throat. "Yeah, uh, just here with a friend."

The crowd laughed, and Henry felt sweat beading on his forehead. Mothers pointed him out to their children.

Beside him, Will whispered, "Andrew Jackson was the first president to be elected by common men. Prior to that, only landowners and rich men could vote for the president. Of course, then those common men nearly suffocated President Jackson at a drunken inauguration party. He had to escape through a window." Will nodded to a nearby window.

"Bro, *you're* suffocating me. Back off with the White House facts." Henry whispered, tugging at his shirt, trying to cool down.

"It *is* a tour of the Executive Mansion," Will said, smiling.

Four Secret Service agents trailed the tour group, muttering occasionally into their mouthpieces.

"This room is known as the Vermeil room. It's a word derived from French, meaning 'silver-gilt,' and has served many functions over the years, such as sitting room and display room. Behind the glass in the cases are pieces of gold-plated silver from antique French and English collections. On the south wall is a New York sofa from 1815."

Henry was beginning to wonder if the tour had been a good idea. He still felt hot and really uncomfortable.

The tour group moved into the adjoining China Room. It had a large fireplace flanked on either side by sculptures. "Each of the presidents, or their wives, chose a set of china. Here, you can see each set from the earliest president's set to the most recent."

Henry pushed against his temples, but Will looked riveted, like presidential china was the most interesting thing in his world. Henry's eyes wandered to two large, comfort-able-looking chairs as the tour guide prattled on. "Flanking the portrait of Mrs. Coolidge are two Chippendale side chairs used by George Washington."

Will glanced at the chairs, then walked toward one and sat down. It surprised Henry that no one seemed to mind and he followed his friend, sinking into a chair that belonged to the first president.

Suddenly, every eye in the room was on him. Several people audibly gasped, and then there was silence. Even the Secret Service agents seemed too stunned to move.

Henry jumped up, wiping his forehead.

The guide cleared his throat and said, "Of course, we'll make an exception to the no touch rule for Henry as he is, uh—" He searched for the words off script "—special." The guide smiled, though it looked a little forced. "This is his house for the next four to eight years."

A few people chuckled, but others grumbled, and several of the parents seemed to be warning their children not to do what Henry had just done. They shot him irritated looks.

The tour guide went back on script. "Many sets of china have been made for the White House over the years. If pieces of the set were broken, the entire set had to be thrown out. Literally. The pieces were broken up and thrown into the Potomac. Or, if White House workers needed a little stress relief—smashed against the basement walls, as was the case when Lady Bird commissioned Tiffany's to design their china with fifty state flowers around the borders and several plates came with big smudges in the middle instead of flowers."

Henry felt like this fact brought out even more grumbling. "I'm sorry," one man said, raising his hand. "Are these expensive dishes that are being so carelessly thrown out paid for with taxpayer money?"

Instead of looking at the tour guide, Henry noticed several unfriendly glances come his way. He turned to Will to tell him it was time for them to go, but Will wasn't there.

Henry paused as the rest of the group walked past military security into the Green Room. He looked down the halls and peeked around furniture as the tour guide said, "This room has been used for lodging, and was used as a card room by James Madison."

Where was Will? Henry looked over his shoulder. He was sweating again and his friend was nowhere to be seen.

Henry started walking back to the Cross Hall, when he heard something that made him stop and listen to the guide. "Here in this room, James Madison signed the first declaration of war by the United States, beginning the War of 1812."

War. The country had just been a baby. And there'd been so much war since. Something about that thought, or those words, or this place made Henry feel dizzy. He rubbed the marble in his pocket that Will had given him. A sudden emptiness swallowed his stomach, and he thought he might get sick.

Henry wanted to sit down again, but didn't feel he could. Which made him angry. This was his house. Why couldn't he sit down without being gawked at? Why couldn't the crowd of people just like him the way they always liked Chet?

Henry gripped the marble in his pocket, feeling something like a cold finger brush his neck.

All of the sudden, Henry felt an intense heat and it seemed that everyone turned to stare at him. The men looked angry, their eyes narrow and fixed. The women were crying, but angry too. They blamed him for something, something horrible. Pressure welled up in Henry's chest, and now he began to feel his own anger toward them, even the children.

Something in Henry snapped, and smoke started to rise from the green carpeted floor, filling the room. The flames crackled, licking the drapes and walls as the room was engulfed with fire, and now void of people. Everything was burning, crumbling.

Henry stood at the center of it. For a moment, he was glad to see it burning, all those hateful people gone.

Then, through the flames, he saw something on the far side of the room. A small casket, wooden, and made for a child. Henry could see a woman standing over the casket. Something struck him as familiar about the woman.

Henry could not see her clearly through the flames and smoke, but he could hear her—loud, mournful sobs that banged against her small frame as though they couldn't come out hard enough.

A deep sadness crashed over Henry. He wanted to offer the woman some sense of comfort, tell her that her loss was not the end. He moved through the smoke, the flames, almost near enough to see the face in the box. Then the woman turned toward him, and he screamed.

Henry's eyes snapped open. He expected to be flat on his back in the infirmary because he was pretty sure he'd fainted from the heat—and from the vision of Mary Todd, whose face had then changed, changed to someone more familiar.

But he was still standing, quietly listening to a tour guide talk about the various shades of green different first ladies had chosen. His Secret Service agent stood a few paces away, looking bored as usual.

Henry wiped his forehead and walked out of the room, listening as a few people snapped pictures.

Twenty-Three

For the second time in less than a month, Henry sat across from his mother as she stood at her desk.

An image from her uVision stretched out on the desk between them, displaying a large picture of Henry's back as he left the tour.

"It's all over the internet," his mother said. "Twitter's having a heyday. And I'm scared to even look at InstaVroom."

"Hashtag best day ever," Henry said.

"It's not funny, Henry," his mother said.

"Mom, I got sick. Legit sick."

"Did you throw up?"

"No, but I—"

"Then it doesn't count. And you don't look sick to me."

"It was like a weird spell. I got hot and…Well, anyway, it's happened before."

His mother paused for a moment. "At least it gives us something to tell the media. When we apologize."

She sat down, a heavy slump into her seat. "Henry," she said, looking him in the eye. "I know this isn't always fun, but you have to be careful. Sitting in George Washington's chair, walking out without a word mid-tour. People freak out if I wear the wrong color dress. It stinks. But the next time I try to wear a different color dress. Not because they're right," she said, holding up a hand so Henry wouldn't speak, "but because the color of my dress is not supposed to attract more attention than the national debt, and I try to keep it from doing so."

"I really was sick," Henry mumbled.

"I believe you," his mother said. "But the internet won't. You shouldn't have been on the tour in the first place; and then to cause such a scene."

"Will wanted to go," Henry protested.

"Who's Will?" his mother asked.

"A son of one of the staff," Henry answered.

His mother paused for another long moment. "Okay. But no more of this. We've got enough on our plates with that whole crazy maid thing. Thank goodness that didn't get leaked."

Henry looked at his mother.

"And, no, it leaking to the media is not my biggest concern," she said. "You are. But it's easier to get information without the whole cyber world getting their piece of the action."

"Has anyone learned anything? About that maid?" Henry asked.

His mother pushed her fingers together and paused so long Henry wasn't sure she would answer. "Yes. But it's not much." His mother took a breath. "The woman was named Concepcion Gonzalez. She's worked at the White House for twelve years with absolutely no incidents. I didn't even know who she was when they pulled up her picture, and I've been trying to get to know the staff. The truth is that it seemed her biggest gift was going unnoticed. Many of the workers have family who've served in the House for generations. Ms. Gonzalez had a cousin who worked here until twelve years ago when she passed away. Ms. Gonzalez was her replacement."

Henry nodded. "So she *wasn't* a member of The Ethereal?"

His mother's face took on a blank look. "The FBI believes Ms. Gonzalez was acting alone."

The way she said it made Henry want to ask if *she* believed the maid had been acting alone.

But before he could ask, his mother continued, "Ms. Gonzalez is recovering well from her injury. You say she fell down and then knocked her head on something?"

It was what he'd said. At the time, it was the only thing he'd been able to say. He couldn't explain that he'd knocked her unconscious with just a touch of his finger. He couldn't say that he'd moved from the path of an airborne knife. He couldn't even say that she'd been begging him to ask his dad for help to save her country or her people. He couldn't say anything except the sparsest bones of truth—that she'd thrown a knife at him.

He tried again now, opening his mouth to say more. Nothing came out.

"Yes," he finally stammered. "Something hit her head."

His mother made a quick note on her uVision and looked up.

"Yes, well," his mother said, looking at him as he looked down. "She conked it good. It took her several days to recover. Although she's still not talking."

"Yeah, well, she attacked a thirteen-year-old kid. How much is there to say?"

His mother replied by tapping on her uVision.

"And you're *sure* she's not connected to the group who kidnapped a bunch of kids and shot at the president during his first hour in office?" Henry asked. "Cause she kind of seems to fit the bill."

"The FBI can find no connection."

"To a group with almost no connections," Henry retorted.

"Henry," his mother said, her voice heavy. "This stuff isn't simple. It's not clear."

"So there's nothing?" he pressed.

His mother hunched forward, typing into her tablet. "Maybe there's nothing. Maybe there's something." She turned the uVision toward Henry. "But there's nothing that connects. And that's what we need."

In its way, it reminded him of something Reylin had said.

The computer projected a picture of a woman's hand and arm with a symbol tattooed to her wrist. "This seems to be a recent tattoo. No one is quite sure where she got it. The chief investigator for this case suspects it denotes some type of affiliation, but we can't identify what it might mean in relationship to her actions here. It may not mean anything. The investigators can't find the symbol anywhere—not on the internet or among any other of the anti-political groups that have made threats to your father in the past."

"Have they looked at flags?" Henry asked. "For countries, or even cities?"

"Yes," his mother responded. "Why do you ask?"

Henry shrugged, unable to find the words he wanted to say. Finally, he replied, "The maid was from another place."

"All our records indicate she was American born, as were her parents." She glanced down at her computer, scanning. "Though I suppose we could check her ancestral heritage."

"I guess," Henry said, trying to remember her exact words. "Do you know if The Ethereal is an American or foreign group?"

"The FBI believes it to be a combination—a group with many types, all of whom have anti-American ideals."

"And the FBI is sure no one claiming to be part of The Ethereal had similar tattoos?" Henry pressed, picturing the arms of the man who'd shot at the Beast as he'd been shoved into a black sedan.

His mother looked at him for a moment, then down at her report. "No," she said after a pause. "None."

Henry looked down at his wrists. "I thought that man

had something on his wrists—the man who attacked Dad on Inauguration Day."

His mother paused, clicking through images on her tablet. "They photographed him thoroughly during the investigation." She shook her head. "There's nothing." She touched a button and the image from the uVision bloomed onto the desk in front of them.

It was true. The man's skin was clean—his wrists had no more than scratches from the scuffle.

Henry stared at the images. He knew he had seen *something* on the man's wrists. But whatever it was apparently hadn't been permanent. Writing maybe? Or scratches that had seemed to form shapes in the horror of the moment.

He shook his head. "Dad's the most important person in the world. It's terrifying."

"It is," his mother replied, reaching for Henry's hand across her desk. "A lot of people worked really hard to get your father where he is. And he intends to do a lot of good and important things with his position. But," she paused, looking at Henry with eyes so intense that he wanted to pull back, "he and I both know that he's not the most important person in the world. You are." Her eyes were so blue. So concentrated.

Henry wriggled his hand free from her grip.

His mother shut her mouth slightly in a way that struck Henry as almost sad, then cleared her throat, turning back to her tablet. "But this," she said, tapping the image of the tattoo and bringing the picture back onto the desk between them. "It's not clearly associated with any of the groups who are against your father. And in fact—" She paused to stare at the symbol. "—it could be a simple coincidence, a pretty pattern some tattoo artist suggested."

She stopped talking, as though thinking. "Still, I wanted you to know, to see it. A child of the president has never been attacked in such a way."

His mother turned to him, holding his gaze. Again Henry had to resist squirming.

"You're a special kid," she said finally. "I've always known this." She smiled for the first time that day. "But others might be taking notice too. This symbol," she said, enlarging it. "Have you ever seen it before? Anywhere? Even in a dream?"

Henry stared at his mother before looking away. "That's a weird question, Mom." He squinted at the stark, sharp lines of the tattoo that projected out from the uVision. It was a golden circle lined in black with four flame-like daggers pointing out almost like the sides of a compass on a map.

His mother shrugged—a surprisingly helpless gesture for her. "Maybe I'm grasping at straws, but sometimes the subconscious notices things we don't, then spits them up in our dreams. You know, Lincoln once dreamed he awakened to a wailing crowd in the East Room, only to be told that they were mourning the president's murder. And on the night before his death, he dreamed he was sailing toward a 'dark and indefinite shore.'" She leaned back, gazing at him.

"Mom, you're creeping me out," Henry said. "I'm not going to die."

"I know," she said quickly. "But my point is that our

minds often process things through our dreams—things we know, but don't know we know; things we see, but can't quite face."

Henry stared at his mother. He'd had lots of dreams since coming here—some in his bed, some when he was at school or on White House tours. In them, he'd seen, or imagined, horrible things. Things he'd told his mother nothing about. But none of them had been tattoos. "Mom," he began. Then stopped.

"The image," his mother said, and Henry noticed that she hadn't stopped staring at him. "Have you seen it?

Henry shook his head. "No," he said, trying to sort through his own thoughts. "Not even in dreams."

His mother nodded and then stood up, rubbing her temples. "Oh Henry," she said. "These aren't the conversations a mother imagines having with her son." She picked up her purse. "Now, come on. Let's go get ice cream before I take you to school."

"Wait," Henry said, looking at his mom. "I think I'm dreaming right now."

His mother laughed. "Do you want some or not?" she asked. "The truth is that I want to get out of this place, and I am in desperate need of some stress eating."

Henry could understand that.

"There's a new ice cream parlor downtown with all kinds of crazy flavors—avocado squeeze, mango passion fruit, chili vanillie—"

"Mom," Henry interrupted. "Can we just go to the Dairy Barn?"

His mother smiled, grabbing her coat and sunglasses. "Heck to the yes."

"That's not what people say," Henry said.

"Isn't it?" she asked, as she pushed a button on her office phone. "Let's go. The Beast is meeting us at the south entrance."

Twenty-Four

Lucy was watching *Ocean's 11*, the reboot. She'd already watched the original. Along with *GoldenEye*, *Broken Arrow*, *Godzilla* and a whole bunch of other movies that had been created around the idea of EMP devices. War stories and alien stories. Even one terrible B movie about six alien warlords trying to consume Earth's energy. A whole galaxy of movies.

Real information was a lot harder to find.

Apparently, EMP devices could be set off with a detonator from a distance and were sometimes called e-bombs. She'd even looked up several images and tutorials for home-made devices. Which she realized probably looked bad in her search history. She'd have to ask Reylin how to hide that. Or maybe hiding it would look worse.

At any rate, she'd learned that EMPs had to be close enough to their target to work. That narrowed the playing field to within a mile or two of the landing pad.

She glanced at her phone. Reylin was supposed to be u-vidding her. Then Reylin would stitch Henry in so that whatever she said didn't show up on the history of their phones.

Even though Henry wasn't happy about it, Reylin was a good ally to have on their team. She was brilliant with this stuff.

And she said she'd found something.

Lucy had gone back to her movie when the u-vid finally came through, making her jump. She looked down and there it was. She could see it spinning as Reylin added Henry to the thread.

"Okay," Reylin messaged. "You guys here?"

"Here," Lucy said.

"Here." Henry's face icon popped up on her phone. "What'd you find?"

"Okay, I don't have a whole lot of time," Reylin began. "But there's a box. A hidden box—the one they'll use to detonate the EMP. If we can find that and disable it, the plot will fail."

"But won't they just hatch another assassination plot?" Lucy asked.

"No. Because the box contains identifying information that could lead authorities to the leaders of The Ethereal. But if one of us reports it." She paused. "Then they'll just change their plans. No one will find the box, or the words on it."

"And the box," Henry said. "How would we even find it? Sometimes this seems too crazy, like it's just better to tell so the plot gets stopped."

"And you could," Reylin said. "But it will just be a temporary fix. The same people in the same positions of power will be able to come up with another plan."

"Okay," Henry replied.

"Do you think if we find that guy's homestead—Burnes—that we'll find this box?" Lucy asked.

"Maybe," Reylin said, "He's got something to do with it." She seemed distracted and was glancing over her shoulder toward her door. "Just keep looking for that box," Reylin whispered. "They've coded it K-0-n-i-g-s-v-0-c-3."

Lucy jotted the letters and numbers down. It looked like Henry did too.

"That's interesting," Henry said, holding up the piece of paper. "Like Konigsvoce. A German/Italian mash-up for the phrase 'King's voice.'"

"Gotta go!" Reylin said as she turned toward her door, and just like that the thread broke.

Lucy was left staring at a completely empty screen.

———

An EMP. A box that could detonate it. Okay, okay. But what Lucy couldn't figure out was how any identifying information would be put on the box.

Lucy pressed her hands against her eyes. They hurt from staring at her screen. She couldn't help but feel that she was looking past something—like she was staring up at a satellite when the real answer was down at her feet.

She looked down. White shoes, brown legs. Nothing else. What was missing?

TWENTY-FIVE

elicate dishes clinked and tuxedoed waiters shuffled past while Senator Masticor sat at a discreet table in the corner, checking his watch, and re-reading the message from his undersecretary about when his superior officer would arrive. He hoped everything would be satisfactory.

Exactly at noon, the limousine pulled up. Masticor watched through the window, waiting. A tall, familiar blond woman exited first, followed by a dark, wiry man. The two of them were flanked by a couple of large men dressed in black suits.

They walked in and the blond found her way to the bar while the bodyguards sat at a table nearby, looking almost casual, though their eyes flew over the crowd without ever glancing at a menu.

Masticor stood and gestured to a seat. The wiry man sat, nodding for Masticor to join him.

A waiter brought a chilled bottle of wine, pouring a glass for each gentleman. The wiry man took a delicate sip, leaned back comfortably in his chair, and said, "We are furious at the attack."

"Yes, sir," Masticor said, not touching his glass. "I know."

The other man held the stem of the glass with his thin, soft fingers, swirling the garnet liquid like gentle waves against the side. "And how did it happen?"

"I don't know," Masticor answered. "Someone from the outside found out. And, apparently, grew impatient."

"Foolishness," the man said as though that explained everything. "What happened with the boy could have compromised everything. These plans, Senator, they are delicate. If something happens beforehand, we will lose a certain weight in our bargaining power."

"Of course," Masticor replied. And when he did, it seemed that the wiry man almost smiled in amusement.

"Of course," he echoed. "You must remember that you are our mouthpiece—the one we rely on to be our voice, our diplomat, to keep these things in check. Gracefully." He took another sip of his drink. "It is alarming that the woman became aware of the situation."

"The president, of course, is a person of interest. Especially after his quick rise to political power. It might have made other groups suspicious," Masticor replied. "Perhaps overly eager."

The wiry man nodded, sipping his wine for several minutes as though Masticor was not at the same table. After a while, he looked into Masticor's eyes and said, "Proceed with the plan. We must continue."

Senator Masticor nodded, understanding that he was dismissed. He rose, having not touched his own drink, and left the man they called Cere to enjoy his solitude.

Twenty-Six

It turned out that Marxma ran fast, killed it at drills, and mentored the boys using both discipline and reward. Plus she could do a back flip.

But she was truly terrible at basketball.

Chet found that he was almost glad. When they'd started their practices last week, he'd worried that Marxma was going to end up as coach, cheerleader, and overall hero, leaving Chet as nothing more than the shiny-pants water boy.

He was relieved when they started shooting to find that Marxma could barely hit the backboard, much less the rim.

Consequently, she had passed the torch to him, or the ball as it were. And with some help from a few of the younger Secret Service agents, they'd whipped the boys into a decent little team.

Now the boys zigzagged up the court, stopping at designated points to do push-ups or wall jumps. The dark-haired

Secret Service agent, Lesa, stood on the sidelines, whistle in her mouth. As opposed to Marxma, she knew her way around a court.

She stood by a row of boys, working with them on free throws. She moved over to adjust the hand position of one of the smallest boys, then stood back as the ball slid across his fingers, then swooshed through the net, never even grazing the rim.

"Yes," the boy shouted, jumping into the air and giving Lesa a high five. She laughed, and Chet wondered why she'd ended up with the Secret Service instead of playing pro ball. She trotted toward another group of kids—slender and tall with wiry tight arms and strong legs. Chet gazed in her direction. She was probably 5'11", just a few inches shorter than he was.

She dropped the whistle from her mouth to talk to one of the boys panting at the sideline. "Come on. I'll do the push-ups with you. And we're not doing any girl push-ups either." The two of them hit the ground, beating out twenty quick pulses, their noses almost touching the court floor.

Chet trotted over. "Nice work, Juan." The boy stood up smiling, and Lesa got up with an exaggerated groan. "This kid's wearing me out."

Juan flexed his bicep, gave it a fake kiss, and jumped back into the other drills.

Chet smiled at Lesa, who put the whistle back in her mouth and blasted it at a few of the other boys who were cutting their sprints short. "Ten extra," she hollered. Chet ran over to them, smacking one on the back. "Come on, guys. If it doesn't kill you..."

"...it can still make you puke," a boy named Edgar finished as Lesa blew her whistle and the boys darted away.

Chet laughed, glancing at Lesa's tall silhouette just as Marxma came onto the court, followed by a heavy man with a camera and a tall Asian man carrying a large box.

"Hey darlin'," she said, reaching out and squeezing Chet's hand. "Christmas came early this year." She gestured to the box. "I thought the boys deserved a little team spirit for all their hard work."

Chet glanced into the box. It was full to the brim with sleek red, white, and blue jerseys. "Cool." Chet reached in to touch the silky fabric.

"Got their names and all," Marxma said, winking. "Now blow that fat whistle of yours and bring those kids over."

Chet paused for a moment. The boys were running in beautiful lines around the court—panting, sweating, focused. He hated to interrupt. But Marxma was standing there, a smile on her face so big it seemed like it really was Christmas.

Chet blew his whistle, waving the boys over as the big man with the camera began to snap pictures.

———

Reylin hunched over her father's computer.

She'd already given them the initial information, plus

Burnes' name, plus more information about the box that would detonate the EMP.

Now it was also her job to find the date for the attack.

Sure, sure, easy peasy. Just crack into the White House database, find information about where the president would be traveling, and with whom. All without attracting notice.

That's what she disliked about Henry. He was always acting like things should be easy. Just because they were easy for him didn't make it all peaches for everyone else.

The attack would happen this spring. They knew that much. She'd told Henry to figure out what dates his dad had things planned when he'd be flying in Marine One. That should help narrow down the options.

Of course it wasn't good enough for Henry Miller. Nope, he wanted all the facts handed to him on a silver platter—right down to the millisecond. Not that milliseconds didn't matter. For this plan to work, they mattered a lot.

Reylin cracked her neck and typed a password into the computer. She hadn't told Henry yet, but she knew from some old papers in her dad's office how they would find the words on the device. That alone would be tricky; it's not like the words were going to be scribbled on it with permanent marker.

But before that, they needed two more things: an exact time when the helicopter would be in the air, and a way to find the precise location of the device.

Each part required very specific information. And each part demanded nothing less than perfect timing. Reylin sighed. Henry didn't even begin to know what he was asking of her. And that was for the best.

The computer whirred. Of course, it would take more than a simple password to get the information she needed. When you were dealing with White House scheduling, that was how it went. They didn't exactly post the president's itinerary on Twitter. *And today the president will be meeting with the Armenian leader, who doesn't like him, and might, in fact, hire a secret band to kill him.*

As for the secret bands, they weren't much more transparent. The ones that did make loud threats online were the least of their worries. It was the quiet groups, the ones you hardly knew existed, that were the most dangerous. Not to mention the hardest to gather information about.

She glanced at the screen, typed in a series of letters and numbers. And waited. All the things she needed were buried in the code, encrypted under a thousand layers that she couldn't yet understand.

A thousand. The number hung in her brain.

If she could just get Henry to find that box, to disable it. It would propel her into something. Make her somebody like she'd never been able to be, like she never would be if she stayed shadowed by her father's success.

Marxma had broken out with her films. Reylin wanted to do something similar, to become a person of power and influence. For that, she needed to do this, to help Henry do this.

She typed in a group of letters followed by a series of symbols. The computer buzzed and whirred. Several lines of code streamed down the screen. And then stopped. The blocky words hung on the screen like a gate.

She tapped the cherry wood of her father's desk with her fingers. Denied or not, she was getting closer. There had been a pattern there, a hint. Soon, she thought, closing her eyes so she could see it in her mind, soon she would find it.

TWENTY-SEVEN

Henry stared at the map on Lucy's phone—trying to make sense of the 1780s Washington D.C. versus the current Washington D.C. It wasn't easy. If it wasn't for the Potomac, Henry might not have believed it was the same place at all.

Lucy was pointing to the Rock Creek and Potomac Parkway. "I think this is north of what was called Goose Creek in the older map." She traced it with her finger.

"Then where is Goose Creek?" Henry asked.

Lucy spun her ring, once, then twice. "I think it's gone now."

Henry squinted at the old map on Lucy's phone, then swiped to the new map. "Crazy what a few hundred years will do."

"A few hundred years plus a lot of development and industrialization," Lucy added, swiping to another tiny image of an old map. "And I think Goose Creek is where he probably would have lived. It ran right through the center of his property; and back then you would have wanted your house near a body of water." She stared at two of the maps for a minute. "For better or worse."

"What do you mean?" Henry asked as she started walking.

"In the late 1700s, this area was barely more than a swamp. They needed the water, but it also brought water-borne and mosquito-borne diseases—typhoid, malaria, yellow fever. I was reading up on Burnes." She paused. "There's not a lot, but his wife and son died of a water-borne disease."

Henry nodded as they walked south. Henry's security detail trailed behind them. Henry had told him he was trying to get in shape.

They walked over the lush White House lawns, past the swimming pool and a stand of trees, along the jogging path Clinton had installed.

"Should we head toward Constitution Gardens?" Henry asked. "There's water there."

Lucy nodded, pinching her lips together. "Yeah, I guess," she said slowly.

Henry raised an eyebrow. "But...?"

"I think it's just manmade. The swamp that was here was drained by Ulysses S. Grant."

"And," Henry said.

"So I don't know that it's water we're looking for neces- sarily." She glanced down at her phone. "Honestly, it's so hard to tell with these old maps at all. It could be just about anywhere. From here to the Potomac."

She put her phone in her pocket and shook her head.

They passed the fountain and walked toward East Street Terrace.

At Ellipse Park, Lucy picked up a pamphlet on its history while Henry watched the pigeons coo and peck in front of them.

"Want to practice the introductions Keikiki's been teaching us?" Henry asked.

"Sure," Lucy said, stuffing the pamphlet in her pocket.

"Give it a go," Henry said.

Lucy took a deep breath and proceeded to stumble over each sound. "Ugh," she said. "It's like all the letters are stuck in my mouth. Like globs of peanut butter."

Henry thought it kind of sounded that way when Lucy tried the language, but he didn't say so. "You'll get it, Lu."

"I know how it *should* sound," she said. "But when I try, I just can't make the sounds come out."

Henry tried to smile, but he was already tired and they hadn't even walked a full mile. Maybe he really did need the exercise. They drifted along the edge of Ellipse Park. Henry liked the wide open space, even if it was hardly D.C.'s most magical tourist location. Maybe that's *why* he liked it. A little dull, often with sections marked off for upcoming events or construction. But it always seemed to hum with a sort of peacefulness in a city that mostly hummed with honking horns.

"Okay. I'm done practicing for now. You go," Lucy said.

Henry shrugged. "I'll work on the parts individually, I think." He practiced the word for 'I' over and over until it felt pretty comfortable.

"I think that's right," Lucy said. "It's like it seems to fit. That language really does draw on patterns, more than just sounds and tones. It's like you're shaping a piece to fit a puzzle and when you get it, you just know."

The 'am' was harder. Henry felt like he had to nail every pitch to the millitone and even then, he wasn't sure he got it.

"Now add it to your name," Lucy said.

Henry did. Putting the tones together was its own kind of challenge. Somehow they needed to connect in a specific way and if they didn't they meant something else. "Dang, Lu," Henry said. They'd gone a mile and a half, almost to the west side of Ellipse Park, and he still couldn't put three words together.

Lucy was looking at him with wide eyes. "I'm never going to learn it, am I? A language that's this hard for you."

"You'll get it, Lucy," Henry said quickly. "You will. We will." As he said it, he closed his eyes and tried to reach in, letting the sounds of the streets fall away, pulling in the steady thrum of the park, connecting himself to the sounds. "I am Henry," he said.

Lucy stopped.

So did the Secret Service agent, looking up and jogging closer to the teens. The few people around them also glanced up and stared for a moment before walking on.

"Henry," the agent asked. "Please try to keep a low profile."

"I..." Henry stuttered. "Um, okay." The agent fell back.

"I think you got it," Lucy whispered.

Lucy and Henry walked farther south, passing a group of homeless people, clustered along the edge of Ellipse Park, standing around old blankets, waving signs about UFOs. A woman glanced up at Henry and stared into his eyes. She smiled—silvery caps over several teeth—and reached out a hand.

Henry took Lucy's arm and pulled her past the crowd of homeless people, through a flock of birds, and toward the center of the park.

Lucy took out the pamphlet. "According to this, Ellipse Park was the site for a ton of UFO sightings in the 1950s."

Henry looked around at the open space. "Well, I guess if I was looking for a spot to land my spaceship, this would be a pretty good one."

"Sure would," Lucy said smiling. "Apparently, the 1950s was the great day of alien craft sightings, but after the introduction of digital filters in the 1970s, UFO sightings on radar dropped off." She paused, looking at the horizon. "Most unidentified object sightings are just atmospheric bends of light. Kind of beautiful really—the way the air can warp light into different shapes and colors—discs, pinpricks, tunnels in the sky."

Both of them paused, their breath coming out in cold clouds as they stared past joggers and starlings. Even in early March, it was its own kind of beautiful.

They walked across the dull winter lawn, sometimes stopping to turn slow circles in the grass.

Burnes' house, of course, if it had been here at all, was long gone. Henry didn't know what they'd been hoping to find—some hint of where it had been—a dip in the ground, an ancient stone, some small, forgotten relic. But too much time had passed. Even the meridian stone that Jefferson had placed at the center of the Ellipse to help with the surveying of the growing capital was covered by turf and basically impossible to find.

If it wasn't for Burnes' voice, he and his story would have been completely forgotten. Maybe that's why he'd bothered to introduce himself at all.

I'm Mr. Burnes. A voice and a name. Lucy was right. It was a strange thing to leave behind.

Henry wandered through the grass, disturbing clusters of bugs from their warm spots. He stared across the wide expanse of the park. All at once, trying to stop the attack on his father by himself seemed really stupid and hopeless.

"Lucy, let's just call the Beast and go home," he said.

Lucy was looking out over the horizon at the buildings and streets in the distance. The Washington Monument cast a long shadow to the east. "It all used to be nothing," she said. "Water and mud and crops and trees. Look at it now."

Henry shrugged again. He felt far away and tired.

"And he was just a man scratching out a living. Old and grumpy. Wife and son gone. Just a speck on this landscape that could eat up a person and you'd never even know he was gone. No wonder Burnes wanted people to notice him, to hear his voice, know his name. Who wouldn't?"

Watching her, she looked every bit the Potowani of her father's family—connected to the earth and the history of the country in a way Henry wasn't sure he could ever be.

"I am Mr. Burnes," Henry said, coming to stand beside her and look across the horizon. And then, on a whim, he said it in Kiribati. "I am Mr. Burnes." The tones lined up like cogs in a watch, clicking into place, singing their song.

And then, there it sat—a dingy white house, wavering in the distance.

"Henry," Lucy whispered.

Near one of the windows, they saw a slim shadow—the silhouette of a man. Slowly, the man turned, his profile becoming a darkened face. Henry could feel his stare, but all he could see was a circular orb that hung from his neck, glowing.

A light burst from the floor, burning a mark into it as the man looked away. He took the orb off his neck, casting it from the window where it fell into a creek quivering in the distance—the bright disc sinking into the depths of the water until it was gone.

Lucy was clutching her chest, not breathing.

"Lucy?" Henry said. "Did you see that?"

"Yes," Lucy said. "A house. A man of shadows. A flame."

"And the pendant?"

Lucy looked at Henry. "I saw him throw something."

"But you didn't see what it was?"

"No," Lucy said. "Not exactly."

"Strange," Henry said. In his mind, the light from the

floor connected to the light of the orb, binding them—drawing him to them, though he didn't know why.

Lucy looked ahead, and murmured, "The light bends, creating discs and pinpricks of light in the sky."

But Henry wasn't listening.

TWENTY-EIGHT

The curator sat at her desk, sorting papers into boxes and folders. The White House had always been, despite its appearance, a dangerous place to work. She closed a box and opened her computer, clicking through file after file, saving those that were important and discarding others.

After 9/11, the staff had been in shock; terrorists had almost succeeded in flying a plane into the House. The staff had gone through multiple de-briefings, dozens of drills. She'd heard stories of it from her mother.

In light of that event, she'd spent hours instructing her own staff on which artifacts were the most worth saving if the chance for saving anything presented itself.

They were, of course, supposed to consider their own safety first, but if the chance arose they were to perform what the staff had taken to calling a "Dolley Madison." They would grab any furniture, artifacts, or paintings that were within arm's reach and take them.

The staff had done these briefings in the East Room, right in front of the Lansdowne portrait of George Washington—the painting Madison was credited with saving, although in reality it was the White House workers who had actually taken it from the wall under Dolley Madison's supervision.

The curator flipped her laptop shut, locked her office, and wound her way to the East Room on the first floor. She paused in front of the painting, studying each line, the heavy swipes of paint in their small hills and valleys on the canvas. It always brought her inspiration and hope when things got confusing. Her grandmother had worked for the White House, and her mother after that.

When she had come into this world, her mother had named her after the fourth president's wife. Not Dolley—that never would have fit. But Madison. Madison Crossley.

She'd given her life to the House—studying history in college, and applying to work here as soon as age and experience had allowed. She was not married. She had borne no children. To anyone from the outside, it would seem that she was nothing more than a relic of the White House herself—old, well-preserved, and brittle.

She smiled. That much was true.

In her time here, she'd come to know more than even the White House walls could contain. Much more. She slipped a small jump drive into her pocket. Someone had been trying to hack in. She would leave what she wanted them to find. Nothing more.

Keikiki might look like the most exotic member of the staff, but she had been to more places than even him.

And she had seen enough to know that safety was an illusion—a bulletproof vest against a fleet of cannons. Terror was terror. Horror was horror. Extremists were extreme. A few snipers on the roof and all the Secret Service in the world couldn't stop the annihilation that would come if enough powerful men and women wanted it to come. They couldn't even have halted a few Islamic extremists during 9/11 if the regular citizens on board United Airlines Flight 93 hadn't interfered.

Ms. Crossley smiled.

Regular citizens. Just like her. But not.

Turns out when you manage thousands of important antiques and artifacts, you begin to understand the traders and bosses that rove and rule in underground markets. It was tempting when you were pulling in a mere $80,000/year to give in to the bribes, gifts, and offers that came your way. And yet she had refused offer after offer. All in the name of history, of art, of integrity.

Well, all except for one. And it had hardly been her grandest proposition.

Crossley glanced down at the perfectly square envelope in her hand, sealed and stamped in wax. She pressed the insignia, tracing the angles formed by four equal lines. Her father had not loved her mother. But he had loved his daughter. It had made his life complicated. She understood. She did not love all the people and all the sides she was asked to support. She did not love all the things she was called to do. But she would do them.

Because when danger came, as danger always would, a few guns and armored cars would do nothing. Madison Crossley understood that better than anyone else. She also knew that, for a woman in her unique position, danger would press the hardest of all.

TWENTY-NINE

Lucy flipped open the ghost book on the desk in the Treaty Room. The ghost of Abigail Adams hanging her laundry in the East room. Thomas Jefferson playing his violin in the Yellow Oval Room. Andrew Jackson swearing and stomping through the halls. Mary Todd. Her young son. Annie Surratt knocking on doors begging for her mother's release before Mary Surratt was executed for her role in Lincoln's murder. And of course Lincoln, Lincoln, Lincoln.

Lots of ghosts. Seen by a lot of people—normal people—from Winston Churchill to Maureen Reagan—most of them deep believers in what they had seen. Lucy tapped the book. She knew that scientists attributed these paranormal events to sleep paralysis or waking dreams—things people see as their minds wake from dreaming sleep.

That made sense for the midnight viewings, but what

about perfectly sane, lucid people seeing ghosts or hearing voices in the middle of a perfectly normal day?

Lucy twisted her ring. She was sure of what she thought she'd seen, and sure she hadn't been asleep. But had it been some other trick of air or light, especially in a place where UFO sightings were common? Were there particular atmospheric conditions in that area that caused "sightings" of various sorts?

She glanced at the brochure she'd gotten at Ellipse Park. Most sightings had occurred between the 1950s and 1970s, people often claiming to see a cluster of a thousand planets. Since that time, the capital had had a few good scares—several during Donald Trump's presidency. Washington, D.C., Myrtle Beach, Iowa, and, coincidentally, Michigan were considered "hot spots"—places where the inversion of air created UFO-esque circles of light in the night sky.

Which didn't explain seeing things on the ground in the middle of the day. And, shifts of light or not, seeing a house with a guy in it seemed weirdly specific, but it was something they had been looking for, something they had really wanted to find.

Mind plus light plus desperation.

Who knows? But, real or not, no one in the White House had ever seen that particular ghost before. And no one in the UFO pamphlets had ever seen light bend into a flame on the floor, or an orb like Henry had seen. In all the books and brochures nothing connected to what they were looking for. Nothing except the voice of Mr. Burnes.

"Lucy," Henry said, and she jumped. "I told you there's nothing in there."

"I know," she said. Another mound of books about White House ghosts sat scattered on the floor around her. "There's nothing about it anywhere."

"Well, then let's look where there are things. Things that everyone can see." Henry bent over his phone, staring at the map of the White House grounds.

"For all the time you've spent reading about ghosts," Lucy said, "I've been looking at those stupid maps. There's nothing there either. Nothing helpful anyway. We searched Ellipse Park up and down, especially where we saw that house. There's nothing there. No box. Or anything else."

Henry sighed, turning to stretch his back before slouching back into his seat. "Where will they plant the EMP, Lu?" he said. "The house is gone; the creek is gone; the land is empty—just trees and grass and tourists."

"And UFOs," Lucy added. "And ghosts."

Henry ignored her. "Definitely no EMP detonator hanging around in a box. And what does Burnes have to do with any of it anyway?" He zoomed the image of the map in and out, swiping quickly with his fingers as though something else would suddenly appear.

"So you're not more weirded out by seeing a ghost house?" Lucy asked. "'Cause I'm freaking out."

"Stress can cause sightings of various types, blackouts, even hallucinations," Henry replied.

"Right. So we were both stressed and happened upon the same hallucination at the same time?"

"It wasn't exactly the same."

"Henry," Lucy said sharply. "Stop being so literal and listen."

"I am listening, Lucy." Henry looked up. "And I don't know why we saw what we saw. I don't know why I've seen —" Henry stopped mid-sentence. "—why any of the weird stuff that happens happens. But it seems to happen a lot here." He motioned to the ghost books all over the floor, to her discarded pamphlet about alien sightings. "And at this point, it's just distracting. What we need to find is that box. And obviously we both want to a whole lot."

"Thus the vision."

"Yeah, or whatever it was. The point is," Henry said, zooming the image of the map out until it looked like a blurry blob, "we need to find the detonator. We need to find what Burnes has to do with it. If anything."

Lucy leaned back, blowing out a deep breath. "Okay," she said. "Let's keep trying, like none of this is crazy at all."

"It's all crazy, Lucy," Henry said. "Sometimes I feel like *I'm* crazy. In fact, I can't tell you how relieved it makes me feel that you actually saw something too."

Lucy gave Henry a brief look. "Henry," she began. And then stopped. He'd been under an enormous amount of pressure. For months. "Try not to stress. We'll solve it. And if we don't, we'll tell. Your dad will be okay." She paused. "You will too."

"I'm not worried about me."

Lucy flipped through her phone. "Well it's all connected. Your dad, his family. This is scary stuff." She swiped again through images of different maps of the city, old and new, several pictures of the south lawn, a picture of the park facing the Washington Monument with its shadow hovering over the lawn, a bird's eye view of The Ellipse.

And then she accidentally swiped too far to a picture Henry had sent her of the tattoo on the maid's wrist. She paused, staring at it. At the center of the tattoo was a circle. A circle surrounded by four flaming points, like a compass— a compass without a needle.

She flipped back to a bird's eye picture of The Ellipse.

Circles weren't some kind of fresh, unusual motif. Circles were really common in tattoo designs. In any designs. It probably meant nothing. Still, Lucy flipped back and forth between the two images, spinning her ring around and around in more circles.

"Henry," Lucy began, looking at the images again and trying to make things connect.

Henry looked up, his eyes unfocused from staring at the screen.

They sat at the large Treaty Table in the Treaty Room, between the Yellow Oval Room and Lincoln's bedroom. Peace agreements had been signed on the wood that made up this desk, and the room held a spirit of safety that Lucy appreciated.

She glanced down at her phone, looking at the symbol from the maid's wrist. "Do you think the maid attack is connected?"

Henry shook his head. "The FBI said the thing with the maid was just random, isolated." Henry looked over Lucy's shoulder at the image she'd pulled up of the tattoo. "That maid was nuts. But nuts happens. Let's worry about the attack on my dad."

"I am worrying about the attack on your dad." Lucy zoomed in on the tattoo, the flaming points like north, south, east, west.

"Seriously, Lu," Henry said. "We're wasting our time looking for that. There's nothing online with any resemblance."

"The Ellipse has some resemblance. And the Ellipse was part of Burnes' homestead."

"The Ellipse is a circle. So are a lot of other things," Henry said, pursing his lips like he was thinking of something else.

Lucy swiped at her phone harder and harder, pushing back the tears that seemed to come out of nowhere, stinging against her eyelids. Henry's dad was in danger—a lot of danger. Henry was too.

But there was something missing—some piece they weren't seeing. She swiped past the bird's eye view, past the one with the Washington Monument, its shadow pointing over the Ellipse. "I'm asking the curator," she said, pushing back from the desk. "About the tattoo. She'll know something."

"I'm sure she's been asked," Henry said. "And she's not exactly sweet as sugar candy."

"Well, I am," Lucy said, pasting on a grin. "And I'm asking." Lucy stood up and opened the door. "Are you coming or not?"

Henry sighed. "Okay, okay. Just why does this matter to you so much?"

"Are you serious, Henry?" Lucy asked.

Henry poked Lucy in the side. "Just wait till you meet *Madame* Crossley," he said, using a fake French accent. "You'll see why I'd rather be attacked by another maid than talk to her."

"Is she French?" Lucy asked. "Should I seriously call her Madame?"

"Definitely not," Henry said. "She's as American as apple pie. Well, if apple pie was made of lemons with no sugar added and then overbaked."

Lucy raised an eyebrow. "That just sounds sexist or ageist or something."

"Whatever," Henry said. "It's just true-ist."

"Hashtag not a thing."

"Hashtag wait and see."

They stood in front of the dark wooden door that led into the curator's office and Lucy paused. The door was large and so perfectly polished it looked like tumbled stone.

The position of curator had been created when Jackie Kennedy decided that the priceless antiques and assets of the White House needed better care and documentation. Anyone able to do the job would have to be a little, well, overbaked as Henry had said.

On a brushed silver nameplate were the words, "M. Crossley." Lucy took a deep breath, held up her hand, and knocked.

"Come in," came a thin voice from the other side.

Lucy pushed open the door to see a small, pale woman in black-rimmed glasses sitting at a clean desk. Most of the room was equally sparse, although to her left was a large cabinet filled with hundreds of delicate, antique wineglasses.

As soon as they walked in, the woman raised a thin eyebrow, which sat like a frown above her glasses.

"Yes," she said. "Can I help you?"

"Um," Lucy said, clearing her throat and starting to understand Henry's hesitation. "We were just wondering if you could look at this." She handed the woman her phone with the image of the tattoo. "Do you know if this symbol has any connections to anything, um, in or around the White House or anything?"

The woman looked at Lucy, lips drawn down, as though they'd never risen into a smile, and took the phone as her assistant came into the room. He glanced at the image Ms. Crossley held up to her face. "Mr. Charles, I am extremely busy right now. If you could come back in a few minutes, it would be much appreciated."

"Of course, Ms. Crossley," he said, scooting out of the room and glancing back at Henry and Lucy as he shut the door.

"I have already seen this," Ms. Crossley said as soon as the door was closed. She set Lucy's phone on her desk. "I did a thorough search of the White House Archives, Congressional Archives, and the Library of Congress. Then of course there's the internet. We have not found anything."

"It kind of looks like a compass," Lucy began, but Ms. Crossley held up a hand for her to stop talking.

"I even had an ancient symbols professor analyze this," Crossley finished. "And he has also come up with nothing."

She looked over her glasses at the two teens.

"Oh," Lucy said, trying not to make eye contact with Henry who, she was sure, was looking pretty smug right now. "Well, if you find something, would you please tell us?"

"I will tell the Secret Service and the head of the Federal Bureau of Intelligence. I'm sure you can talk to them if you have further questions."

"Oh, well, thank you," Lucy said. Sometimes she was glad she had a Japanese grandmother. They taught you to bite back words when words needed biting back. Overbaked didn't even begin to describe this woman.

As they walked back down the hall, heading toward their lesson with Mr. Keikiki, Lucy refused to look at Henry.

"Come on Lu," Henry said. "Don't be mad."

Lucy almost laughed. "I'm not mad. I just don't want to have to tell you that you were right."

"Hashtag true-ist," Henry said, just as Ms. Crossley's assistant slipped into the library. For a moment before going in, he locked eyes with Henry. Then he pressed his lips tight and shut the door.

Thirty

Henry scanned the Solarium. Mr. Keikiki was not there, which was a first.

Usually when they got in, he was sitting at a table, still and composed as though he'd never left the Solarium in his life. Today was their first lesson since the maid attack two weeks ago. "Maybe he's not coming," Henry said, standing up and heading to the door. "Maybe he cancelled. We can go look for more information on—" Henry turned and nearly smacked into the head usher.

"Hello children," Mr. Keikiki said, moving to the front of the room.

Henry looked to the door, plotting an excuse to leave. He could say he was sick, that his grandma had died, that...

Lucy nudged him in the side, and whispered, "Your mom will freak out if you ditch."

Henry gritted his teeth. This was such a stupid, pointless punishment.

"It's only sixty minutes," Lucy murmured, pulling out her notebook and making a lot of noise with the pages. "And it's better than you getting grounded. Besides, we don't even know what direction to look right now."

"Might be nice to find out," Henry whispered back. "Instead of sitting in here, trying to make tonal vibrations with our throats."

"Please take a seat," Mr. Keikiki said. Henry plunked down and Lucy laid her notebook down as Keikiki set up the whiteboard. "Today's lesson will begin with a myth from my people's history." He walked around the solarium, stopping in front of the feminine figure in a cloak.

"For a thousand years across a thousand suns reigned a thousand princes of a thousand peoples." He paused. "Their lands were lush; their bellies full; their children fat. Among them lived only one who was not happy. She watched the skies in a way that most others watched their counting chambers. And for each trip around their sun, she noticed it grow a little dimmer. In time, the voice of her warning grew louder. There was not, she cautioned, energy enough for a thousand more years of such indulgence.

"Her warnings, as such warnings do, fell on deafened ears.

"Until the year came that the crops grew thin. Until the year came that the water ran murky. Until the year came that the fires began—straight lines of heat, hungry for ground that still ran with brambles and meat.

"The Sky Watcher found she couldn't turn her back on her people, any more than a mother could turn her back on a greedy child. And so—as the people around her grew thin in both body and spirit—she gazed to the heavens, to the realm she understood better than anyone else.

"And so it was that the Sky Gazer discovered a bit of light in a faraway place—a hope for grace in the burning landscape—a distant world whose positioning was unique in that its energy could feed a thousand other worlds."

Henry sighed again, more quietly this time. How could he be stuck in this calm, sunny room when it seemed everything was crumbling down around him? If it hadn't been, he might have given his mother a good, slow clap. She had chosen her punishment well. Learning the language was painful. Listening to Mr. Keikiki was worse.

Henry stole a glance at Lucy, who had abandoned her notebook and was staring at the statue beside Mr. Keikiki, her expression focused, almost rapt.

Keikiki turned back toward them, a huge smile on his face. "Now. Let's begin." He began making slight clicking noises with his tongue, followed by a humming that varied slightly in pitch and duration, but the differences were so subtle that it was really hard to hear a difference at all. Henry looked down at Lucy's blank notebook.

The language just didn't make sense. Maybe it wasn't even a real thing. Maybe in a few more weeks when they'd suffered enough, his mom and Mr. Keikiki intended to come in with cookies, laughing, and say, "Ha, we got you."

But that wasn't going to happen, not if Marine One went down in the meantime.

Henry tapped his finger on his desk, glancing at the

clock while Mr. Keikiki clicked away. Henry looked at him, the subtle sounds barely moving Keikiki's mouth. Henry had never learned anything like this. He was taking Japanese at Sidwell, and after a few lessons and some audio casts, he was practically fluent. But this...

"Now, it's your turn, Mr. Miller," Keikiki said, turning to him.

Henry stole another look at the clock and cleared his throat. Mr. Keikiki clicked. Henry tried to repeat it. It wasn't the same. Keikiki clicked again. And again.

Henry tried to focus, find the place in his mouth where the sound seemed to be—soft and near the back teeth, not the front.

"Not bad," Mr. Keikiki said, cocking his head to the side. "Ms. Hawk. Care to give it a try?"

Lucy did, but Henry could tell she just wasn't getting it. She could tell too. She stopped clicking and looked down at her desk, cheeks flushed.

Keikiki pinched his lips together, and Henry almost thought Mr. Keikiki was going to tell her it just wasn't the right fit. He willed his teacher not to. The only reason any of this was even kind of okay was because Lucy was here.

Lucy looked up. "I..." she began, but Mr. Keikiki interrupted her.

"Do you remember how you felt the first time you heard this language?"

"Yes," Lucy said quietly, looking down at her still-blank notebook. It sounded like she wanted to cry. Which made Henry hate the language that much more.

"Good," Mr. Keikiki said. "Keep remembering, and eventually I do believe this language will serve you well."

"Yes, sir," she said, still not making eye contact.

Keikiki made a song-like tone, and when he did Lucy looked up, right in his eyes.

"What word is that?" Lucy asked.

"*Remember*," he responded.

"I," she began. "I think I knew that." She smiled.

Mr. Keikiki smiled back. "Now, Henry." He paused. "As opposed to Ms. Hawk, who is truly challenged by this language, I believe that you are actually stopping yourself. You don't want to be here."

"It *was* a punishment," Henry replied, looking again at the clock.

"And an excellent choice for one," Mr. Keikiki said cheerfully. "But if you would let it, it could be more than a punishment. Ms. Hawk's assignment is to remember. But your assignment is to feel. You must allow yourself to feel the words. It's a little like singing, or even acting—the tones come out better when you actually feel what you're saying. There's more nuance that way."

"How am I supposed to feel what I say?" Henry asked.

"Well, you did it just now," Mr. Keikiki responded. "You were annoyed, and I could sense that. You could have used any number of different words and I would still have sensed the annoyance. And since it seems you're feeling the tiniest bit combative, let's go with that." He stopped and thought for a moment. "The word 'attack,'" he said. "Try saying it."

Keikiki said the word, and when he did, Henry did feel it

—the nuances. Danger, a bit of adrenaline. Strangely, Henry felt it so much that he found himself not wanting to try to repeat the word. It brought up too many memories and feelings, and he hated the way they stirred in his stomach.

Henry mumbled the word.

Mr. Keikiki raised a bushy eyebrow. "This is a feeling that I know is fairly fresh for you and perhaps it's not fair to ask you to say such a word, but I think that if you do, it might help you to understand the language. And perhaps some other things. Now try again." Mr. Keikiki repeated the word.

Henry said it again, knowing it was incorrect the moment it left his mouth.

"Close your eyes," Keikiki instructed. "Feel any emotions that come to the surface. The more you do, the easier it will be for you to connect to the words, their deeper meanings."

Henry closed his eyes and said the word. Still nothing. He opened his eyes. "I'm sorry, Mr. Keikiki. It's just too hard to form the tones."

"No," Mr. Keikiki said, a slight edge to his usually calm voice. "What is hard is that you don't want to remember how you felt. Think of the woman who attacked you. Think of how it felt, how you felt. Picture her hands, the knife. And say the word."

Henry scowled at Mr. Keikiki. "I will not. And I won't let you bully me like this. I don't know what you're trying to do, but this is a language class, not some psychotherapy session. If I don't want to say the word 'attack'—" Henry stopped mid-sentence. Without thinking, he had spoken the word in the language. The whole room seemed to shiver and pulse—danger, fear, thrust, power. All those feelings, all that energy bound up in that one word. It faded as it hit the edges of the room, as though swallowed up by the statues that surrounded them.

"Oh, Henry," Lucy said.

"I am sorry to have bullied you," Mr. Keikiki said, back to his perfectly mild tone, "but I do admit that I was hoping you would feel a little attacked and that a bit of that might—if you'll pardon the pun—translate."

Henry shrugged, looking away. Kiribati was weird. He didn't like it. In fact, right now, he hated it. In that one word, he'd felt so many things: the whir of the knife from the maid, the hands of the thug who months ago had tried to get him into the black car, the sight of the man with two shapes scraped or drawn onto his wrists as he'd shot at the Beast, the threat of Ethereal, Reylin's tear-streaked face, the risk of the EMP plot. He'd felt everything.

The stupid word. The way Lucy had suddenly looked at him like she'd pitied him when she didn't even know how strong he could be, how strong he'd been when he was attacked.

Mr. Keikiki was looking at him, his forehead deep with lines. "Henry," he said. "Have you been attacked before? Before the incident with the maid?"

"You mean, that whole shooting-at-the-Beast incident."

"What I mean is, have you been attacked personally?"

Henry shrugged again, trying to smile. "Chet attacks me all the time."

Mr. Keikiki pinched his lips together. "Would you say the word again?"

"Actually, I'm kind of tired," Henry said. "So I probably can't. Besides, it's Lucy's turn anyway."

Mr. Keikiki met Henry's eyes and held his gaze for a moment. Henry could see every line etched in the old man's face. Then Mr. Keikiki took a deep breath and the lines almost seemed to clear. "Of course. As you say, this is not a psychotherapy session. It's just somewhat helpful when learning this language to connect with the words on a more intimate level."

Mr. Keikiki smiled, the scar on his lip dipping down as his mouth went up. "You've both done wonderfully today. Why don't we dismiss a bit early, so you can enjoy this gorgeous weather?"

Henry didn't need to be asked twice.

THIRTY-ONE

Alex Charles stumped down to the White House Mess in the basement of the West Wing.

He usually went out for lunch, but today Her Majesty Crossley had too much for him to do. Maybe he should have felt like the luckiest guy alive to be in the White House, just out of college, and working under one of the most prestigious White House historians of all time. But he was already tired of doing the same thing every day. And Crossley got on his nerves.

He ordered some pasta from the Mess and stopped at the pick-up counter to get it just as a sweet smell and soft blouse brushed past him.

Marxma Frey stopped just shy of the door that led into the Mess and turned. "Well, hello, Mr. Charles," she said, the slow sway of her accent almost hypnotic.

Alex nearly dropped his food. How did she even know his name?

"Do you have work upstairs or do you want to come in?" she asked, gesturing toward the Mess door. "Chet is meeting me in a few minutes."

Alex felt like he couldn't move his mouth. "Well, I…"

"Oh, come on," she said. "I'll have Chet add you to our table." She tapped a quick message into her phone.

"Okay, sure," Alex said. "If you think it's"—he paused—"if you think he'd be cool with that."

"One thing about Chet," Marxma said, looking up. "He's always cool." The phone in her hand beeped and she glanced at it.

"There," she said. "He's got it all taken care of. Now come on in." She pushed open a door and walked through.

Alex held the platter with his pasta awkwardly in front of him and followed. The Mess was normally reserved for senior officials, cabinet members, commissioned officers, and the guests of all those people. Marxma seemed to fit in just fine, but he definitely didn't.

He tried to straighten his tie without dropping his pasta while Marxma strode over to the maître d' and asked for Chet's table. The maître d' stood, leading the way, and Alex found himself stumbling after them. By the time he set his food down, Marxma had already settled in and put the napkin on her lap. She glanced at him.

"I hope you don't mind me saying so, hon, but it looks like you've had kind of a hard day."

Alex wasn't sure he could mind her saying anything to him. "Well, um, I guess I kind of have a lot of hard days. Just trying to get the swing of things and stuff."

A member of the staff brought them waters with lemon. Alex held his fork awkwardly above his food, unsure whether he was allowed to eat it or not.

"Well, I'm told Ms. Crossley can get a little crusty," she said, smiling.

"That's for sure," he said, trying not to stare. Marxma was probably two inches taller than he was with light blue eyes that shimmered like an arctic ocean. He cleared his throat.

"Don't let it get to you," Marxma said.

He shrugged, looking down.

Marxma seemed to notice his food and waved a hand toward it. "You better dig in before it gets cold."

He stabbed his fork obediently into a piece of bowtie pasta, as Marxma delicately squeezed lemon juice into her glass.

"I mean, Crossley's okay and all," he said. "She's just really brusque." He popped a sun-dried tomato into his mouth. "And not just with me. She's that way with everyone —janitor, senator, president's son. At least she doesn't discriminate." His phone blinked and he glanced down at it.

"Well, that's a way to put it." Marxma pushed her water to the side and leaned closer. "Just between you and me, I don't think Chet is a big fan of Crossley."

Alex fumbled with his phone. "I doubt his brother is either." He clicked the image closed just as Marxma glanced down at it.

"What makes you say that?" Marxma asked, taking a croissant from the basket the waiter had set down.

"Well," Alex said, shoving his phone into his pocket and picking up his fork. "Any time Henry comes in with a question, Crossley just brushes him off. Happened today, actually."

Marxma shook her head, flaking off thin bits of bread and chewing thoughtfully. "That's a shame. Honestly, I'm surprised Henry is brave enough to come to her with questions at all."

Alex stared. How could someone make eating look so beautiful? "Yeah," he said, realizing that he wasn't quite sure what she'd just said.

"Seems to me," Marxma said, "that the curator's job is to give information, not withhold it." She took a sip of her lemon water.

Alex touched the phone in his pocket.

"I mean, yeah," Alex said. "I agree. Crossley's just not very forthcoming. Or," he said, taking his phone out and glancing at the image again, "very helpful at all."

Marxma glanced toward his phone as the screen flicked off and raised her eyebrows. "I mean, it's definitely none of *my* business. But it is Henry's and, well, maybe it would earn you some points with the first family to talk to Henry and answer the questions she wouldn't."

Alex put the last of his pasta into his mouth. "You know, maybe I should," he said, watching her slender fingers slip down the cold glass.

At that moment, Chet Miller hurried through the doors and to the table. "Hey, Marxie. Sorry I'm late." The two of them held hands as he sat down and a waiter bustled over with menus. Alex looked at his empty plate. His phone beeped again.

"I'm Chet," the president's son said, holding out a hand.

"Hi," Alex said.

"And how do you guys know each other?" Chet asked, glancing at Marxma.

"Actually, we just met," Marxma said, smiling into Chet's face in a way that made Alex blush.

Chet looked mildly confused, but smiled back. "Well, great." He opened his mouth like he was going to ask another question just as Alex's phone began to ring in earnest.

"I'm so sorry," Alex said. "But I think I'm going to have to go. Crossley keeps calling. Those miniature coffee mugs from 1942 aren't going to index themselves."

Chet laughed out loud. "I don't envy you, man. She's probably slithering around the White House right now making sure no one breathes close to the antique sconces."

Alex smiled. "Thanks for inviting me. It was cool."

Chet just shrugged. "Hey, you play basketball?"

"Um," Alex said. "I kind of do a little. I mean, I'm not amazing or anything."

"Well, we're looking for staff who'd like to scrimmage against a little team I've been coaching. If you ever want to play, just let me know."

Alex nodded and headed toward the door. Maybe working at the White House didn't have to be the worst job in the world after all.

Henry and Lucy walked in from the courtyard, silent. They had talked through every possibility they could think of for locating the EMP device and had no ideas, no leads.

As they walked down the hall, Henry noticed Ms. Crossley's assistant standing near the flower shop, holding a stack of papers like he had something important to do and chewing on his cuticles like he didn't.

Henry nodded at him as they walked past. Mr. Charles fell into step behind them.

They walked quickly along the basement hall and Mr. Charles walked more quickly to keep up. Henry gave him a glance, remembering the maid. He clenched his jaw.

Lucy seemed to read his mind. "Hey," she said, stopping in the hall and looking at Ms. Crossley's assistant.

"Um, hi," he replied.

"Do you need...something?" Lucy asked.

Mr. Charles looked at both of them in silence for a minute before blurting, "Did Crossley tell you anything about that photo of the tattoo?"

Henry swiveled around to stare at him.

"Nothing at all," Lucy said. "According to her, it's just a pretty picture."

Mr. Charles sucked on his lips in a way that made Henry uncomfortable. His shirt collar was flipped up on one side and there was a tiny splotch of pink near the right pocket, as though he'd dripped ketchup there at lunch. Henry took a step back.

The curator's assistant looked at both of them, glanced at the White House library, then waved a hand, gesturing for them to follow him in.

Lucy looked at Henry and shrugged. They walked into the White House Library, which was just east of the curator's office. Bookshelves lined the walls, with a fireplace positioned on the northwest side. Above the fireplace hung one of Gilbert Stuart's famous paintings of George Washington. Two security guards stood near leather seats, and that made Henry feel better.

"Listen, this might be a dumb thing for me to do, but I just thought I should say something."

"Okay," Henry said. "Shoot."

"That picture you brought Ms. Crossley. I did a little of the research for it. It's true that there's no information about it. But I did find an image that looked like part of it."

"Really?" Lucy asked.

"Yes," he replied. "Crossley seemed surprised when anything turned up and she said it was too different to be related, but it didn't seem like it should be totally discounted."

Henry looked sideways at Lucy.

"Is it a compass?" Lucy asked.

"Well, no," he said, giving her a strange look. "Here, let me show you."

Alex Charles held up his phone. It showed a fuzzy picture that looked like it might be a gravestone. The lettering was almost impossible to read, but at the top of the stone Henry noticed a symbol. It was true that it didn't match the one on Concepcion Gonzalez's wrist. Her tattoo had elaborate flame-like designs arching out from the round center. But near the top of the crumbling gravestone was a similar circle, a few faint lines forming a square in its center.

Henry stared at it. "Whose gravestone is this?"

"It's hard to make out all the lettering in this picture," Mr. Charles said. "But it looks like David something. The dates are clearer."

"David Burnes," Lucy whispered, her voice tipping up in a question.

"There's something else written," Henry said, taking the phone. "You can just see the tops of the letters."

"Look, I have to get back to work," Mr. Charles said, reaching for his phone.

Henry slowly handed it back. "Do you know where this is? This headstone?"

Mr. Charles clicked back a few times on his phone. "It's at the North Town Cemetery, two miles from here. A bunch of old graves are there."

"Have you been?" Lucy asked, although Henry practically had his foot out the door and was tugging on her arm.

"No," Mr. Charles said, smiling. "I do computer research. Not real history. But I knew Crossley would brush you off, and—I don't know—it gets annoying."

"Well, thanks," Lucy said as Henry tried to leave.

"Yeah, thanks," Henry said over his shoulder. He was practically running down the hall.

"It could still be nothing," Lucy said as they bolted up the steps toward the exit.

"But it's as much of something as we've got," Henry said. "I mean, maybe the device is where Burnes is buried. Maybe it's in some coffin. Or mausoleum. Maybe there's a connection there, some identifying information near the tomb."

"Those all sound like a bit of a stretch," Lucy said.

Henry sighed, slowing. "What isn't? But there is a connection. There has to be."

"Well, there doesn't *have* to be," Lucy said. "But it *is* something."

Henry could tell she was mulling over things—trying to connect the dots. He'd seen that look a hundred times in a hundred classes. A puzzle. Lucy was working to put it together.

"Circles circles everywhere," Lucy finally said. She looked at Henry. "And, you know that thing you said about connections—I basically said something along those lines earlier today about the Ellipse. And you were all like, 'Whatever, everything's a circle.'"

"Well, not all circles are created equal."

Lucy squinted down at her phone. "Maybe."

Henry bumped his shoulder playfully into Lucy and smiled. With this new information, he felt lighter, just a little hopeful. Maybe they could do it. Maybe they could help his father. "So I guess we were both right. I mean, you have to admit, everything *is* a circle."

"And you have to admit that all of this is a bit of a stretch."

"Wait, weren't we on different sides of this argument this morning?" Henry asked.

Lucy rolled her eyes as they stepped out of the east exit into the sunshine, wandering through the Kennedy garden toward the south lawn.

"But how do we do it?" Henry said.

"Do what?" Lucy asked.

"Leave," Henry replied. "I can't exactly go look at some old grave with my posse following me around." He nodded toward his security detail who was standing outside, following them casually. He realized that he barely noticed them anymore—their presence like his own shadow.

Lucy nodded.

"We could go in the night," Henry said.

"Seriously, Henry?" Lucy said.

"What?" he asked.

"Well, for starters, this plan—so called—would require a certain very obedient girl to figure out how to sneak out of her high security house and past her own family's security detail."

"Come on, Lu," Henry said. "Don't you think you could channel just a little bit of rebel without a cause?"

"We have a cause," Lucy replied matter-of-factly. "And, no, I couldn't. And also, even if I could, it would take more than a little. Security guys are definitely out of my league." She paused. "Besides, what am I supposed to do? Wander through the streets of D.C. at midnight?"

"You could take the city bus."

"Okay, now I just feel like you're trying to get me killed without having to hire a hitman. Hashtag cheapskate."

"I wasn't," Henry said, straight-faced. "but...now I'm thinking about it. Anyway, to preserve your own skin maybe you should propose a different solution."

Lucy sighed and pressed her hands against her eyes. "I mean, is there a time when they would be really busy and not notice us that much?"

Henry lifted an eyebrow.

"It might *help* at least," Lucy said.

"Chet's having a party this Friday to celebrate our three-day weekend. There will be lots of kids, lots of noise, and probably security guys distracted by some of them bringing in, um, stuff they shouldn't."

"Okay, that could work," Lucy began. We could—" She stopped and looked up. They were at the front entrance of the White House, which was flanked by several Secret Service agents and two butlers. As they left the building, four Secret Service agents formed a small square around them.

Lucy sighed. "We could nothing," she murmured. "Maybe get to another room." They slid into the Beast as the Secret Service agent outside the door said something into his phone. "But, yeah," Lucy whispered. "There's no party—or anything else that I can think of—that will get us, unseen, out of this place."

Thirty-Two

Masticor opened an old notebook with several papers clipped inside. Strangely enough, old notebooks had become much safer places to keep important information than any computer or backup drive.

He stroked the crinkled pages with a smooth hand. No one thought of paper anymore. And even if someone had picked this up, it would look like nothing but old letters and articles. He fingered the edge of a yellowed piece of paper and smiled.

Some of the information was as old as the Revolutionary War. Priceless in so many ways. Yet any thief or spy would pass over it without a thought, hunting out account numbers, passwords, or cold, hard cash.

Masticor flipped through the pages, though he'd long ago committed the words he needed to memory. The words had come hundreds of years ago from a messenger sent from

Georgetown to oversee the construction near the new capital city. A messenger who'd met an old woman as she'd wandered the grounds, looking for coins.

Masticor read the account as it had been recorded and catalogued.

The old woman scavenged through dirt and debris beyond the old Burnes homestead, winding her way to the base of the Washington Monument, as yet a half stump of a building. I watched her for a spell before making my way toward her as she stooped over a patch of discarded stone. "You will not find much by way of riches there," I told her, removing my hat.

"Bah," the woman said, her old teeth capped in metal. "This land will grow riches like weeds. Watch and see, old man."

I smiled at the woman and offered her a crust of bread. "It isn't gold," I said. "But 'twill fill a belly better than coins."

"Indeed it would," she said, picking at the ground, but ignoring the bread. "But bread cannot feed the soul." She stopped, then looked toward the unfinished edge of the monument. "Iron," she muttered. "That is how they should finish it off. Powerful stuff, that."

I nodded genially, returning the bread to my satchel. "I've heard talk of aluminum."

"Aluminum!" The woman laughed.

"It's quite valuable," I replied, fishing in my pocket for something. "Worth more than gold."

"Well," she spat. "One day it will be thin as paper and worth just as much, that's what I say."

I raised an eyebrow and found what I was looking for in my trouser pocket. When I held forth a thin silvery coin, the woman licked her lips. "My sisters," she began. "They are quite ill."

As she reached for the unusual coin I drew it back. "You claim to know much of the future. I'd like just a piece." I held the coin up to the sky so she could see it clearly—a disc shining like a planet hung from my fingers.

The woman narrowed her eyes. She must have known me then. Or suspected from whence I came. "Agreed," she said, "but only a piece."

"Pieces," said I, "will do for the present."

The woman laughed, an ugly sound, then reached for my palm, and began to speak.

Masticor scanned the paper to its end. That messenger had been his sixth great grandfather—on a mission for information in the new world that was forming up around them.

But information hadn't been enough. They'd needed a certain person with a certain heritage. And that they hadn't been able to find.

Until now.

Masticor closed the book. *He who speaks to determine will have words revealed at his coming.*

From a book of old papers, they had the *how*. From the

experimental technology at the office in Kansas City, they had the *who*. Now they just needed to figure out the *where*.

————

Henry grabbed a tray and headed for the shortest line in the school cafeteria. The food at Sidwell Friends wasn't half bad —nothing like the lunches he'd had at public schools. It was one of the privileges that made his mother uncomfortable with the opportunity of having sons who went there, one of the things that made her uncomfortable with being the president's wife in general.

Henry tried to do his part in lowering the privilege bar by eating the least healthy foods they had to offer. Today it was fries and a burger. Home fries and grass-fed beef, but it was the best he could do under the circumstances.

Henry bit into a thick fry, the grease and salt sticky on his fingers. His mother used to make fries like this for them, baked in the oven because she'd said they were healthier that way.

Henry broke the fry in half. His mother had grown up the only daughter of a steel worker in Michigan. When she graduated from college and became a librarian, it was a major socio-economic step up. Her parents were proud of her. Her brothers teased her. When she met his father, who was studying law, she leaped another rung up the ladder. Her brothers stopped teasing. When his dad became governor, some of the family gatherings almost started to seem strained—factory or auto workers and then his parents. No one was mad. No one was mean. But a divide had formed. It was a divide that his mother still felt keenly.

Henry poured some extra ketchup on his burger. Grandpa Morris would have approved of that. Even if it was organic ketchup.

Henry was dabbing his finger in a blob of ketchup that dripped from his burger when Reylin came up to him. "I need to talk to you," she said as Henry licked off his finger.

She shoved a stack of napkins his direction and looked away. Henry smiled. At least they both hated being allies. He slid the napkins back her direction and made loud chewing noises. "Shoot," he said between sloppy bites. (Grandpa Morris would have approved of that too, though Henry wasn't sure his mother would.)

Reylin looked away, wrinkling her nose. "A couple of things I gathered. One, the attack has to be before the beginning of May because at that time Boeing will have the new Marine One fleet ready. The EMP device can only work on the current fleet because its electrical parts aren't hardened to the device."

Henry nodded, though he wasn't quite sure what all of that meant. Looking at Reylin, he was pretty sure she didn't know either. Where was Lucy when he needed her? He looked around the cafeteria. Ms. Smith walked among the tables wearing spiky heels and a pristine white pantsuit.

She spotted Henry with Reylin and smiled at them. Henry tried to smile back, but he really just wanted to find Lucy. Finally, he saw her at the far corner of the cafeteria at the end of a long line, waiting for the stir fry, Gerome standing behind her, staring at her hair.

He turned back to Reylin. "We already knew it would probably be this spring, though, right?"

"Right," Reylin said, taking a deep breath. "There's an area on the White House grounds that is out past the main landing area, but you can see Marine One from there. I think that might be kind of where we'll need to look, but I should be able to get some more information on that soon," she continued, an even tone to her voice, as though she'd been practicing what to say.

Henry guessed she probably had. Neither of them liked talking to each other, and to talk about this stuff was extra bad. Henry looked at Reylin. She was actually taking a lot of risks to do this. "You want a fry?" he asked, holding out the basket.

"No," she said, holding up a hand. "Thank you." She paused and looked to the line where Lucy was. "Now, focus. I've done a little digging. On March 28th an anti-drug delegation will be coming from South America. Columbia. I think that's when the attack will happen."

"March 28th?" Henry said. "That's in just over two weeks."

"Right," Reylin replied. "I think the attack will be sooner than we anticipated because I'm pretty sure the attack will correspond with that visit."

Henry squinted at her, chewing slowly. "Why?"

"Because," she said as though it was too obvious. "Whoever takes down Marine One will want to have somebody to blame. If your dad is working with an anti-drug delegation, then it will be easy to blame the drug cartels who aren't happy about that."

Henry nodded. That did make sense. You take down the president and a few anti-drug Columbians, and it would be easy to send the blame to the drug lords.

"Okay," Reylin said, standing up. "We need to find the location of the device before then."

"Thanks," he mumbled, shoving the last fry into his mouth as Lucy came over and sat down.

"That took forever," Lucy said, waving at Reylin as she walked off.

"You should have gotten a burger," Henry said. "Line was shorter."

"I don't even like burgers," Lucy said.

"I know," Henry added, trying to lighten his own mood with a joke. "Your parents have ruined you."

Lucy clicked her chopsticks together. Henry watched her hands, the long fingers as nimble as a pianist's.

"Did Reylin have anything to report?" Lucy asked.

"Actually, yes," Henry said, using his napkin for the first time that day. "She thinks it might be soon. And I'm worried she might be right. Do you still have that map on your phone we used to find Burnes' old stomping grounds?"

"Yeah," Lucy said, taking her phone out of her purse. "Why?"

"Because," Henry said. "We need to have a look at the area south of the landing pad for Marine One, which is close to Ellipse Park."

Lucy opened an image on her phone. "But in the opposite direction of the gravesite we haven't figured out how to get to."

"Yes." Henry stared for a moment at the map while Lucy chewed thoughtfully.

She looked down at the map. "Ellipse Park to the White House to the graveyard—they fall into a line. Do you think that means anything?"

Henry shrugged. "All of D.C. is kind of in lines. The Jefferson Memorial, the Washington Monument, the White House. Lines lines lines."

"And circles circles circles," Lucy murmured, pointing to the walking paths, the promenade around the park.

Henry squinted at the map. It was really hard to see. Everything was just too small until you zoomed in enough that you lost the big picture.

He was having trouble placing it all in his head. And Lucy was right—the graveyard was in the opposite direction, *north* of the White House, and there was no clear connector. It was hard to picture how any of it fit together. If it fit together at all. And they only had two weeks.

Henry pushed away the twisty feeling in his stomach. Two weeks wasn't a lot. But it was still enough. And if it wasn't, they would tell someone.

Henry held to that shred of possibility like a cancer patient hangs to a life vest. It was the wrong thing. Deep in his gut, he knew that if they couldn't find the EMP detonator with the identifying information, they wouldn't be any long-term help for his father. They would just be kids yammering about some conspiracy theory with no sound evidence that a real threat existed.

He chewed on his cheek, trying to imagine Burnes' old property boundaries transposed over modern-day Washington, D.C. "Maybe we should get a paper map of the whole city. These little ones don't give much perspective."

"Yeah, I'll go get my time machine," Lucy replied, flipping to different maps on her phone. "No one does paper anymore."

Henry slumped back in his seat. "Hey, Lu," he said after a minute, "remind me what it means that something is 'hardened' against EMP?"

She set down her phone. "It means that the electronic components are wired specifically to defend against an electromagnetic pulse. Otherwise, if an EMP device is activated, the electronics will fry."

"Fry," Henry said, looking at his empty fry basket and trying to think.

"Right," Lucy said. "And when the electronics in an aircraft go down, the whole thing goes down."

THIRTY-THREE

Henry rolled over in his bed for the millionth time, his thoughts swirling through facts and theories, stories and maps. A woman got a tattoo that may or may not connect to a symbol on the grave of David Burnes. David Burnes—a name and a voice, a shadow that Reylin had given them as her only clue.

A warning cat.

A desperate maid.

A ghost voice.

His missing house.

The White House.

Marine One.

His father.

That symbol.

Lines.

And circles.

Henry pulled his pillow over his head, wishing he could suffocate his thoughts into silence. It was nearly ten o'clock, Thursday night. Henry sat up and slid his feet into the slippers by his bed. Then he called down to the usher's office. "Do you have any movies I could watch in the theater?"

"Well, dear, let me see," the female voice said on the other line. He could hear the slight click of computer keys and then her response. "Looks like you're in luck. A film studio just dropped off a movie that you could pre-screen. It won't be out to the public for two more weeks. Sound alright?"

"Yup," Henry said.

"We'll get it set up for you," the woman said. Henry could practically hear her smiling through the phone. Aside from Keikiki, he really liked most of the ushers. A movie to distract him was just what he needed right now. Maybe afterwards he could think straight.

Henry sat in the large easy chair, wearing 3D glasses, chomping on handfuls of popcorn and drinking a large soda, wishing he could be an ordinary kid without a care in the world, or maybe a super kid who could figure all this out.

He nestled deeper into the soft red cushions in the theater room and focused on the opening credits.

Just as the movie started, Henry saw someone coming down the aisle toward the front of the theater. He was also wearing 3D glasses and was dressed in plain brown pants and a white button-down shirt.

"Hey Will," Henry said. "Been to any tours lately?"

"None at all, actually," Will answered, missing the sarcasm entirely. "You?"

"No," Henry said, shaking his head. "You totally ditched me on that last one. And then people took pictures."

Will nodded, as though that was the most natural thing in the world.

"Where did you go? That really wasn't cool."

Will looked at him through the blue and red 3D glasses. He shrugged. "I can't remember. I go here. I go there." He paused, a small smile pulling up on his lips. "Actually, I heard your brother was gone, so I wondered if I could show you something cool."

Henry looked at him skeptically. "Like George Washington's chairs?"

"Cooler," Will said, missing the sarcasm again.

"Fine," Henry said, pausing the movie and taking off his glasses. "But you better not ditch me this time."

Will smiled. "Have you spent much time in the Queen's Bedroom?"

Henry sank back into the plush theater chair. "Seriously, Will, your idea of fun needs an epic do-over."

"Come on," Will said.

Henry dragged himself out of the chair, pouring the rest of the popcorn into his mouth before following the younger boy out of the theater and up the stairs.

The Queen's Bedroom was painted pink, the walls

covered with various paintings and a paneled mirror that Henry thought was particularly ugly.

"Dozens of queens and dignitaries have stayed here," Will was saying. "The queen of Great Britain, the Netherlands, Greece, and Norway. Not to mention other people like Winston Churchill."

"Yeah, great," Henry said, fingering his 3D glasses and wishing he'd just stayed watching the movie.

"This room is really pretty unusual," Will said.

Henry shrugged. "Seems the same to me as all the rest—antique furniture, chandeliers, priceless this and that."

"Of course," Will said. "But it's more than that. Do you know about the Truman renovation?"

"I did go on the tour, you know. And unlike you I didn't run out early. Or—" He paused. "—as early."

Will cocked his head to the side. "*Thus let bygones be bygones. Let past differences as nothing be.*"

Henry raised an eyebrow. "So now we're talking in memes, are we?"

"It's just something my father used to say." Will grinned. "Anyway, in 1946 when Bess Truman was showing the Daughters of the American Revolution the Blue room, the huge chandelier that hung in the room started to sway back and forth, almost coming down on the ladies. People whispered about ghosts in the White House." Will shook his head. "As if. It turns out, it was President Truman upstairs taking a bath and the floor was crumbling beneath him. Truman said he almost fell through the floor in his tub, wearing 'nothing more than reading glasses.' That might have been a joke, but the truth was that the foundation of the White House was crumbling. It was built in the 1790s and presidents kept adding more and more stuff to the house. Then, as technology improved, with plumbing, heating, air conditioning, and electricity—the walls were just getting too heavy."

"Dude," Henry said. "I'm missing the pre-screening of a movie to listen to you talk about plumbing."

"It gets even more interesting," Will said.

Henry didn't know if Will was trying his own hand at sarcasm, or if he was serious. Either way he kept talking.

"The house was falling down around their heads. They even thought about demolishing the whole place. That would have been disastrous. Anyway, when Margaret Truman's piano leg came through the floor, it was time for a major renovation." Will paused. "You know Margaret had a very pretty voice. They say."

"Will, I'm sorry, but I really don't care." Henry regretted the words as soon as they came out. Will was just a kid—a weird kid who got excited about weird stuff. But Henry *was* still a little miffed at being ditched at the tour. Plus, he was tired, and he'd gone to the theater room in the first place because he was trying *not* to think about the White House, or anything else.

Henry took a deep breath and dragged his hand through his hair. "Will, I'm going back to the movie. You can come too, if you want."

Will looked pale and sad. He still had his 3D glasses on

his head, but they sat crooked over his blond hair, which cowlicked up in the back. "Wait. Just hear me out."

Henry paused. It wasn't easy to stay mad at Will. He was just too eager, too earnest, too sincere. Henry sighed and rubbed his eyes, feeling the tired ache behind them. "Okay, okay. I'm all ears, bro." He tossed his 3D glasses in a garbage can nearby as a peace offering.

Will smiled, his face brightening. "So at the time the President's Mansion was being rebuilt, they found this old passageway, probably created after the British burned the House to the ground during the War of 1812. Most people wanted to fill the passage in, but Truman—well, actually his wife—thought it might be prudent to keep it, so he had it reinforced in case of, well, an emergency."

Henry stared.

"Look at this," Will said. He pulled the bottom of a painting of flowers away from the wall, then reached behind it and flipped a small switch.

A light beamed from the ceiling, shining like a small spotlight toward the mirror. Will moved the mirror outward by a few degrees so that the light reflected off of it, hitting a small circle of blue wallpaper positioned in the southeast corner of the room. Henry watched the spot as a tiny hook came out of the wall where the light had hit. Solar activated? He had no idea.

Will walked to the mantle above the fireplace and picked up a silver placard, about the size of a baseball card. "An inscription," he said, pointing to the back. "From the brink of collapse I was rebuilt." 1952 was written underneath.

Will took the plate and latched it onto the hook. When he did, the light reflected off the silver placard to another spot on the wall. "See that patch of light," Will said. "Push on that."

"You're kidding," Henry said.

Will just shook his head, the faint light in the room causing his features to look almost white.

Henry walked over and pushed the spot on the wall marked by the small swath of light. To his astonishment, the wall folded inward. Henry crouched down and looked into the hole. Inside was something that looked like a door handle. Henry turned it, and the previously seamless wall opened into a tight passageway that led to a dim hall.

"Where does it go?" Henry asked, staring into the dark passageway.

"It's an escape. It takes you out under the north lawn, then under the city. About two miles north from here."

Henry paused to stare at Will. "Two miles north?"

"Yes," Will said. "You can use it if you want to get out of the President's Mansion undetected."

Henry turned to look at Will, who still seemed to be glowing from the slight light. Henry had thought of him as a little brother. Suddenly that seemed all wrong. In this moment, in this light, something about Will struck Henry as very old. "Why do you call it that? The President's Mansion?"

Will shrugged. "That's what most people call it."

"No," Henry said. "No, they don't. They call it the White House."

Will didn't respond. He closed the door, turning the handle, and the wall sealed up like there had never been an opening. Then he put the silver placard back and turned off the light.

"Who knows about this?" Henry asked.

"You," Will replied.

"Secret Service?" Henry said.

"No," Will answered.

"My mother, father?"

Will continued to shake his head. "Just *you*."

Henry stared into Will's blue eyes. He was tall for his age, almost the same height as Henry. "Who are you?" Henry asked.

The other boy blinked. "I'm Will."

Henry pursed his lips. He could feel his forehead getting hotter, his hands sweating. "Okay. Then *what*—what are you?" Henry suddenly felt like he was seeing Will for the first time—the old-fashioned clothes, the shaggy blond hair, his slight frame, strange way of talking, the unusual band around his wrist.

"I...," Will began, stepping back from Henry. "I'm here to help."

Henry stepped forward, speaking a little louder, unaware that his voice had changed, that his words had changed, shifting from the comfortable English to the song-like tones and the only syllables that seemed to fit. He took Will's arm. "I am Henry," he said in the language Mr. Keikiki had been teaching him. "Who are you?"

"I," Will said, his own words changing, swaying. "I am Will. And I am a *Convincer*."

The word brought images of Henry's home in Michigan, of his friends and family, of many of the beautiful things he'd seen in his life.

Henry closed his eyes as if to savor the word.

When he opened them, Will was gone.

Thirty-Four

When Henry arrived in the Solarium, Lucy was already there. Mr. Keikiki stood in front of a new iron statue of a smirking king or emperor of some sort. It was huge.

"This is representative of some of the history of my people," Keikiki said, turning to face them. "I thought bringing it here might give you a little inspiration. And keep our lessons contained as your skills improve." The statue was at least seven feet tall, freshly polished, thick, and dense. It looked like it weighed a million pounds, and it was connected with a thin iron chain to all the other statues. Henry had no idea how Keikiki had even gotten it into the Solarium.

Henry shook his head as Keikiki launched into a story about a malevolent advisor to a great council. The advisor convinced them to seek after gold and jewels, entertainment and fashion, while he himself acquired fertile lands, flowing rivers, seed, and minerals.

Henry wasn't really listening. Tonight when Chet was having his party, he'd show Lucy the passageway he'd found. Well, the passageway that Will had shown him. If there was a Will.

Henry rubbed his eyes. He was so tired. He'd spent several hours the night before looking through the ghost books for a servant boy. Nothing. Which meant that Will was probably just a White House kid using insider knowledge of hidden passageways to mess with him. Right?

It sounded like a decent explanation, but even Henry didn't really believe it. Something was wrong with Will.

Or, well, something was wrong with Henry. Ever since coming here. No. Ever since being attacked in the park, something had been wrong. Wrong with his body? Wrong with his mind? He wasn't sure. The things he was seeing didn't feel like hallucinations or dreams. They felt almost like visions. Which is what every psycho cult leader thought about his craziness. Henry felt sick.

What if the original attack in the park hadn't even happened? What if he'd blacked out and imagined it? What if it had happened, and they'd drugged him with something that would give him permanent hallucinations?

Keikiki droned on about government. Lucy's pen scratched on the paper.

Henry pushed against his temples. Some things had been real. Which was comforting. His phone had been broken for sure. And The Ethereal had legitimately nabbed nine other politicians' children the night of that first attack. Also, Henry had definitely been almost stabbed by the maid. A real flesh and blood person with a real metal-sharp knife. Legit.

Henry took a deep breath. If Will was a ghost, then fine. Henry wouldn't be the first person to see a ghost in the White House. Not even close. It wasn't even crazy. Just cool. But if Will wasn't real, were the things he had shown Henry still real? And if those things were real, well, then what did that say about Will? Henry's head hurt trying to wrap itself around the questions.

Mr. Keikiki was finishing his story about the huge statue. "He did not govern his new people any better than he'd counseled their previous leaders. With his wealth and his power, he kept them fed and busy, but low and lean enough that they would always feel their need, that they would know not to overtake the one who was giving them life."

Henry shook his head, looking out the window at the group of tourists waiting to come in for the next tour. Weaving among them was a small woman who seemed to be looking for something. He watched her for a minute. She was a little bent, with dull gray hair that coiled over her shoulders like tarnished wires. Just as Mr. Keikiki began the lesson, the woman looked up to the broad window of the Solarium, and stared.

Henry squinted. She couldn't possibly have seen through the window, but her gaze didn't waver. Henry turned his own eyes away, feeling a sense of something. Not danger, but not safety either.

Lucy flipped the page of her notebook and Henry shook the feeling away, trying to concentrate on the day's lesson.

They had learned some basic conversational phrases, and Henry had managed to acquire a fairly rudimentary use of some of the spoken language. But he was still frustrated at the highly regular irregularity of the tones and sounds. Today, after a month of lessons, Keikiki was just barely introducing the written alphabet. "These letters, if you can call them that, are arranged in an order counterintuitive to most known language," he told them. "They are arranged according to the vibrations, the sound waves."

Mr. Keikiki paused. Lucy was taking notes as usual, but Henry found he just couldn't. He was staring at Keikiki like the chief usher was a lunatic. "I'm sorry," Henry said. "I'm not following." He was kind of ticked about it too. Was Keikiki making this purposefully ridiculous? Henry had more important things to do than worry about this useless language.

"You realize that all matter consists of some sort of mechanical or electrical waves, right?"

Henry nodded.

"This language is the same," Keikiki said as if that explained it all.

Henry shook his head. "Still not—"

But Lucy interrupted him. "Is that what makes it so musical?"

Keikiki smiled. "Yes. Although it is so much more. It's

not just tone, but timing. Pulse and resonance. Think about the common light bulb. If the pulse is too slow the lights flicker, if it's too fast, the current doesn't flow properly. This language is very much like that. It is not so much about the sound as the tones, the vibrations, the air movement, and the communication between...people." He looked at Henry. "You're starting to get it, so let's just try it."

Henry bit back a snide comment. He definitely did not feel like he was *getting it*, but Mr. Keikiki had already begun talking to him.

Henry gave short responses at first, but after a minute, they grew longer, more detailed. Some of the words he couldn't even remember learning, but the more he spoke, the more he seemed to lose himself in the language.

His muscles relaxed; his mind gave way to the reverberations and tones. Maybe he *was* starting to get it. And Mr. Keikiki was right; it was pretty cool. It literally seemed to resonate.

"I feel," Henry began, speaking in the language, "I feel amazing."

The word seemed to fill the room, almost tremble with happiness.

Mr. Keikiki smiled widely, his scar narrowing to a point as he did. He scribbled more letters on the board—the words they'd just said. "Write and then say the words."

They took turns writing on the board. Lucy tried to speak the corresponding words, but Henry could tell that she always had the wrong pitch, or that the duration of the sound was off.

"In the language," Mr. Keikiki said, "the length of the sounds matter. Truthfully, everything matters."

Lucy blew a stray hair away from her face. "No kidding," she said, as Mr. Keikiki patted her on the shoulder and she sat down.

"There are actually more than ten thousand symbols for sounds in the language. And unlike English, the sounds have a pitch and duration that change the meaning drastically in many cases."

Henry sighed, feeling his headache return. It had taken them hours to learn just a few. Well, for him to learn just a few. Lucy was still struggling.

"I'll practice writing this at home," Lucy said, as she looked at her work on the board. "At least I can write it."

Mr. Keikiki looked at her and then at Henry before he erased the board and touched the arm of the statue that he'd brought in. "That is ambitious of you, Ms. Hawk, but I have a somewhat odd request. I'd rather you not write or speak this language anywhere, except here in the Solarium when I am with you. There is so much to learn, and it would be so easy to learn it incorrectly. Until you both have a better handle on it, it's best to keep the writing and speaking of the language to the times when we're together in the Solarium."

"You're kidding?" Henry said.

"You mean, you don't want us to practice?" Lucy added.

"Not just yet," Mr. Keikiki said with a smile. "Now promise me that you'll keep it to this room."

"Sure," Henry said. It was one less thing to worry about.

"Okay." Lucy sounded like all the air had gone out of her sails.

Mr. Keikiki wished them good night and left the two of them sitting in the Solarium.

"That was weird," Lucy said.

"Ah, Lu, don't be mad that he told you to do less homework."

"Come on, Henry. You have to admit it was strange."

"What does that man do that isn't strange?" Henry said. "I'm just glad that this time there's some small benefit to me. This language is giving me nightmares. Literally. I'm always stress-dreaming it. Maybe now that will stop."

Lucy sighed. "Not for me. I'd feel better about it if I could practice it—even writing the letters. We've even got Monday off for that teacher in-service thing. I could have practiced a lot."

Henry shook his head, and Lucy looked down at her hands. "But maybe he's right. Maybe I'd just practice it wrong."

"Well, it is like having a language with 10,000 letters instead of just a meager twenty-six, so the margin for error is pretty high." He smiled.

Lucy closed her notebook and set it down. "Anyway, my algebra homework is calling to me, so I guess that will just have to be enough."

"Yeah, rough life," Henry said. He stood up and looked at the board Keikiki had erased just before he'd left. "That guy is a little crazy though. The language is bizarre enough, and then to slow us down just as we were getting it."

Lucy gathered up her things and the two of them walked from the room, pausing as they passed the huge new statue. "Just as *you* were getting it," Lucy corrected. She sounded kind of irritated.

Henry reached out and touched the statue, feeling the energy and connection from the lesson leave in a rush when he did. "Look, Lucy, you don't have to come to these classes. I mean, it's totally your choice. It's not mine." The words came out all wrong. He hadn't meant for them to sound mean, and he didn't want to make her feel dumb. Besides, the person who would lose the biggest if she left was him. He'd be stuck alone with crazy Mr. Keikiki, learning a language he'd never use that was going to take the rest of his life to master.

"I guess I don't have to come," she said, staring past Henry at the wall. He couldn't tell if she was angry or sad. "And I can't even figure out why I still do. Hanging out with you definitely doesn't make it worth it." She gave him a sideways scowl. "But there's something special about this language. I can't help but love it. It's like the difference between a two-dimensional picture and a three-dimensional sculpture. Both are visual and beautiful. But one has more... fullness to it. Honestly, even if I never learned to speak it, I'd feel happy enough just being able to listen." She paused, looking annoyed again. "Which, apparently, is something that will only ever happen in this classroom."

"Lucy Lucy Lucy," Henry said. "You are seriously the biggest nerd I've ever met."

"Thank you," Lucy said. They walked out of the room

and down the hallway. "Speaking of, I got you one of those maps. Paper style. I didn't even know that was still a thing, but they had them at the visitor's center."

She pulled the folded rectangle out of her backpack and handed it to Henry, who took it, his hands starting to sweat.

"Tonight?" he asked, looking at Lucy.

"You're crazier than Keikiki," she replied. "But, yeah, I'll be here."

THIRTY-FIVE

Friday night turned out to be a big night in the White House. Kids from Chet's party filled the game room and spilled into the halls, the Solarium, and the porches outside.

Henry wandered around, listening to music blaring from speakers in different rooms. He paused to watch Chet and Marxma playing a game of pool. Marxma was incredibly good, and Chet was concentrating on his shot.

"Give up while there's still time," Marxma cooed, her southern accent lilting. Henry half expected that voice to throw Chet off, but his brother wasn't going down without a fight. He sank one ball and then another.

"You know President Lincoln loved a good game of billiards," Lucy said, coming up behind Henry. "He called it a 'health inspiring, scientific game lending recreation to the otherwise fatigued mind.'"

Marxma sank her final ball. "Lincoln was a brilliant

man," she said, her voice a slow drawl. "I'm certainly feeling inspired right now."

Chet glared. "Lucy, I'm blaming that loss on you. I thought my mother had come up to hang out."

Lucy shrugged. "She is the one who told me. When she gave me the White House tour."

"Lucy and I are going to watch a movie," Henry said quickly. "Better luck next time, bro."

"Actually," Marxma said. "I ought to be heading out too. We're filming bright and early tomorrow morning, so I can be back in time for your mom's charity tea party."

"You're just scared to play again," Chet said.

"Maybe. Maybe not," Marxma smiled and pulled Chet toward her. "You *are* pretty terrifying."

Henry paused on his way out of the room. So did Lucy. In fact, it seemed that suddenly the whole party had frozen as Marxma leaned in and kissed Chet right on the mouth.

Hoots erupted and cameras went off. Marxma and Chet laughed as Henry tugged Lucy out the door.

"Twitter's going to go nuts," Lucy mumbled.

"Mom's going to go nuts," Henry said. "But it's not like they haven't been making out for weeks now anyway. They just decided to go public."

Henry and Lucy reached the Queen's bedroom and Henry took a deep breath, trying to remember each thing Will had shown him. First, move the painting. Flip switch. Henry executed each step with Lucy watching him like he'd gone crazy. Light onto mirror, which spotlighted a place on the wall. The hook came out.

Lucy gasped.

Henry hung the silver placard on the hook, and the light reflected to another spot on the wall. Henry pressed that point, and the hole opened, the door handle barely visible.

"Henry," Lucy asked. "Who showed you this? How do you know about it?"

"A kid showed me. A kid from the White House."

"How?" she asked.

"I...I don't know," Henry said.

Lucy opened her mouth, but he cut her off, not wanting more questions he didn't have answers to. "We have to leave our phones," Henry said, holding out his hand.

Lucy shook her head, almost imperceptibly. "Why?"

"Because Secret Service could track me. And your parents could track you."

Lucy handed over her phone, although it was obvious that she didn't want to. "I feel like you're somehow making this more dangerous than it needs to be. How will we navigate? How will we see?"

Henry smiled, holding up the map she'd given him, as well as two metal flashlights. "Old school."

"Fine," she said, bending down and ducking into the hidden door. "Let's just get this over with."

The two of them entered a small space with a platform that could barely hold the both of them. As soon as they closed the door, Henry thought he heard a small click in the Queen's room behind the wall, like someone had just come in.

The area was cramped and damp, and Henry found it a little hard to breathe. "You okay?" Lucy asked.

"Yeah, good," he mumbled, turning on his flashlight and staring down from the platform at the dozens of crumbling steps that led to a tight, dark tunnel. "Okay, let's go."

Lucy followed him closely, stumbling once and grabbing the back of his t-shirt to find her balance. The bottom two steps had completely crumbled and Henry jumped to the hardwood landing below, dust spewing into the air.

"Nice," Lucy said, waving her flashlight around. "I hope these things have good batteries." They followed the narrow tunnel, heading north. Wooden beams supported the tunnel. They passed one every ten feet or so and Henry felt relieved each time. Above them, heavy wire mesh webbed along the ceiling of the tunnel, which couldn't have been more than six feet tall and was just over two feet wide.

"You know people die in places like this," Lucy said. "Gasses, cave-ins, who knows what else."

"Probably worm monsters," Henry replied.

"Probably," Lucy said.

"That'll be Marxma's next movie. *Escape from the Great Dank Deeps.*"

"Dank is right," Lucy replied, then stopped.

"What's up?" Henry said.

"I thought I heard something behind us," she said.

"You're just creeped out," Henry said.

"Can't argue with that," Lucy mumbled. "Give me a heads-up before the worm monster sneaks up behind me and eats my head off."

"They've got to knock off at least one character in those movies," Henry joked. "Better you than me."

"You always were a gentleman," Lucy replied, glancing behind her.

They moved slowly and steadily north. It was hard to know how far they'd gone without their phones, but Henry was pretty sure the cemetery wasn't far away. Every few minutes he shined his light ahead of them, looking for the end.

"You sure it doesn't just go on forever?" Lucy asked.

"Nope," Henry said. "But at least we can't get lost. This place is just one straight line." Henry's flashlight flickered. "Which I guess is good since we might be walking home in the dark."

"Not funny," Lucy said, turning off her light. "I'll save mine so we have something."

As she said it, Henry shined his light onto an old, rickety ladder that led to what appeared to be a small hatch with a lever. Henry climbed up and pulled the lever, which turned with a hiss, releasing the hydraulic pressure as the hatch popped open.

"I never thought I'd think Washington D.C. smelled so good," Lucy said as they both took a deep breath of the fresh air.

They stepped out into an area designed to hide the hatch —a round patch of gravel, surrounded by brush and small trees. Henry and Lucy used twigs and branches to cover the open hatch so they could return the way they came.

They walked through the dark to the nearest intersection, trying to orient themselves. Henry pulled out the map. The cemetery was just north of them. A perfectly straight line up from Ellipse Park.

The tunnel had been creepy, but Henry wasn't entirely sure this was better. The roads weren't really roads at all— more like driveway type paths that surrounded the plot of land that made up the old cemetery.

Everything seemed empty, abandoned. Which, in a city like D.C., was almost more disconcerting than a cramped secret tunnel.

Even the cemetery wasn't much of anything. Henry could tell it had been preserved on account of it being so old, but it was also obvious that not too many people found reason to come here. A simple stone wall surrounded the cemetery, three small bricks leading through an otherwise unassuming entrance. Hanging off of an old post a sign read, "Closed to Visitors After Dark."

Lucy paused and Henry walked ahead of her. As he did, a dark lump on the ground suddenly moved.

Henry and Lucy both jumped as a crumpled beggar held her arms overhead, stretching. "Well, hello children," she said, dabbing at iron-colored eyes that continuously watered. Her hair was thin and gray, matted and wiry. Something about her looked mildly familiar to Henry. She scooted a battered tin cup toward them.

Henry raised an eyebrow. "Is that the cost of entrance?"

Lucy nudged him in the side and dug into her pocket. "Here, ma'am," she said, handing the old woman a few dollars. "You have a good evening."

"What are you doing?" Henry hissed.

"What's it look like?" Lucy whispered back, gesturing toward the woman. As she did, the woman caught hold of her hand and said. "Thank you, my child. And for your kindness, you have earned a palm reading."

Most of the color fell out of Lucy's face, but she took a deep breath and said, "That's very nice of you, but—"

"Ah," the woman said, interrupting her. "I see many deviations." She looked deeply into Lucy's palm. "Your days will not always follow a smooth line."

Lucy tried to politely pull her hand back. "Thank you," she began.

"But don't worry, my child. Goodness will always follow the good." She smiled into Lucy's face. "Sooner or later."

The woman gently released her hand and turned to Henry. "As for you, young man."

"You can't even see my palm," Henry pointed out.

"Nor do I need to for those of your line," she replied. "But you are right. I cannot see your future. For the future is yours to decide."

"Yes, well, thanks," Henry said, shaking his head.

The woman held out her hand, as though expecting payment.

"You just told me something I already knew," Henry said.

"Hardly," she replied. "I just told you something you still don't know."

"Oh," Henry replied. "Well, thanks for that." He began to leave.

"Please, child, my sisters are so very sick."

"Henry," Lucy whispered, stopping him. "My grandpa always told me that we don't give to people only to get something in return. That's not giving; it's trading business."

In the darkness, Henry glared, but dug into his pockets. Turning back to the old woman, he found that she had already fallen back to sleep. He paused, then dropped a few coins into the woman's limp hand.

"Happy?" he whispered as they walked away.

"Honestly, Henry, I think that the son of the president can afford to give that poor woman a few cents, even without receiving an accurate palm reading."

Henry didn't reply. He didn't like having his future told —or, well, not told—by some homeless woman.

"You probably want to get some hand sanitizer or something," Henry mumbled, looking back over his shoulder at the sleeping woman. He squinted, unable to see the lump in the darkness. Had she gotten up and moved?

"Right," Lucy said. "I'll just go get some. I'm sure they've got a dispenser on that mausoleum over there."

"At least wipe your hands on some leaves," Henry said.

"No," Lucy said, looking down at her palms. "You know, the lines really do stop and start a lot."

Henry shook his head. "Glad you think it was money well spent."

"Never had a doubt about that," Lucy shot back.

The argument was cut short by a crackle they heard in the distance.

"Look, let's just find the tombstone," Henry said.

"Deal," Lucy replied, looking back down the dark path they'd walked.

The night went silent again as they stumbled over tombstones older than the United States. Many were hidden by weeds and dirt, only an edge or corner poking out. Henry and Lucy had to pull the debris away to read names and dates. Or try to. Often the words were so faded that they were left staring at nothing more than a piece of pitted stone. To make it worse, the stones were all different sizes and shapes, arranged haphazardly throughout the cemetery, as though someone had tossed them into the air, letting them fall wherever they would. Of the ones they could find and read, many were crumbling or broken. Ahead of them, a cross lay toppled in the dirt.

Lucy shuddered.

"Come on, Lu," Henry teased. "This is history."

"That's the truth," Lucy said. "Though I think it's the type of history I'd rather learn in the daytime."

Henry shrugged. He found that the darkness didn't bother him as much as the silence. He could hear the city alive in the distance, but here it felt like there was a cover over the dead. "It is creepy," Henry said. "So quiet."

"Lonely," Lucy added.

And at that moment, they came to a small plot at the top of a grassy hill, bordered to the north by a thick stand of trees and surrounded by a long-dilapidated picket fence. Henry shined his light into the area while they climbed over the broken pieces of fence to get a better look.

Overrun by tall grass, with poison ivy creeping up the

back and sides, stood a simple gray stone, the etchings shallow, but visible.

David Burnes.

Beneath the death date was the round symbol similar to the center portion of the maid's tattoo. It did look a lot like a compass, a compass without a needle. Another image tapped against Henry's memory, but he couldn't quite grab it. Henry leaned forward, trying to get a better look under the dull light of the flashlight.

In the distance, they heard the crack of twigs. Henry looked up just as his flashlight flickered and died.

"Glad I saved mine," Lucy said, turning hers on and shining it through the cemetery. They both looked back at the stone. Beneath the circular symbol they could see an epitaph followed by another strange symbol.

Henry cocked his head to the side. "You know," he said, "that almost looks like some of the Kiribati letters Mr. Keikiki was showing us."

Lucy shook her head. "That's not possible. This guy was a Scotsman." Quietly, she read the words next to the symbol, "For man, who chooses."

Henry looked over her shoulder and began sounding out the strange symbol as if he were reading Kiribati.

"We're not supposed to practice it, remember?" Lucy said.

"Relax," Henry replied. "You're the one who said it wasn't Kiribati."

And then, just ahead of them the air shifted and a loud crack sang through the silence as a huge branch fell from one of the trees. Lucy screamed, jumping back just as Henry looked up to see a cloaked figure leap down between them. In an instant, he and the figure were standing face to face.

The figure was shrouded in black. Henry couldn't see anything through the cloak, which blurred as it flowed, eerie and indistinct. And yet, looking at it, Henry felt sure that the creature was not a ghost. He reached out a hand to touch it and as he did, the figure struck him, trying to break his wrist.

Henry pulled back, the air slowing as his body sped up, so that the cloaked attacker only hit the tip of his finger. It still stung, and in the next moment, the figure kicked Henry in the chest. He stumbled back. Whoever was hiding behind the cloak was definitely not an apparition. Henry wished that it was. Ghosts couldn't kick like that.

Henry sucked in a deep breath, and the figure crouched, ready to pounce. Henry spun around, and the darkness seemed to fade as though the air was drawing light from the stars and moon. He could see clearly now. Each twig. Each stone. The blades of grass as they swayed and bent under his feet. Above him, he heard bats fluttering through the air, sensed their sonar emissions. Near the tombstone, he felt Lucy shaking, the quick movements of her body and breath as they shuddered in and out.

The cloaked figure flicked a hand, sending a small, metallic projectile toward him with incredible force. He responded by throwing his head back. The weapon whizzed by within inches of his forehead. He continued to bend back, his body twisting, flipping through the air. And then he ran, almost flying, toward the cloaked figure. The creature threw with both left and right hands—several small daggers like thin, metallic arrowheads coming at him in quick succession.

He dodged and turned, able to calculate where they would land and how quickly. When his attacker threw the final one, Henry reached up and grabbed it. His movements were so controlled, so precise that it felt like he was plucking a dandelion seed from the breeze. Then, with all his force, he flung it back at the figure.

The cloaked figure dodged out of the path and stopped. Henry couldn't see its eyes, but he got the sense that the creature was staring at him.

"Who are you?" Henry demanded. The figure didn't answer, lunging, fist extended. Henry swung his body to the left to evade the blow, but it grazed his right cheek. Henry felt the bruise blossom on his skin almost immediately.

He spun, never feeling the slightest bit dizzy, then raised his leg, kicking the wispy figure in its head and knocking it away from him.

The figure recovered quickly, jumping, spinning, and punching in rapid succession as Henry stepped back, then reversed course and ran forward. He leaped over the creature, landing on his feet. In the distance, Lucy gasped.

He turned just the slightest bit to make sure she was okay. As he did, another metal tip hurtled toward him, tearing his t-shirt and scratching his chest. He held his hand to the skin, blood warm between his fingers.

He ran toward the figure, jumping over its head. Only

this time, he kicked his legs so that they struck the creature on the back of the head twice, knocking it face forward into the dirt.

He turned again and ran two more strides toward the downed figure. The creature looked up, flipping backwards, then thrusting in Henry's direction.

Henry swiveled and ducked, avoiding the hit, his muscles aching from the fight. Despite the pain, maybe even because of the pain, his body seemed to react with more strength. He leapt quickly, striking blow after blow to the creature—head, back, neck, face.

The creature withstood the hits with surprising agility, though Henry could see that it was getting tired. Finally, it fell backwards into a wounded position, then turned, running like a fox into the night.

Henry paused, the cut on his chest a dull pulse. To his right, he heard Lucy running. He knew that to her the fight must have happened in an instant. "What?" she said, her voice nearly a shriek. "What was that? And what—" She stopped. "—What happened?" She stood directly in front of Henry, staring at the blood that was congealing against his skin.

Henry found himself suddenly exhausted. He sat on the ground, right next to Burnes' tombstone. "If I'm not mistaken," Henry said, staring into the darkness where the cloaked figure had fled, "that was The Ethereal."

Lucy sat next to him. "And you...?" she began. "How did you move like that? What happened to you? Who...?" She stopped as though she didn't know how to ask the question. "Henry, who are you?"

Henry shrugged. "I'm me... I think, but..." Again the words wouldn't come—not the way he wanted them to.

He leaned against the tombstone, trying to catch his breath. *Who was he?* It was a question he'd been asking himself for months, ever since he'd been attacked that September night in the park. It was a question he still couldn't answer completely, but turning to his left and tracing his finger along the symbol that looked like Kiribati, he pronounced the word slowly. Around them, the air seemed to tighten and bend.

"This," he said. "This is who I am."

Lucy stared at the stone, placing her finger directly over Henry's, their two hands tracing the word as one.

He knew she could not understand the word he had said. She didn't know the letters or the sounds he'd produced, but when the word twisted the air, a light came into Lucy's eyes, like a memory that wasn't her own, swiped from the air and pocketed.

She looked up into Henry's eyes. "For man, who chooses. *Determiner.*"

Thirty-Six

"Call me," Henry vexted Reylin as soon as they got back from the cemetery. "It's about our, um, history project."

It was well past midnight and she didn't reply. He and Lucy sat up in the Queen's bedroom, trying to figure everything out. "But what does it mean?" Lucy said. "*Determiner*, the grave, the symbol?"

"I think when we find the people trying to kill my dad, we'll find out," Henry replied, scouring the map and the symbol on Burnes' grave. "I think maybe..." His words stopped again, choking in his throat as he tried to push them out. He wanted to say that he thought maybe he'd been given a certain type of drug when he'd been nearly kidnapped. But all that came out was, "Maybe a drug..."

"You mean the drug cartel that might be trying to kill your dad?" Lucy asked.

Henry shook his head. "I can't quite say what I mean, I

guess." Though even if he had been able to speak his theory, he still couldn't explain *why*. None of it made any sense. "Let's just work on a plan."

Lucy nodded, staring over his shoulder at various places on the grounds and in the White House until deep in the night when they finally collapsed into sleep on the couches.

The next day an usher came looking for them. Henry made up an excuse about falling asleep watching a movie and Lucy vexted her mother the same story.

"I'm in big trouble," Lucy said. "Even if she believes me."

But her mother vexted her back, saying that the chief usher had already contacted her and that security would drive her home after Mrs. Miller's charity tea that afternoon. "Next time," her mother vexted, "please text me that the Millers have given you permission to stay the night and don't leave it to the chief usher to do. We're having a dress sent over for the tea."

Lucy replayed the vext three times. "That's it?"

"You sound disappointed to not be in trouble," Henry said.

"If you think being attacked by a cloaked figure in a 300-year-old cemetery is weird," Lucy said, still staring at her phone. "Well, let's just agree that this is weirder."

Apparently, a bunch of kids from Chet's party had stayed the night, crashing in the theater chairs and Solarium couches. The staff had contacted their parents. The teens were now wandering, sleepy-eyed, down to the kitchen to find some food. Henry and Lucy fit right in.

Henry vexted Reylin again just as an usher showed up with a dress for Lucy.

"Oh, um, thank you," Lucy said, casting a troubled glance at Henry as the usher led her away to get ready.

He vexted Reylin two more times, then sent her a text for good measure. Nothing. His mother's charity tea was starting in minutes. He wouldn't be able to do much more until it was over.

———

Marxma slipped the small envelope into Chet's pocket. Men always loved it when she did that. She'd developed a bit of a reputation as being one of the few celebrities who still wrote actual letters in response to her fans. Her publicist took care of almost all of her social media, but every week several lucky fans would receive a small, pink envelope in their mailboxes.

If you were much luckier than a fan, you got a letter in your pocket.

Chet looked straight ahead at the small group of people beginning to fill the ballroom for his mother's charity party, but Marxma saw the rise of color along his cheekbones as his hand brushed hers and held the piece of paper.

Marxma squeezed his hand, looking around at the chandeliers, the crystal glasses, the diamond bracelet that hung from her own wrist—all of them reflecting the light, like bits of sun captured in stone.

She had never told Chet, but her roots were in poverty. When she was young, her mother had moved them to a trailer park in the back woods of Tennessee. Most people wouldn't think of that as a step up, but through that step, they had escaped a life in another place that had been even worse.

Images burned into Marxma's memory of starving children, polluted water sources, food crawling with worms and rot. And the fires—red blazes filled with the screams of all those caught in their paths. They had been like flash floods, those fires—catching unexpectedly, tearing along a dry path until finally petering out, leaving ash and bone in their wake.

All her life, she'd hoped to be able to help her people, to give them some of the prosperity that she knew this earth could bring.

But to do this, she would need the help of the president's son.

From across the ballroom, she looked at Henry. Lucy was at his side, her face close to his, whispering intently. Henry was moving stiffly and looked a little rumpled, which wasn't unusual, but Lucy also looked tired, dark circles under her eyes, which seemed to deepen the more she talked. Marxma could relate. Although she hid it better, she also felt exhausted; and her head was killing her.

"Look at those sweet kids," Marxma said, winking at Chet. "I suppose we ought to dance our way to them." She took Chet's hand in hers, and he pulled her to him, his body warm and strong as he wrapped his arm around her waist.

It wasn't a bad life, this one. Unfortunately, it was something she knew couldn't last forever.

———

A car had arrived to whisk Lucy home right after the party. "I'll call you," she'd said.

Now, alone in his room, Henry held his phone, looking at the string of vexts he'd sent to Reylin. He hadn't said anything about the cloaked figure or the strange name that had connected to him in a way he couldn't define or understand. But he'd been bugging her to contact him, and she hadn't. Finally, he pulled up his email and sent her a message.

She replied within the minute. "Don't ever vext me in the middle of the night unless you want my dad to think something is going on. Luckily, he didn't hear you, but I had to block you just to be sure you wouldn't keep vexting. Lucy too." Even without the vext, Henry could imagine her whiny voice through the words. "I've emailed you seven times."

Henry clicked on his phone. She had. He never used email except to send a teacher an assignment. Although, of course, it made sense if you wanted to talk more discreetly. His history project excuse only would have gotten them so far. "There's been a development," he emailed her.

"That's interesting," she messaged him back. "There's been one on my end too."

"Details," he typed.

"My driver will drop me off at the North portico. 6:30."

THIRTY-SEVEN

Reylin showed up in leggings and a running jacket. "You ready for our run?" she asked, smiling.

Henry looked down at his jeans and loafers. "Uh. I'll go change."

Reylin rolled her eyes and Henry leaned close and muttered, "You forgot that detail."

"Just get your shoes," she whispered back. "We'll walk. Hurry."

Henry did.

They ran off ahead of Henry's security detail. Reylin kept trotting ahead, antsy. She'd turn around and scowl when he didn't keep up. Impending disasters or not, it made him want to walk slower.

"Hurry," she said. "Let's get some distance from your security guy."

Henry was huffing and puffing by the time she slowed

down. "Okay," Henry said, leaning over. "What's your development?"

"Keep walking," Reylin said, her eyes narrowed at the security guard.

Henry did, but he said, "Listen, do you have something to say or are you just trying to make me look like an idiot?"

Reylin seemed to pinch in a sarcastic comment as they walked farther. "I was right about the drug delegation," Reylin said, glancing back at the security agent.

"Okay," Henry said, still breathing hard and trying to hide it. "Good for you."

"But I was wrong about the date." Reylin started to jog again.

Henry's breath caught and he hurried to keep up. "How wrong?"

Reylin pursed her lips. "It's tomorrow."

Henry stopped and she circled back to him. "I'm sorry," she said, gesturing for him to keep walking. "I just found out."

"Are you sure?" he asked.

"Ask your mom if you don't believe me." She looked over her shoulder at the Secret Service agent. "Apparently, she said something to Chet at the tea party. I'm surprised you didn't hear."

"I was a little distracted," Henry said, walking again, though he wasn't sure how his legs were still moving.

Henry started walking again, although he wasn't sure how his legs were still moving.

"Henry?" Reylin said, walking just a bit faster. "It's okay. Don't freak."

"Yeah, why would I do that?" Henry asked. "It's just a little assassination plot with a bomb we can't find. No biggie." He walked ahead of Reylin, who had finally slowed. Then he stopped.

"The reason I vexted you in the middle of the night," he began, "is because I went looking for Burnes." He glanced back at his security guy and started to walk again. "At his grave."

Reylin walked closer to him. "And?"

He opened his mouth to tell her about the fight, the speed and skill, the powers of the thing that had attacked him. None of those words would come out. "I got attacked," he stammered. "By a cloaked figure."

Reylin's eyebrows bent inward. "You're kidding?"

He shook his head, still trying to catch his breath while walking far enough ahead of his security detail. "I think it was The Ethereal. Or someone connected to The Ethereal."

Reylin stopped right on the path.

For the first time, Henry had to backtrack and nod for her to keep following him.

"That *is* a development," Reylin said, picking up her pace again. A line of sweat had broken out above her lip and her cheeks were flushed. "A really bad development."

She looked so worried that Henry felt a small twinge of guilt for all his irritation at her. Maybe they would never be close friends, but it was obvious that she cared about this.

They both began to jog again, each of them lost for a moment in their thoughts as they tried to outpace Henry's security.

When they'd gotten a bit of distance, Henry shook his head and said, "It's not enough time. It's just not. We'll have to report it."

"No," Reylin said, grabbing his arm, pulling him along. She looked sad, almost desperate. "We can do it. I think...I think I've found a map. I can get it tonight and bring it tomorrow. They don't fly until tomorrow evening. We've got time."

"Barely," Henry said.

"Yes," she agreed as they both walked along the path. "But barely is still time. To quit is to take a big risk with your dad's life. Maybe with your whole family. Let's wait until barely is up."

"Okay," Henry agreed, turning back, wiping the sweat off his face. "Okay."

"I'll be here by noon," Reylin said. "Map in hand. Or we call it."

"Deal," Henry said, turning back to the White House. "Twelve o'clock." Somehow the number felt like a gamble when he said it—a couple of dice thrown out as he bet on his father's life. But deep down, he knew that to quit before their time was up was just as big a gamble with an even bigger cost. If they could do this, they could stop a terrible thing, nail the assassins, and protect his family. That was worth a smaller gamble on Reylin. For now.

He stopped at the west entrance, pulled out his phone, and set the alarm for noon the next day.

That was the first important time. The second would be when the helicopter was set to take off. 4:00 pm. They would have just four hours. That fact dug into his gut like a knife. He vexted his mom that he wasn't feeling well enough for dinner and was going to stay in his room. Then he vexted Lucy. "Be here at 12:00 pm tomorrow. Urgent."

Before she could reply, he turned off his phone and walked through the hall, up the stairs to his room, where he pulled out the paper map Lucy had gotten him, memorizing every detail he could.

———

Chet took out Marxma's letter and read it again. She was leaving him. Well, she wasn't exactly leaving *him*, but she was leaving. Heading to some tiny country in some remote place for a shoot. It would only last a few months, but she wouldn't have reliable internet. Or phone service. Or even mail. She would still write, she promised; the letters just might be delayed.

Chet crumpled the letter and stuffed it back in his pocket. Sure, she'd write—until she bumped into this or that cute co-star. Until she got too busy. Until she realized she hadn't cared that much about him. Until a million little things got in the way like they would when you were a million miles apart.

But she needed him. That's how she'd put it; that's how she'd assured him. Needed. He grasped at that word—one of the final ones she'd written—grasped at it as though worried it would drown in the tangle of all the other words she'd written.

———

The curator, Madison Crossley, made her way to the East Room. Its oak floor, artwork, and simple furnishings were some of her favorites in the House. Classic. Almost delicate. She crossed through a hallway with a picture of Lincoln and his son, Willie. She paused to look at the young face, so much more attractive than his father, then shook her head, hurrying on to the East room.

Once there, she stood in front of the Landsdowne painting, then carefully began her inspection.

Taking a small, white handkerchief, she wiped the top of the frame, followed by the bottom and sides, each ridge dusted more thoroughly than any of the maids would ever consider necessary. After that, she began her inspection of the canvas and frame, careful to note whether or not any scratches, fingerprints, or other markings were on it. This simple procedure was what her mother had taught her to do all those years ago. It was a legacy she carried on. For her mother. And others.

And for her troubles, she received an extra five thousand dollars every month. Not a bad deal, but she could have gotten more, much more, from other underground offers if she'd chosen to take them. Still, the risk was low. Or the risk would have been low, had she not been propositioned by another organization. That request had come on a plain, white notecard, beginning with the words, "As a favor to the people of your late father…"

Requests from the friends and family of your late father were always hard to turn down, but they were particularly imperative not to deny when your father's friends and family had the sway they did within certain governments.

The request had been simple. All they wanted to know was if any groups had shown a particular interest in any artifacts at the White House. It was like getting paid a hundred grand to leak to the news what the president's favorite ice cream was. So easy. So harmless.

Except that it wasn't.

A foot in both worlds—the same as her life had always been. If only she could have chosen a side. Instead, she straddled her life. Inspecting the Landsdowne painting for one group, then sending an email to another group, the letter X in the subject line, the body of the text filled with boringly correct facts. "The original Gilbert Stuart painting is on display at the National Portrait Gallery at the Smithsonian, though I would be more than delighted to show you the replica the White House has displayed in the East room, especially as it has received renewed interest as of late, and is in impeccable condition. Each replica was painted with certain barely noticeable idiosyncrasies, and this one is no exception, as you can see in the attached image."

That should be enough.

Except that when they responded, as she was nearly certain they would, she would send a similar email to the other group. At least she would if she ever found the scratch on the frame they were so very concerned with preventing.

Thirty-Eight

Mr. Keikiki had warned them against using the language outside of class. Warned. Lucy paused on the thought. Yes, that's what it was. He wasn't worried that they would practice it wrong. He wasn't worried about their pronunciation or grammar. He was worried about something else, something in the tones that did something.

Something. But what?

Lucy stared at her notebook—the one with the notes from Kiribati. She was trying to keep the rule not to study, really she was. But something was off about that. Off. Not just weird. She glanced through the pages, through the stories about the kings and rulers—Keikiki's people and myths. Or that was what he'd said.

On the last page, she glanced at several of the characters Keikiki had written. So different than any other language she had known. Even Japanese. Like drawings, or maybe more like flat sculptures. More than words. These were words that connected. 3D instead of 2D—isn't that what she'd told Henry?

She moved her mouth along with the words, not making sounds, but trying to form the words. The words her mouth couldn't make, had never been able to make. Even though she knew she wasn't dumb. She was no Henry, but usually she was pretty good at learning things quickly. And with her grandmother, she'd had exposure to different sounds from early in life. It shouldn't be this hard.

Lucy opened her laptop, thinking about the word on the gravestone they had found—the word that somehow *felt* like Henry. Determiner. What did that even mean? She'd spent the whole evening after the charity tea searching for a similar symbol online and had found nothing.

This morning she scrolled through page after page hunting for more information about Kiribati. Maybe she couldn't speak it. Maybe she wasn't supposed to write it. But the chief usher had said nothing about not listening to it, and that was what she was going to do.

Finally, she came across an obscure uView channel. Eleven views, no followers. She clicked PLAY and a dark bronze man who looked much like Mr. Keikiki came onto the screen and began to speak. Beneath him were the English words close-captioned. "Hello. My name is Tiomon. How are you?" *Mauri. Arau Tiomon. Kouara?*

Lucy sucked in her breath. The words were challenging, the tones and pronunciations difficult—rich and deep. But they were neither impossible, nor were they the strange, symphonic language Mr. Keikiki had been using.

Lucy opened her mouth and spoke. "*Mauri. Arau Lucy. Kouara?*" She played the video several more times, repeating along with the man. Looking in the mirror, she said it again. "*Mauri. Arau Lucy. Kouara?*" The air didn't shiver; her mind didn't open. And she knew she had spoken it perfectly.

She clicked through to the end of the video where an alphabet was displayed. It was a little different, but also not the strange symbols they'd been learning. Not the powerful, musical thing that had entered her life just over a month ago, that had changed things.

She snapped her laptop closed and looked at the clock. "You won't believe this," she vexted Henry, including a link to the uView page.

Mr. Keikiki had some questions to answer, but—looking at her phone—Lucy realized they would have to wait.

Henry's vext scrolled across the screen. "Can't look now. Reylin is almost here. We've only got four hours."

Four hours. To find an EMP device and disable it before Marine One left the ground. To find a way to make all the things that didn't make sense click tight.

THIRTY-NINE

Six minutes past four. That was when the EMP device was timed to activate. It would be exactly six minutes after Marine One left the ground. The helicopter would be high enough in the air to crash, but not so high that the pilot could maneuver the blades in any way to stop it from crashing.

Henry looked at his watch. 11:58 AM. He took a deep breath and waited for Reylin and Lucy at the North Portico. He reminded himself that if they couldn't figure it out, they could tell Secret Service. They could stop the flight. This time. But what about the next time, or the next?

Reylin arrived first. "Henry, hurry. We don't have a lot of time. I was finally able to dig into my dad's computer and got this." She held up a picture on her phone. "Now, come on, let's go."

"We have to wait for Lucy," Henry said.

"Are you kidding?" Reylin asked. "She can catch up. Let's go."

Henry let himself be dragged inside. He stopped and spoke quickly with one of the ushers, telling him to bring Lucy when she showed up. Then he took Reylin's phone and stared at the picture as they walked. It showed an image of a book with red binding and the words *Constitution and Laws of the United Sates* on the binding. "What good is a book going to do?" he asked.

"It has a map. Or leads to a map. Or...something," Reylin said. "All I know is that this is the thing they're using to communicate with an informant in the White House."

"They use this book to communicate?" Henry asked.

Reylin bit her lip. "Somehow, yes. I'm not sure how. I'm not sure if there's something in the book. Or if it's just in a room that we need to find. All I know is that it's how they communicate with their informant in the White House."

"And how do you know? Where did you even get this?"

Reylin lowered her voice, even though in the White House, Henry wasn't being trailed by security. "I hacked into a chat thread. People were using bogus names. But I found this image. And they called it the 'key,' as in the key to a map. If I'd had more time, maybe I could have gotten more clues about them and the informant. But I didn't."

"The spy," Henry said, thinking of all the ushers and maids, mechanics and technicians who worked at the House. All at once, he stopped.

The White House contained hundreds of workers. And thousands of books—shelf after shelf, not to mention entire walls of books in the library. Henry looked down at the picture. "Reylin, we'll never find it. It could be anywhere, and we only have a few hours. If this is all you have, let's just tell the Secret Service." He looked up from her phone. "They'll ground Marine One and they'll heighten security and maybe there won't be a next time."

Reylin made a face that Henry thought looked like a silent growl. "There will definitely be a next time. And I've already taken some huge risks just getting this for you." She waved her hand at the image on the phone. "Not to mention the fact that with no evidence at all, Secret Service might —*might*—ground Marine One this time, but they'll most likely not take anything you say seriously enough to heighten any security for next time. Plus, it's easier to stop a *known* threat than to try to predict and stop an *unknown* one in the future. Come on, Henry, it's time to step up and at least try."

She reached out to grab his arm and pull him along to the next room, just as Lucy came up to the two of them, panting.

"Thanks for waiting," she said, glaring.

Henry was sweating. He shoved the picture at Lucy. We have to find this book. It has—" He stopped. "A map, we hope." Then he looked at Reylin. "Seriously, if it doesn't, I'm done. I'm telling someone. This is already just too close."

Reylin shrugged. "It's your family. Do what you want."

Henry gritted his teeth.

Lucy took the phone from him. "The words 'States' is

spelled wrong," she said. "On the binding of the book. It's spelled 'Sates.' What does that mean?"

Henry took the phone from her. "That's strange."

"Curator," Reylin said. "She'll know."

Henry and Lucy both exchanged a look, but they couldn't argue. If anyone knew where to find a book with a misspelled title, it would be Ms. Crossley.

When the three teens arrived at her office, she didn't even look up from her computer. "Can I help you?"

For one brief moment, Henry considered smashing one of the antique wine glasses that lined Crossley's shelf. That would have gotten her attention, but it probably wouldn't have gotten them much help. Instead, he tapped the glass that encased the curio cabinet as if inspecting it.

"Mr. Miller, please," she began, finally looking up from her work. When she saw the three kids, Henry noticed that she stared for just a moment at Reylin before looking back at him. "Those are very valuable. And they are from my personal collection, not the property of the White House."

"Oh, uh, sorry," Henry said. "We were just wondering if you might know where this book is." He held Reylin's phone up to her.

She studied the image for several minutes.

"We noticed that the word 'States' is misspelled," Reylin interjected.

"Of course," the curator said curtly. "I noticed that immediately." Setting the phone down, she began to type into her uVision. "The original portrait is not here, but we do have a copy of the portrait from the 1700s."

"Portrait?" Henry asked. "Isn't this a book?"

Ms. Crossley ignored him. "Gilbert Stuart did not sign or number the copies he made of his own original portraits. Instead, he made the paintings each slightly different, changing tiny details that most people wouldn't notice. Here," she said, projecting the image across her desk so the children could see. "This copy is in the East Room, marked by a spelling change on a book in the painting. Instead of 'States' he wrote 'Sates.'" She paused, glancing at the image on her computer again. "With a few other alterations as well." She looked up at them. "It's from the Lansdowne Portrait, painted in 1796, showing George Washington renouncing his third term as President—a gesture that allowed the American democracy to flourish where European efforts had failed. This particular portrait was the one saved by Dolley Madison when the White House was burned during the War of 1812." She paused, glancing at all three of the teens. "May I ask why you are looking for this particular portrait?"

No, is what Henry wanted to say, but before he could Lucy piped in.

"Thank you so much," she gushed. "We're doing a group report on White House oddities for school, and this is one of the things Reylin found in her research." Lucy gave Ms. Crossley her biggest smile. Reylin did too. Henry wasn't sure he smiled, but he managed to refrain from sneezing on her face, and that would have to do.

———

As soon as the three teens walked from her office, Ms. Crossley picked up the phone, dialing the number that would connect her to the chief usher. "Hello, Taake. I know that we don't always see eye to eye politically, but you might want to know that the president's son has become peculiarly interested in the Lansdowne portrait."

She paused. "Yes, the one in the East Room."

The usher's voice rose just a bit on the other line, but Madison Crossley interrupted. "The portrait is still in pristine condition. I inspected it only hours ago as part of my daily routine. But I might advise you to check after the boy makes his visit. It's no secret that the president's children don't always leave things in perfect condition."

She paused again. "Yes, I did tell him where the painting was. If he should not yet be there, that's your concern."

Again the voice rose. This time she waited for the chief usher to finish. "It's my job to know things about things in the White House, and to protect them. It's your job to know things about people in the White House, and to protect them."

Finally, she added. "Yes, I thought he was too young." She paused, wondering whether she should include the final detail. There was only one thing in life that both her parents had agreed on: It was difficult to serve two masters. She took a deep breath. "You might also want to know that the young Masticor girl is with him."

And with that, the other line went dead.

FORTY

"So it's not a book," Lucy said, examining the portrait carefully. "With a book they could have tucked something between the pages, or even sketched or drawn in it. But this..." She stood as close as possible to the painting. Henry hung back, looking from her to Reylin, who glanced nervously at the doorway where a security guard stood.

"Where's your mother when we need her?" Lucy asked. "I bet she could tell us even more than *Madame* Crossley about this painting."

"Yeah," he said. "She could." He pulled out his phone and vexted, "Hey Mom. Doing some research for school. Tell me about the portrait of Washington in the East Room?"

"It's very famous," his mother vexted back, an emoji that had hearts for eyes scrolling across the screen. "The artist, Gilbert Stuart, painted many replicas to sell so he could support himself. The original is on display at the Smithsonian."

Henry waited impatiently. Even with vexting, his mother was slow. And they'd already lost some time wandering the White House and talking to Crossley. Henry glanced at his watch as his mother's vext came through.

"It's full of symbolism," she said. "A pen and paper draped with red cloth to show the rule of the law. A window in the back with both a storm and a rainbow, representing the storms of war giving way to peace. The sword in Washington's hand symbolizing the victory of democracy over dictatorship."

Henry glanced at the painting. "Know anything about the books in it?"

"Books?" his mother vexted. "I don't think so, but this is the painting Dolley Madison ordered to be removed from its frame in order to save it during the War of 1812."

"Removed?" Henry vexted.

"Yes," his mother replied. "It was bolted to the wall, and they were running out of time. You know, the British invaded D.C, took the White House, fed themselves dinner there, and then burned it to the ground. So the painting is original, but the frame has been changed."

"Really?" Henry vexted back, then said to Lucy, "Check the frame. Maybe there's something there."

His phone dinged again. "That help?" his mother vexted.

"Thanks, Mom." Henry said. "You're the best."

His mother replied with a series of heart emojis, but Reylin was going nuts.

"It's got to be here," she was mumbling. "Put your phone down."

Henry almost vexted his mother back just to spite Reylin, but instead he started looking along the frame with Lucy, taking the bench from the Steinway piano and standing so he could see the top better. The guard's beeper buzzed and he held his hand to a piece in his ear, walking briskly away from the room. Henry was glad.

Reylin was still focused on the books in the painting. "I really don't think it's the frame. Why else would it have been a picture of the book?"

"Maybe just to show us where to go," Lucy replied.

"Maybe," Henry replied, but he wasn't seeing anything. Stepping down, he inspected the book with the misspelled word and then glanced at the book beside it, one that hadn't been in Reylin's picture.

He stopped. "Lucy, these letters…" They were tiny, and almost looked like scribbles to an untrained eye, but to Henry they were unmistakable. "They're Kiribati."

"Henry, I—" Lucy began, but before she could finish, he sounded out the two symbols. The tones hung in the air, and something shifted as a quiet high-pitched sound almost like the buzzing of a bee began to come from the portrait. As they watched, a small slit of wood was cut out of the lower left corner of the frame, a paper drifting to the floor.

All three of them stared.

Henry bent to pick it up and Reylin looked over his

shoulder. On the yellowed back of the paper, they could see a circle drawn in fine black ink. Just like a compass.

"It's a map!" Reylin exclaimed. "Let's go.

Lucy didn't move. "Henry, that language—" she began, but Reylin was pushing him out of the room, staring at the parchment.

———

Lucy glanced back at the empty sliver in the 200-year-old frame. She should have been worried that her parents would kill her. Instead, she was worried about something bigger.

"It's like," she whispered to herself, trailing after the other two. "It's like the material *responded*." To a command, to a voice. As though Henry's words had been read into some invisible supercomputer. And the matter in the world had obeyed.

FORTY-ONE

Mr. Keikiki's black wing-tipped shoes made almost no sound as he walked from his car, past his office and through Cross Hall. He hurried past portrait after portrait of different presidents, across the long, red carpet to the subdued amber oak of the floor in the East Room.

Sound first, then color. That was how his father had taught him to organize the world. In general, it had served him well. Many first ladies had relied on him for those skills, dignitaries appreciated it, government officials needed it. But occasionally, he wished he had learned better from his mother to feel the world. "Sometimes," she used to say, "it trembles. And then you will know things before they happen." Which is what he had needed since the boy had come to the White House.

Mr. Keikiki stopped in front of the East Room. He paused, drawing in a breath before going through the door to meet the painted blue eyes of George Washington. Mr. Keikiki glanced down at the bottom left corner of the frame. Then he pulled out his phone and began to run.

———

Henry looked at the map, the *compass*—north, south, east, and west marked by what appeared to be small openings. "I think it really is Ellipse Park," Henry said.

Lucy peered over his shoulder, muttering, "Circles circles everywhere." She'd been distracted ever since they left the White House.

"But this time it has a line," Henry said. "A needle." A sketch of the shadow of the Washington Monument stretched to the south, as though pointing.

"That only happens a few times a year," Reylin said. "I expect it's giving us a sort of coordinate."

They looked up toward the park, the Monument, the afternoon sun.

"Let's hurry," Henry said, glancing at his watch. They only had two hours left and everything was taking too long. The White House grounds weren't small. He picked up his pace and turned to Reylin. "The name you told us that first night—Burnes. This is taking us to his homestead."

"South of the landing area for Marine One. That makes sense."

"But where?" Henry muttered. "We've already looked there. It's empty."

Reylin shook her head and pointed to the tip of the

Monument's shadow on the map. Henry took a deep breath and glanced at his watch again. They had nothing to go by but this map, and considering it had been hidden in an antique frame, it seemed like a decent bet. Decent or not, it was their only bet.

They tore across the south lawn. Three red discs with white X's had been set up to mark the points on the ground where Marine One would soon land.

For now, the air was still, the late afternoon sun setting away from the long shadows of the trees. Lucy was staring at the sunlight as though thinking. They followed the simple line of the map across E. Street Terrace and to the edge of the Ellipse on the east side. There they stopped near a small stand of trees.

Reylin looked across the park. "If we follow the trajectory of that line, it should be right about there," she said, pointing a quarter mile across the field.

"Nothing's there," Henry said, looking at the spot, then at the map, then at his watch. It'd taken them almost thirty minutes to get here.

"I see that," Reylin said, taking the map.

Henry listened for the chitter of birds he'd noticed when they first came to the park, but around him, the world seemed to have stilled. He thought of what Will had said about animals noticing things that people don't. Something about the memory and the silence made him nervous.

Yet through the silence, he could feel the pulse, the energy he always felt when he came here. "It's underground," he said suddenly. "I can feel it. The pulse from the device."

"I don't think—" Lucy began.

"Perfect," Reylin said. "Now how do we get underground?" She turned the map in different directions.

Henry took the map from her. He walked south, slowly like he was feeling his way in darkness, following the pulse more than the line. He paused at the southeastern edge of the park, pacing back and forth several times, and then stopped. Stomping on the ground, he smiled. "Something's underneath the sod, right here." Bending down, he dug at the grass, then into the dirt until his fingers scraped a large, flat stone. "We need to move it."

"It's huge," Lucy said, kneeling beside him and pushing away dirt. "And I don't think you're feeling any pulse from the EMP device. You can't. It's not activated."

"Well, I'm definitely feeling something," Henry said.

He dug his fingers in around the edge of the stone. Reylin joined him and before Lucy could help, the enormous stone flipped open to the side, revealing a small, dark opening, like the entrance to an underground cave.

"That seemed too easy," Lucy muttered, looking into the darkness.

"We're so close," Henry said, just as the sound of a helicopter in the distance broke the stillness. He glanced up, then plunged into the small cavern, waving for the girls to follow. "Come on. I think we might be able to do it."

Small, rotting steps led down into a damp passage beneath the rock. Above them, the vibrations from the helicopter increased as it neared the ground, shuddering in landing.

Henry ignored it. He felt more excited the closer he got, more alive than he had ever felt. Twenty-five minutes left. They could do this. They walked forward through the darkness, deeper into the heart of the cavern. It took longer than Henry expected—a lot longer, but it felt steady and sure. The pulse thrummed, pushing into his veins, louder and clearer than the far-off whir of the helicopter blades. He would be able to save his family. They were going to do it. The feeling burned like an ember inside his chest.

At the end of the long, narrow cavern, they came into a room—small and square, surrounded by walls of dirt and root. At the center stood a blunt stone table and on that table rested a blue box. It seemed to pulse like a beating heart. "That's it," Henry said. "Now, how do we disable it?"

"*Words revealed at his coming,*" Reylin muttered, glancing at an image on her phone of an old, yellowed page. Her hands were shaking like she was excited.

Henry glanced at his watch. Ten minutes. He caught his breath.

Reylin cleared her throat. "I thought it was supposed to have some words on it or something—words that would tell us how to do it and also prove who is behind this."

She walked toward the box. "Henry," Reylin said, looking down at it, a touch of panic in her voice. "Do you see anything?"

Lucy flicked on her phone light and Henry bent to inspect the box, muttering, "Come on, come on. Words.

Where are they?" He touched the top of the box and when he did, he felt a small pulse.

The box lit up.

"It's activating," Reylin muttered, her teeth clenched.

Several letters on the side of the box illuminated as the box whirred to life.

"That's it," Reylin said. "The code to stop it. But it's in another language." She looked at Henry. "Do you speak it?"

"It's Kiribati," Henry said slowly. He glanced at his watch. Seven minutes.

"No," Lucy said. "That's not Kiribati. It's something else, a different language. Listen, I don't know what we've been learning, but it's not what Mr. Keikiki says we've been learning. Something's not right about it. Something's not right about everything." She stared at the strange letters on the box. "Henry, I know you're gonna think I'm crazy, but I don't think you should say the words."

Henry shook his head. Five minutes. "Then what else should I do?"

"Call your dad," Lucy said. "Tell him not to get on the helicopter, but don't say those words. Something's wrong about them, about everything."

"There's no time," Reylin said. "He needs to stop the device. He needs to read the words. Maybe Keikiki is the guy behind this."

Lucy shrugged, then shook her head. "No. Maybe," she murmured. "But if Keikiki was behind it, why would he teach Henry the language he needed to disable the machine?" Lucy stepped forward and looked at Henry. "Something's not right. Call your dad."

"He won't even be able to hear it ring. If we even have reception down here," Reylin said. "He's getting on a helicopter right now. Henry, please, just say the words. This thing is going to go off."

Henry looked from Reylin to Lucy. He put both hands to his head, trying to think. Everything Reylin was saying made the most sense to him, and he wanted to save his dad, his family. He wanted to stop this device; he wanted to make a difference. But Lucy. Why was she worried?

"Give me your phone," Lucy said, her voice rising. "I'll call."

Reylin was getting angry. "Stop it. You're wasting Henry's time. You're distracting him." Faintly, they heard the whir of the helicopter as it left the south lawn.

Lucy grabbed the phone out of Henry's back pocket and pulled up his dad's number.

"Stop it," Reylin shouted, grabbing at the phone and accidentally knocking it to the ground where it hit with a sickening crack on the rock bottom of the cavern. "Oh no. Henry, I'm so sorry. So so sorry. Just read the code. Stop the device. It'll be okay. Please. They're in the air. You've got to stop it."

Lucy's face had paled, and behind her Henry noticed an even whiter face. Will had come down the stairs. He looked sick, thin. He shook his head, whispered, "Stop."

"Henry," Reylin pleaded. "Just try it. Please."

Lucy shook her head. Henry looked at his watch. One

minute. He felt like he couldn't breathe. His dad was in the air. The helicopter was gaining altitude. Fifty seconds. There was nothing else to do. He could read the words. He could stop this. He looked at Reylin and nodded.

Slowly, so he didn't make any errors, he sounded out the words, perfected the tones.

The air went blank.

Not still, not soft. But dead. Henry staggered back. He looked to Lucy, who had stepped toward him, then to Will who held out a pale, fading hand. In his palm rested a small circular stone, four faint lines inside it. Henry blinked at the symbol that matched Burnes' grave.

And then Will, and the stone, were gone.

———

Taake Keikiki had run north, choosing a direction at random and hoping to find the boy. He'd run past the fine houses and then into the darker back roads and alleys when he felt the air suddenly suck out of his lungs. It felt like dying, this emptiness. Like an end that wouldn't be followed by a beginning. His head throbbed, his joints hurt. He felt his age in every bone and blood vessel. And he knew he had chosen the wrong direction.

"Henry," he whispered in the tongue he'd learned from his own father. "Henreau of Avocatia." He could not feel the boy, his pulse, his presence.

Step by step, he turned and retraced his steps. He didn't want to. He wanted to sit down, to lie in the cold alley and go to sleep. He wanted his mind to go as empty as that feeling, but it couldn't. And so he followed it—the hollow of that feeling. One thing about that emptiness, that void. It, at least, was something he could feel, something that would lead him to the child.

From his pocket, he pulled out his phone, took a deep breath, and pressed a number. "Hello, Mrs. Miller." Years as chief usher helped him to stay calm, even when his body felt like it would crumple. Still, she must have heard something in his tone, as her own voice rose on the other end. "Yes," he replied. "I have to hurry. We don't have much time."

Through his phone, he could hear her beginning to weep, followed by a faint beep like an alarm. He took a deep breath, searching for something to comfort her, but he found nothing. She had known what was at stake when she took Henry in. "I think I know where he is now," Keikiki said into the phone. "But I have to get there quickly."

Forty-Two

Something was wrong with Henry.

Lucy bent over him as he held his head. He kept muttering, "Did it crash?"

"No," Lucy murmured. "There was no crash. It's crazy quiet out there."

Henry nodded, still slumped over. Which was all wrong. He should have been up and jumping around. He should have been whooping and screaming and checking the box for names and calling his security. Lucy stopped on the thought—where was his security—just as Henry muttered, "Will."

"Will what?" Lucy said.

"Will," Henry repeated. "Where did he go?"

Lucy shook her head. She had no idea what he was talking about. "Henry," she said. He looked at her with glassy eyes, like he was having trouble focusing on her face, like he was somewhere far away. He leaned his cheek on the cold floor of the cavern, looking pale, almost gray. Lucy thought he might throw up.

"He must be sick," Reylin said. "I'll go get help."

"No," Lucy said, her voice rising. "Tell me what happened. What's wrong with Henry?"

"How should I know?" Reylin responded. "Maybe it was all the stress, the adrenaline."

"What did the box say?" Lucy asked, standing and staring at Reylin. "It wasn't a name. It wasn't the people who'd plotted this. Where are those names?"

"It was a code," Reylin said. "It stopped the device. And maybe there were names too."

"They weren't names. You said names would be on that thing," Lucy said, her voice rising. "Who were the people who did this? Who is The Ethereal?"

"I have no idea," Reylin replied, the turn of a smirk touching the sides of her mouth. "All I knew was that the box would make things clear, save the president. And it did. I can't read the future. I can't say what all those words mean. Ask Henry what the names are. Tell him to read it. You guys were the ones who were learning that language, not me."

"How would you know about that?" Lucy asked.

Reylin scowled. "It's not like Henry never bragged about himself. I'm going for help." She turned and stomped back through the tunnel.

Lucy bent down to Henry. She helped him to his knees, then his feet. Slowly, like his mind was a million miles from his body, he staggered forward. She draped his arm over her shoulders and helped him through the tunnel, up the steps, across the grass of the dark, empty park.

As they dragged toward the White House grounds, crossing E. Street Terrace onto the southern border of the lawn, Lucy expected to see swarms of Secret Service, lights, police.

She didn't.

In fact, as she helped Henry stumble along, Lucy wondered again what had happened to Henry's security detail. The agents usually blended in so well that she hadn't thought about them, and then they'd been in such a desperate rush...it was easy not to notice. But usually as soon as they left the White House, someone followed. Today, no one had.

Thinking about it now, Lucy realized that she hadn't seen any security since the guard near the Landsdowne painting. She looked behind her to the street. It was empty. So was the dark park beyond it. "Something is *so* wrong," she whispered to herself, reaching into her pocket to get her phone and call her parents. It wasn't there. Lucy paused. She'd had it in the cavern. Had she just left it there?

Around them, the grounds were deserted and perfectly quiet, no birds singing, no flies buzzing. Henry slumped onto the earth and Lucy helped him up again. She'd have to go back for her phone later. "Come on, Henry," she said. "I know you feel sick, but I can't pull you the whole way."

As they got nearer to the south entrance of the White House, a black luxury sedan cruised toward them. "Finally," Lucy muttered, waving it over. In the distance she could see that Reylin sat in the passenger seat next to a driver dressed in black. The car pulled onto the lawn in front of the White House. Lucy saw the driver get out and open the back door.

A woman stepped out, wearing a shimmering red dress, though as far as Lucy knew there were no events at the White House tonight. Quickly, the woman began walking toward them.

Lucy tugged Henry toward the woman. "Can you help me?" she called. It took a minute for Lucy to realize who it was—their principal at Sidwell Friends. "Ms. Smith," Lucy said. "I'm so glad to see you. Can you call Secret Service? Or...anyone? Henry's really sick."

But Ms. Smith ignored her and stepped directly toward Henry. She reached out for him with a long slender arm. Then, with an ease Lucy hadn't expected, she lifted him up. "Determiner," she said. "You've done well. Now come with me and I will show you your destiny." Looking into his eyes, she reached out a delicate hand and touched him on the cheek.

———

Suddenly Henry felt light again. His breathing came easily. He could run a million miles if he wanted. The empty White House faded away and in its place was a vision of a beautiful city where the sun shone, the air hummed, and the ground radiated a warm, red heat. Someone was touching him— long, sleek fingers, soft skin.

He looked around and realized the streets were lined

with people. They wore expensive clothes in fashions he'd never seen before. Around him, a cheer rose up. Shouts and whistles. Applause. For him.

Henry beamed, head held high. He deserved it, he realized—this praise, this rejoicing. He had done something for these people, something no one else could do. He had saved them from the *Ravaging*. The word came to him in the language that he couldn't place. Ravaging. A word he didn't understand.

The woman spoke in a gentle voice. "The Ravaging is the end of many worlds—faraway places. Planets that need Earth."

Henry smiled, glad he could help.

But in the distance, he heard another voice, someone calling his name. Someone he had known for a long time. He shook his head, confused. Who needed Earth? And for what?

The crowds were throwing flowers at his feet. A band of ornate silver instruments began to play.

"We have needed Earth for a long time," the gentle voice said. Henry looked at her hand. Everything else around her was red, shining, but her fingers gleamed white, warm, beautiful.

"Earth is in the perfect location," the woman continued, "with just the right balance of resources."

Henry nodded. Of course Earth was needed. They had no other way to save all these people.

In front of him, the world of his vision seemed to expand as he came to a large terrace on a high porch, overlooking an expanse of people. "Hail, Henreau, son of the High King," they all cheered in unison. Thousands of people stood below the terrace, applauding. White mountains surrounded the lush valley, which was lined with white buildings cast out of stone and filled in at the edges with gems of various sizes and shades.

Henry reached out an arm. He wanted this, this praise, this power. But the other voice kept calling him, saying his name. It was a voice he liked, a voice that had brought him joy for many years. His elation faded slightly and he turned to the woman with her hand on his cheek, one he somehow knew was of the Six, the Setrarch—a word he had not known, but somehow now did. The woman's eyes were lined in black, like a mask.

"What of Earth?" he asked the woman, the cheers dimming below him. "What of its people?"

She did not answer. She did not need to. Henry saw it, as he had seen it before. Great fire covered the earth, her people burned. There was no other way. To save the Thousand, he had to sacrifice the One.

Through the flames, a voice called to him, like she was in pain, like she was crying. The flames became the red dress of the woman, swirling in front of the voice, suffocating it.

"Lucy," Henry said, his throat so dry it felt as though it had been scorched. "Lucy."

He saw her face now, to his left, one side shadowed by the woman. Suddenly, he stood, using the strength of his own legs. The woman struggled to keep her hold on him.

"Let go," he said, tugging away. In the distance, the

White House came into focus again. Through the trees he saw birds and bugs, though nothing moved. All of it paused, waiting for him to speak. "This is my home."

"This is not your home," she said, her fingertips grazing his skin.

Henry felt the hollowness come back into him. He slumped, feeling weak.

Until another hand reached out to hold his, pulling him fully from Ms. Smith's grasp.

Henry looked at Lucy. She had been crying, the wet streaks still dark lines on her cheeks. She squeezed his hand. Her hand was not as soft as the woman's, not as strong, not as beautiful. But Henry squeezed it back and when he did, some of the hollowness went away.

Thinking of the flames, seeing them swirl through the woman's dress, through the gray-black smoke of her eyes, he spoke. "I am the Determiner, and I cannot accept that destiny."

As he said it, she reached for him again. "You will not give a mere Piece to save the Thousand?" A single finger brushed his skin, darkening Henry's vision. He saw the faces of the people again, their cheering dropped into silence, their clothes thin, their faces gaunt with hunger, pocked from malnutrition. Flames burning like rivers behind them.

He paused. "Is there not some other way?"

"If there was, Determiner, we would have used it millennia ago."

Henry leaned toward the warmth of Lucy's hand, the pulse of her wrist. Again, he broke contact with the woman, drawing away from her. "I cannot give what is Good to meet what the Six demand." He was surprised at his own voice, the command in his words.

"Ah, but you think Earth is Good?" Ms. Smith reached out to touch his cheek again, but Lucy pulled him away, dragging him toward the car.

"Stop," Ms. Smith said, stepping toward them with strides that seemed impossibly long. "There are two ways this can happen. The Determiner can freely offer up the planet to the Setrarch. Or the Determiner can die and fail to make a determination."

All at once Lucy's hand jerked out of his. Henry turned to see the driver of the sedan with a gun against Lucy's head. The driver nodded to Ms. Smith who came up in front of Henry, boxing him in.

"You can't hurt me," Henry said, twisting both ways to look at them. "People have tried to before, but when they do, I grow strong, unbeatable."

Ms. Smith's hand snapped out, her fingers tight around his arm. His shirt kept her from touching his skin, which meant he didn't get any more visions. Just the brute force of her incredibly strong hand. Henry pulled back, trying to get away.

From the car, Reylin laughed, slowly opening the door and stepping out.

"You're an idiot, Henry," Reylin said, ignoring Lucy. "Any protection, any *strength*, you ever had wasn't you at all." She snorted. "It was from your father, the High King, who left his power through his Kingsbox to protect you.

When that power triggered, the Six used a new technology to trace you. But now that voice is gone. Just a few minutes ago, you disabled it yourself." She batted her eyes, switching to her southern drawl. "Way to go, sugar. Aren't you glad you had such an *impact*?"

Henry looked at the driver, who still held his gun to Lucy's head. Henry heaved away from Ms. Smith's grip, struggling, waiting for the feeling, for the world to slow down while he sped up. He kicked at her legs, which she moved gracefully away from him as she grabbed his other arm, twisting him so that he tripped, dangling in her grip. She held him with her impossibly strong fingers. Henry found his footing, trying to scratch at her as she held him. Nothing happened. He couldn't so much as budge Ms. Smith's slim hands from his forearms.

"You tricked me," Henry said, looking at Reylin.

"Wasn't hard," Reylin said. "I don't even feel bad about it."

"You're part of The Ethereal."

"Not at all," she said, looking troubled for a moment.

"Then who are The Ethereal?"

She pressed her thin lips together before answering. "Just a scapegoat. Nothing more."

"What about the bomb? Is my dad safe?"

"There was never a bomb—just a ruse to capture *you*. Feel important now?"

Henry scowled, pulling against Ms. Smith's steely hands.

"And your dad?" Henry asked.

"My father, as you could have guessed if your brain

moved any faster than your fat body, is one of the Six. They need the earth."

"How much was he involved?"

"Well," Reylin said, "do you think all of the White House security just decided to take a nap? It takes a pretty good ruse to pull off the kind of code red that will empty the White House for the evening." Reylin smiled. "He figured Mannivera and I could handle this part."

Near her, Ms. Smith smiled, her grip softening on Henry's arms. "Henry, we are not on different sides."

Henry tried to pull away, and her grip tightened. He gritted his teeth, his legs weak, his head still foggy from whatever had happened in the cavern, from trying to figure out the difference between the truth and the visions.

"Right," Reylin said, "because the part that you still don't seem to get is that my dad is one of the *good* guys. The Six need the earth to help a thousand other planets. Help that you won't give unless you are forced. Help that you won't give because you have food to eat and a fancy place to sleep and people around you who take care of your every need."

"Look who's talking," Lucy mumbled.

The driver pushed the gun harder against Lucy's skull, but Reylin ignored her and looked only at Henry. "It's easy not to care about billions of suffering people when you're at the top of the food chain."

Henry shook his head. "There has to be a way to save people without sacrificing others." He looked at Lucy, her head tilted sideways from the pressure of the gun.

Reylin smiled. "Well, I don't know about that. But I know that there is a way to save people simply by sacrificing *you*."

Suddenly the gun flew out of the man's hands and smacked Reylin in the head. Ms. Smith jumped back as Reylin sank to the ground.

A blue-cloaked figure was running toward them.

FORTY-THREE

The cloaked figure held up his palm, muttered a word, and the gun flew through the air into his hand. He raced toward the driver and, with the blunt side of the gun, he struck the driver between the eyes.

The driver fell back against the car and the cloaked man kicked him twice in the gut, then again in his ribs. The driver hunched down, gasping for breath and groping for the door handle of the car. The cloaked figure hummed out a few words Henry couldn't understand and —with no one controlling it—the car roared suddenly to life.

The man cursed, hoisting the unconscious Reylin into the car. The cloaked figure muttered a word and the driver-less car lurched forward, then sped away, dragging the man along the ground as he clung desperately to its side.

Ms. Smith staggered toward them.

"Hello, Mannivera," the cloaked figure said, pulling

down his hood to reveal a dark face with a deep white scar on the left side of his lip.

Henry could hear Lucy suck in a breath.

Ms. Smith ran at Mr. Keikiki, grabbing his hands with her long white fingers and pressing against him.

He dropped the gun he'd used against the driver. His body seemed to bow backwards until he pulled in a deep breath and uttered a word filled with undulating consonants and sighing vowels. The words shifted the air, which threw Ms. Smith back. She landed in a heap several yards away.

Mr. Keikiki stood tall, his cloak blowing in several directions at once. When he breathed, his form blurred and Henry recognized the wispy, undistinguished visage, so similar to what they had encountered in the graveyard.

"Was it you?" Lucy whispered. "You taught Henry the language that destroyed the box. You attacked us at the cemetery."

The man squinted. "I taught Henry the language, not knowing he could destroy the Kingsbox, not even knowing myself where it was. And a cemetery? No."

Lucy opened her mouth to say something, but Henry grabbed her arm and pointed. Ms. Smith had dragged herself up from the ground, her red dress falling like a river around her legs. She looked larger than normal, taller, broader than she had before.

"You know," Henry whispered, "I'm not really sure she's a middle school principal at all."

Lucy snorted. "Like Keikiki here isn't the chief usher."

Beneath the cloak, Mr. Keikiki almost seemed to bristle.

"But of course, I am," he said. "It's just that it's a bit of a side job."

Lucy folded her arms and turned from him.

"Lucy," he said. "Remember. Remember how you first felt when you heard the words I spoke. Remember how you feel when you hear them now. *Remember.*" He repeated the word in the language. The tones rang through the air, and Lucy let her arms fall to her sides.

Mr. Keikiki turned to Henry as Ms. Smith lumbered toward them. "Please pay attention," Mr. Keikiki said. "Some of this will be important."

Henry nodded, looking at Ms. Smith who was now as large as an ape and moving quickly in their direction.

"My job—" Mr. Keikiki held out his arms as she got closer. "—My *real* job is to teach. But also protect." He said that word in the language as well. And when he did, the music of it flowed around him like a shield. The woman in red banged her body against him and fell back again.

Ms. Smith definitely looked different now, her body and muscles bulging out of her dress, her teeth growing long, gnarled, sharp. Her dress tore with a crack almost like lightning. But even in her transformation, she looked beautiful— white hair flowing past her waist, feminine voice in sharp, straight tones, her body strong and sleek. And her hands— so slender and long, nails platinum—glistening and hard.

"Run," Mr. Keikiki said to the children. He did not have to speak in the language for them to obey. They scrambled to the east side of the White House, pushing through a patch of sharp, twiggy bushes before looking back at the chief usher.

Mr. Keikiki's mouth moved, uttering something inaudible. Small objects lifted from the ground and shot at the woman. She batted them away with her hands and feet, slicing stones and branches with her nails, hitting wildly yet precisely at each thing the usher hurled at her.

Keikiki flipped through the air and she moved to the side, striking him in the thigh, so that he crumpled to the ground. He twisted back up, pointed, and uttered a word. A huge rock flew at Ms. Smith. She ducked and rolled, the rock grazing her back.

"Is he using magic?" Lucy whispered, shifting in the bushes, trying to see.

"I don't think so," Henry said, listening as hard as he could, then slumping beside a bush. "But what do I know?"

"It wasn't your fault, Henry," Lucy said, kneeling beside him, still watching Keikiki and Ms. Smith through the bushes.

"It was," he replied.

"No, it wasn't. You got tricked," she said.

"Yup," he replied. "And Reylin was right—it was easy."

"It was only easy because you care about people."

"It was easy because I wanted to be a hero, someone that mattered."

Ahead of them, the woman picked up the gun the driver had been using. She fired several shots at the chief usher. Mr. Keikiki uttered a word that was quiet, but clear. It sent a wave through the air that they could feel. For a moment, the bullets hung, hovering at eye level.

Mr. Keikiki spoke again and the bullets reversed their course, gaining speed. Ms. Smith lunged behind an oak, then threw the gun at Keikiki. It moved so fast that it grazed his cheek, leaving a long line of blood that dripped to his mouth. Through the blood, they could see his lips moving.

Ms. Smith could too. She stood, watching the movements of his mouth. And then she smiled, picking up a small round stone with her slender hand. Mr. Keikiki continued to speak and the Beast came careening around the corner of the White House.

"It's about time," Henry said as it pulled up to the place where they were hidden.

Just as it arrived, Mr. Keikiki widened his mouth to speak. As he did, Ms. Smith flicked her wrist forward, almost casually. The stone flew from her hand, straight into Mr. Keikiki's mouth. His words caught as he raised a thin hand to his throat.

In front of Henry and Lucy, the engine of the Beast stuttered and cut out.

Forty-Four

Ms. Smith walked forward. "There are few ways to kill a god," she said, coming closer to Keikiki. "But you're not a god, are you? You're just a weak, old man, dependent on those even weaker than you for your power." She glanced to the place where Henry and Lucy were hiding. "Since you could speak, I knew he hadn't gone far." She bent down to the silent old man, both of his hands at his throat now, his skin changing from brown to gray.

"He's choking to death," Lucy whispered.

"Yes," Henry whispered, trying to put it all together. "Because he can't talk. The language is what gives him power."

"No," Lucy said, shaking her head. "The language *is* the power." She was staring at Keikiki and Ms. Smith, who now held a small, thin dagger above his throat.

"I'd make it quick," Ms. Smith whispered, "but I have a

feeling that throat of yours will go for a fortune. Not to mention this cloak. There are people who study these things, you know. Hoping to learn how to replicate them."

"Come on," Henry whispered, staring at Mr. Keikiki through the bushes. "Cough it out."

Lucy turned to him, her own face impossibly pale. "He's not going to, Henry. He can't speak." Tears collected at the corners of her eyes. "But you can."

"No, I can't," Henry said. "Not well."

"You found the map and disabled the box just by sounding out those words—words you hadn't seen before."

"Right, Lu. And it ruined everything. Remember?"

In front of them, Mr. Keikiki rolled away from Ms. Smith, but it was obvious that he was weak from the lack of breath. He pushed at his stomach as though trying to dislodge the stone himself. Ms. Smith grabbed him by the shoulder and pinned him to the ground.

"*Attack*," Lucy said. "I know you can say that word. I know you know how it feels."

Henry pinched his lips together. He did know how it felt. A terrible word. And now he felt he knew even more about it, as though the word itself had changed somewhat through his experience. Now he knew the word as not only a physical event, but also as a trick, a plan, a conspiracy against someone. He thought about the word, the layers under it, the different things it could mean, the different ways it could feel. He looked at a small thorn on the bush in front of him, and under his breath, he muttered the word in the language.

"Attack." The air around them shivered, grew hard. The thorn trembled.

"Good," Lucy murmured, her eyes trained on the chief usher. "Now, say it *outward*."

Henry nodded. He knew what she meant. It was like going from a defensive position to an offensive position, from holding your hands in front of your face to punching someone else's face. Henry held the word in his mind. And then he turned it.

"Attack," he murmured in the language he had thought was Kiribati.

The thorn flew from the bush and embedded itself in Ms. Smith's cheek. She reached up as though slapping a bug and turned to stare in their direction.

"Do it again," Lucy whispered. "Do it bigger."

Henry took a deep breath, focusing on more thorns. "Attack," he whispered, his voice rising, repeating. "Attack, attack, attack." The thorns ripped from the bush—dozens of miniature arrows released from a bow.

Ms. Smith let go of Keikiki and held her hands in front of her body, trying to shield it from the thorns, which embedded themselves into dozens of points across her skin.

"Keep going," Lucy hissed. "And bigger." She ran forward, straight toward Keikiki as Henry continued to shout the word, standing up from behind the bushes, sending not only thorns, but sticks and rocks toward the bleeding woman.

She backed away, looking at the ground for something to use as Lucy raced toward Mr. Keikiki. He was still conscious, but gray. "Come on," she whispered, helping him up and standing behind him. She wrapped both of her arms around his waist, made a fist, and squeezed. His body jerked. She did it again, and this time, he leaned forward, coughing out the rock and then vomiting on the ground.

Henry glanced at the vomit and squinted his eyes. "Attack," he shouted and the bile rose from the ground, then splattered across Ms. Smith's face and dress.

She howled, small pinpricks of blood mingling with the mess, just as Henry sent a large holly limb toward her. It struck her leg before she bent over and picked it up.

"Focus on her hands, Henry," Keikiki shouted, his voice gravelly, "not her body." To Lucy, he said, "Into the car." Lucy helped him toward the Beast as Keikiki mumbled another word. The soiled cloak fell from his shoulders, folding itself into a tiny square as the engine of the Beast puttered to life.

Keikiki climbed into the driver's seat, shifting it into gear and muttering more words in the language. Lucy dove in beside him.

The Beast drove toward Henry just as Ms. Smith hefted the large branch over her head and threw it at Henry. Keikiki swung the car in front of him. It fishtailed and the branch crashed against the window.

Henry turned toward them and the back door flew open. "Definitely a Beast," he muttered, jumping in and slamming the door behind him.

With a word, the car lurched forward toward the

woman, then stalled. Mr. Keikiki cursed, his voice still hoarse.

"The car isn't running smoothly because your voice isn't running smoothly." Lucy said, frowning.

Mr. Keikiki nodded, took the wheel, and pressed the gas.

The woman launched into the air, landing on top of the Beast. She began to pound into the roof of the car, her fists hammering like they were neither skin nor bone.

"My voice is weak," Keikiki said. "So we will do this a more traditional way." He drove right, then barreled left, trying to shake Ms. Smith loose.

Above them, Ms. Smith began to peel off the metal roof.

Lucy looked up and murmured, "Impossible."

"Hit the floor!" Keikiki barked as the woman tore open the roof and reached her hand into the open space.

Henry and Lucy crashed to the floor while Keikiki pulled a gun from a compartment in the car and shot. Without the language, his aim was terrible.

Above them, the woman laughed, reaching down and grabbing Keikiki's wrist. The gun clattered to the floor as the car careened to the left.

"Henry," Lucy screamed.

Henry stared at the gun that had fallen to the floor. He focused on the pocked black metal, thought of the sleek shiny bullets within. "Attack," he shouted and a bullet sang from the gun.

Still holding Keikiki's wrist, the woman hovered behind the bent metal of the roof, using it as a shield. The bullet pinged against the thick metal and fell harmless to the floor.

Ms. Smith pulled on Keikiki's wrist, trying to drag him up and out of the car.

Keikiki yanked back, muttering, his foot barely on the accelerator, as the car sped and slowed in spurts.

Henry looked through the mangled roof at the woman's angular face, her muscular chest, her long, Herculean hands.

His mind tore back through the language lessons, the introductions, the alphabet, the stories—searching for something useful, something powerful. He looked at Keikiki, whose lips were almost white, his face scratched and dirty as he continued to mutter and fight. For what? For some kid who hadn't even bothered to smile at him. Or listen or cooperate or try very hard during their lessons. For a kid whose desire to be something had blinded him to the true plot against those he cared about the most.

And then the word came to him—spoken by Keikiki only minutes ago. Henry had never said the word before, but it was one he now understood in layers that dug deep into his gut. "Protect," he whispered, all his energy channeled into the tones, into the push and sway of the word.

From its place on the floor, the gun moved, then fired—straight up, not toward Ms. Smith's face or heart, but toward the hand that held Keikiki's wrist. The bullet struck, precise, cracking the bones of her hand, tearing the flesh apart.

The woman screamed, pulling her arm back and swaying unsteadily from her spot on the roof.

Keikiki thumped into the driver's seat, the car lurching forward as he did. He took the wheel, his hands shaking.

"May the Cerulean bless you, child," he murmured hoarsely, leaning forward and hitting a button. It activated the defense mechanism of the Beast, sending an electric shock to the outside of the vehicle.

The woman screamed again as the voltage struck her skin. She lost her balance, fell from the car, and rolled to the side.

Keikiki drove them over the grass and onto the road as the woman sank into the small, delicate form that had been Henry's middle school principal. Henry stared at her. She hunched forward, an ugly blotch of darkness spreading up her arm from the mutilated flesh and destroyed bone that used to be her hand.

FORTY-FIVE

"You lied to us," Lucy said.

"I did," Mr. Keikiki replied.

It was all the two of them said for many minutes as they drove deeper into the darkness. Henry—exhausted from whatever had happened to him in the cavern and then from fighting off Ms. Smith—had fallen asleep as soon as they'd gotten buckled into the car.

"We almost died." Lucy spoke again as they left the city, the trees growing thicker and taller.

"You did." Mr. Keikiki turned onto a two-lane highway, maneuvering the Beast around shadowy curves as a fog settled over the road.

Behind them, Henry slept deeply.

Lucy spun the ring on her finger, around and around, her thoughts circling with it. "Is Henry alright?" she finally asked.

"Depends on what you mean by alright," Mr. Keikiki said.

"Will he get better?" Lucy asked.

"Yes," Keikiki replied.

"What won't get better?" she said.

The old man sighed. "Oh, many things."

Henry stirred in his sleep, then sat up suddenly, rubbing his head as though he thought he'd had a really bad dream.

"Wasn't a dream," Lucy said before he could even ask. "And we've been kidnapped."

"I prefer the term 'rescued,'" Keikiki said.

Beside him Lucy shrugged. "Is there a difference at this point?"

"No," Mr. Keikiki replied.

"We can't go back?" Henry asked, shaking his head as though trying to get things to fall into place.

"Back to what?" Keikiki asked.

"To my parents, my home." His words came out slowly.

"Henry," Mr. Keikiki began. "I think you better have a soda. I got you one of those Purple Octopus drinks—the ones with extra caffeine."

"Bottoms up," Lucy grumbled. "You're going to need it."

Mr. Keikiki sighed as Henry popped open the can.

"This drink," Henry said. "It's not going to make me like what you have to say."

"Correct," Mr. Keikiki replied. They were driving into the country now, passing fields and hillsides.

Lucy stared into the darkness at the livestock sleeping on the grass. She had stayed awake the whole time, slowly sipping the Purple Octopus, her anger finding the surface as her terror had subsided. And now she was ready for Keikiki to talk.

———

"Where are we going if it's not back home?" Henry asked as soon as he'd polished off his drink.

"We can't go back to the White House," Keikiki replied. "It's too dangerous."

"It's the safest place on Earth," Henry said.

"Not anymore," Keikiki said, then paused. "It's also not your home."

Henry squinted into the darkness, trying to separate what had really happened from some of the things he had seen. "That's what Ms. Smith said. Those same words." He shook his head, trying to remember the pieces, trying to put them together. "I know it's not my real home," Henry said. "But it's where I was living. It's where my parents are. And Chet. My *family*." He stopped on the last word. It felt different now—true still, but with a hole in the center.

"Is it?" Keikiki asked.

"Yes," Henry said, quickly, slamming his empty can into a cup holder. "Of course."

Lucy stared from one of them to the other.

"It is where people live who love you, that much is sure," Keikiki said, turning onto a gravel road that bumped as they spoke. Fields of dry corn stalks stretched out on either side of them.

"Right," Henry said. "*Family.*"

"Henry," Mr. Keikiki said. "Tell me about your father."

"Well," Henry said, his voice rising, sharp like the tip of a pencil pressing too hard. "He's the president of the United States. Maybe you've met him." Henry held the sarcasm up like a shield. "Born and raised in southern Michigan, the youngest of four kids. He worked as a bookkeeper, assistant, then as a lawyer before he became the governor."

"Good," Mr. Keikiki said, switching to the language. "Now, tell me about your father in this language."

Henry opened his mouth to speak, but couldn't. "I...I can't," Henry said, startled. "I've forgotten the words."

"No," Keikiki said. "You haven't. You simply can't say what you're trying to say in a tongue so pure."

Henry sat quiet for several minutes until he finally murmured, "What are you saying?"

"Many people in this world are raised by those who are not their biological parents."

"But this is different," Henry said.

"It is more complicated," Keikiki responded. "Yes."

Henry saw it then, the way his family clicked together without him, the way the pieces that had never seemed to fit didn't. In his mind, he pictured the photographs—the photographs of the dying baby in the hospital. A secret his parents had kept from him, a secret he'd kept from everyone else, even Chet. He had always assumed that baby had been another, an in-between, a memory too painful to share. And maybe that part was true.

But it had been more than that. It had been a hole into which he could slip.

"How?" he asked, barely able to make the word come out of his mouth.

Keikiki pressed his lips into a pale line. "We had only a few days to find a suitable family in which to place you. That is the way with the Determiner. A family with deep intelligence would be ideal, and one in which your physical characteristics would not stand out too much."

Ironic. Henry had always felt like the odd one out in his family. It was strange to think that his family had been chosen because nobody could plunk him down in Taiwan and have it go unnoticed.

"Hundreds of thousands of babies are born every day on Earth," Keikiki continued. "We narrowed it down to a few suitable families. Your Earth mother's pregnancy was at risk. We knew that. And your parents were a very good match for our needs."

"How great for them," Henry said sarcastically.

"Oh my gosh," Lucy said, holding her head with both hands.

"It is not as though we killed the child," Keikiki said solemnly. "But when he died, we were ready. We had already positioned one of our doctors nearby. Your parents went in to the hospital to have a baby. They came out with a baby."

Henry couldn't say anything, couldn't ask the question he needed to. But Keikiki must have sensed it.

"They were not happy to lose a child. But you were a salve, not a dagger, if that's what you're wondering."

Henry supposed that was what he was wondering. Though he still didn't like the answer. A salve is better than a dagger. But a salve is still not the same as having the child you wanted.

Mr. Keikiki continued. "The Millers love you as their son. But they always knew you would leave them in the end."

Had they loved him as a son? How could they when he had just come in to take the place of the one they'd planned on, hoped for? He wished he could see them, ask them, watch their faces when they answered.

He beat away the thoughts. "Why would I..." Henry began. "Why will I leave them?"

For the first time that night, Keikiki seemed unable to form an answer. Finally, he said, "Henry, please tell me about your biological father in the language."

Henry shook his head. "How could I? I don't even know him."

Keikiki waited without answering.

Henry looked down at his legs that had once dented a car, at his fingers that had once knocked a woman unconscious with a tap. He thought about the things he'd seen, Reylin's words, Ms. Smith.

"He protected me. His voice."

Mr. Keikiki nodded. "And..."

"Now he is silent." Henry paused, muttering in English, "I killed him."

For the first time, Mr. Keikiki almost smiled. "No, Henry, you did not kill him. But you did silence his voice in this world, which in your case—in our case—might be just as bad."

"Now tell me about your mother."

Lucy stared at Henry, her eyes so dark in the night they looked black.

"I..." Henry began. "I don't know."

"Correct," Mr. Keikiki said. "Little is known about your mother. She was brilliant and brave and beautiful. But she died giving birth to you. It is a rarity for a Queen of Avocatia to die in childbirth. When it happens, a gate opens up to a host of other worlds. And that is considered a sign that her son will become the next Determiner." Mr. Keikiki continued to switch between English and the language so Lucy could understand.

"That word," Henry said, speaking it in the language. "Determiner. It is my name."

"More of a title," Mr. Keikiki replied. "The name you were given at birth was Henreau."

"Not a name then," Henry said. "But more than a title. It is a piece of me, of who I am."

"Yes," Mr. Keikiki said. "It is your mission. You are *the* Determiner." He quieted, turning into one of the fields with nothing more than a few tractor marks leading the way. "Or you were. The one who was appointed to decide whether Earth would stay alive, or be—" He paused. "—used."

"What do you—" Lucy began, but Henry interrupted.

"Was?" Henry asked.

Mr. Keikiki turned off the headlights, letting the Beast creep along the path with no more than moonlight to show the way. "When a Determiner is appointed and sent to Earth —a very rare occurrence that has only happened a few times in the years since Earth has been inhabited by intelligent human life—he is given the power to decide whether Earth will stay or whether it will be used as a power source for many other planets. One thousand other planets, to be precise."

Henry thought about the crowds of people he'd seen in his mind when Ms. Smith had touched him. They'd been celebrating him, the power of his determination, his ability to give them what they needed. He remembered them, too, as he'd come back to consciousness, to an awareness of Earth—their clothes and faces had become ragged, thin, destitute.

Mr. Keikiki slowed even more as the road got rougher. "Earth's positioning is unique to its sun, as well as other suns —ideal for channeling huge amounts of energy to places that, at present, have very little energy left to them. It is the one place known in the universe that might have enough energy to rescue the Thousand."

"That's..." Henry began, "...not good news."

"It is not," Mr. Keikiki responded. "There is no way to save the Thousand *and* Earth. And that is where you come in. The people of Earth raise the Determiner, showing him much of the world, and then—at a time appointed by the King—he is asked to give his determination. Will Earth continue to live, or will its energy be used? This determination he speaks to the voice of the King in a place he is shown. But if that voice is silenced…"

"No determination can happen," Henry concluded in the language, then switched to English. "Okay, so Earth goes on. That's what I would have determined anyway." Henry looked at Lucy.

"You have silenced the voice," Mr. Keikiki said, "the voice of the King. And you are correct, no determination can happen. But by law there are two ways Earth can be channeled as energy."

"You mean destroyed," Lucy interrupted.

"Yes," Keikiki answered. "I mean destroyed. In the way humans destroy trees to create paper or homes or fuel. It is destroyed, but it is used for something people have deemed necessary. *Channeled*," he repeated again in the language, looking at Lucy before continuing. "First, Earth can be channeled, destroyed, if the Determiner deems it appropriate. Second, Earth can be destroyed if, for any reason, a determination doesn't happen. The Determiner can be killed; or the day of determination can pass without the Determiner speaking to the voice of the King." He paused. "And you have silenced the voice of the King."

"So when this day passes, if Henry can't talk to this voice, then the earth will be destroyed?" Lucy asked.

"Correct," Mr. Keikiki said.

"Then why in the world, or thousand worlds, did no one tell me this?" Henry said, his voice rising. "Why was I left to wander around like some stupid little kid until I accidentally de-voiced the King?"

"It was clearly not an accident," Mr. Keikiki said. "You were led there with intention by those who work for the Six."

"The Six," Henry said. The Setrarch.

"Yes, those who are appointed as diplomats over the Thousand Planets. They very much want you to determine against Earth. Since it seemed increasingly unlikely that you would do that, they decided to do something else—trick you into silencing the King."

Lucy turned around to look at Henry.

"And why," Henry continued, getting angrier, "did the box with the voice come with the equivalent of a self-destruct button?"

Mr. Keikiki shifted into first gear, the engine a soft grumble. "That I do not know. The Kingsbox did not have those words on it originally. To be honest, I'm not sure how they came to be there at all." He turned the Beast, running over a small patch of corn as he left the path. "I'm also not sure how the Six found out where the map for the Kingsbox was located. It is known only to a few loyal and elect. Even I did not know exactly where it was, though I had an idea of where the map would be found."

"So it wasn't a chat room," Henry said, remembering Reylin's explanation.

"Definitely not," Keikiki replied.

"Then how did you find us?" Lucy asked. "Without knowing where the Kingsbox was."

"I could feel the silence," Keikiki replied, glancing at her, "when the voice went dead. And I followed that silence."

Mr. Keikiki pulled into a muddy field. "The truth is that the Six should not have even known you were there, in the White House. They should not have known which, of all the billions of earthlings, the Determiner was. That has always been part of the arrangement. In that way, the Determiner can make his decision without the pressure of the Thousand."

"Then how did they find me?" Henry asked.

"Well, you are prone to be a bit of a show-off," Keikiki said, the corners of his mouth barely turning up. He cut the engine, opened a compartment in the Beast, and pulled out an old map, several canteens, water purification tablets, and a bunch of energy bars. "But I believe that it was a little more complex than that. I believe that they, likely with the help of their undersecretaries, found you when you were attacked— the first time. Before the maid."

"Before the maid?" Lucy asked, turning to stare at Henry.

Henry looked at Mr. Keikiki. He'd never told Keikiki about the first attack. It seemed like ages ago that a man had followed him into the park and tried to drag him into a car. "You think the Six hired those men to attack me, not The Ethereal?" Henry asked.

"I do not think it was the Six," Mr. Keikiki said. "I don't think at that point they knew of your whereabouts. However," he added, "the Kingsbox was created in part to protect you, to keep all your bones in one piece. When you were attacked, likely for political gain—possibly by the actual Ethereal—the Kingsbox activated to protect you. You received added strength and agility. And it seems that the Six and their undersecretaries have developed some technology for tracking that, uh, shift."

"It *was* a shift," Henry murmured, "like the whole world slowed down and I sped up. How did you know about it?"

Mr. Keikiki shrugged, looking through the windshield to some dark mountains ahead of them. "I didn't for sure. As I said, it was a theory. I saw what happened with Ms. Gonzalez. It was rather obvious that she hadn't just tripped and bumped her head. But it was also obvious that she had somehow known who you were. Which meant something had likely tipped someone off before, and she'd found out about it."

"So The Ethereal attacked me, which allowed the Six to find out about me."

"That is my guess," Keikiki said, looking to the dimming stars as the night tipped toward morning.

"Then who is The Ethereal?" Henry asked.

"Another unknown," Keikiki said. "It could be a hostile group from Earth, of course."

"Or...?" Henry said.

"The Six is *not* the only group wishing for energy from Earth. Others might want the Determiner to be destroyed before the day of determination. In fact, the Six might well be the most diplomatic, since they hope to use you and not just kill you. But there are others, others with simpler aims: destroy the Determiner before the day of determination."

"Great," Henry muttered.

"Why didn't you tell me?" Lucy asked, still looking at

Henry. "When you were attacked the first time."

"I couldn't," he said. "The words wouldn't come out. Literally."

Mr. Keikiki nodded as though that made perfect sense. "Without the language, he couldn't have described it. It was a protection of the Kingsbox, meant to keep people from finding out about Henry beforehand. A protection the Six somehow circumvented." He paused. "The good news," Mr. Keikiki continued, quietly opening the door of the car, "is that now that the voice and its protections are silent, the Six will have a harder time tracking you." He got out of the car and motioned for the children to follow. "And we're going to need that."

"So the Six are looking for us. And when the day of determination passes, Earth will be destroyed. And we're... hiding?" Henry asked, getting out of the car and looking over the fields at the empty countryside. "Which won't do much good anyway. Because soon the whole country will be looking for us."

Mr. Keikiki pinched his lips together.

Lucy stepped from the car and stared at him suspiciously.

"No, they will not," Keikiki said.

"Because...?" Lucy asked.

"Because you are dead," Mr. Keikiki said. "All the major news channels should be relaying the information by now. The son of the president and daughter of the secretary of state were caught in a terrorist plot and murdered before they could escape the White House." Mr. Keikiki paused.

"In an ironic twist, the fact that Richard Masticor successfully evacuated the White House last night made the story all the more believable."

"But I don't want to be dead," Lucy whispered. "I want to go back and be with my family. Especially if the earth is doomed to destruction anyway." Her voice was getting louder. "Henry has a role in all this. You do too. But I'm just here by accident. No place, no purpose. Just stuck."

Mr. Keikiki bent down and looked into Lucy's eyes. "My child. Last night much was lost—taken, if I'm going to be honest. By those who have much to gain if the world is destroyed. However, all is not quite lost. There are ways, well, one way, to determine without the Kingsbox."

"But...?" Lucy said, hearing the pause in his voice.

"But if such a thing is possible, it will be difficult—so difficult it is almost a myth." Mr. Keikiki cleared his throat.

"Say that in the language," Lucy said.

"It is a myth," he said.

"I thought so," Lucy replied.

Mr. Keikiki paused. "How much of this language do you understand?"

Lucy shrugged. "I don't understand the words of it at all. I just get the music of it."

"The meaning?" Mr. Keikiki said.

"Yes," Lucy said. "I guess so. I think what I really get is the heart."

"Then," Mr. Keikiki said, "you may have more purpose here than you think."

Lucy pressed her hands against her eyes. "I still don't

want to be dead."

"Don't worry, Lu," Henry said. "We'll fix this and you can go home. And maybe I can too. If I can even figure out where home is." He shot an accusing look at Keikiki.

Keikiki looked up at the stars and Lucy followed his gaze.

"Home," she said, looking to Keikiki. "You have another home, too. On another planet, not another island."

"Yes," he responded. "Though I haven't been there for many years. My mission was, and is, to train Henry. The language of the King can only be spoken by the royal line. And a few choice others who are called Z'astra. That is me—*Z'astra*, a teacher. When in the presence of a king or prince, I can speak."

"And only then?" Lucy asked.

"And only then," he replied.

"Wait," Henry interrupted. "So without me nearby, you can't speak the language? Like, at all?"

"Correct," Mr. Keikiki replied.

"Great," Henry mumbled. "So the bad guys are looking for us. That's awesome. And to save Earth we're looking for a myth. Double awesome. And you and I have to stay together for you to have powers. Triple awesome."

"The good news is that Ms. Smith was willing to kill you," Mr. Keikiki said.

"Wait," Henry said. "That's the good news?"

"Yes," Mr. Keikiki said. "If she didn't believe that one could determine without the Kingsbox, she would have just let the day of determination pass and not worried about you at all. The fact that she got desperate enough to try to kill or kidnap you means that the Six are nervous. It means that they believe it's still possible to determine without the Kingsbox." Mr. Keikiki smiled. "And it means they haven't found a way to do it themselves. They haven't found the piece of the myth we're all looking for."

"Which is?" Henry asked.

"A small stone—plain enough, faintly orange with four white lines within, creating a square."

Lucy looked at him. "Another circle. Like the one on Burnes' grave where Henry got attacked. Like the center of the maid's tattoo."

"*The* circle," Keikiki said. "That all the others are fashioned after."

"Aaannnd..." Henry said, drawing out the word. "Quadruple awesome. We're looking for the same thing as the people who want to kill me."

"Of course," Mr. Keikiki said. "We find it, and the pieces that go with it; we get to Determine. They find it. Well," he said, "then the determination is in their hands. And it probably won't be in Earth's favor. That symbol, that stone. It's our myth. It's our Guide." He fidgeted with his bag, tightening the straps. "Or part of it."

"That's not the only place I've seen that symbol," Henry said, looking at the small footpath that wove through the trees up the mountainside. "It was on a gravestone. But also —" He paused, looking at Lucy. "There was this boy. His name was Will."

Lucy tipped her head forward, listening.

"I think," he said. "I think I was the only one who could

see him. Anyway, he had something kind of like this on his wrist. I didn't really pay attention at first—he was always kind of a weird kid. But right before he, um, went away, I saw it again; and I think it was the same."

Mr. Keikiki nodded, like none of this surprised him.

"The boy called himself a Convincer," Henry added.

"Yes," Keikiki said. "There are some in this world who have come to value it, respect it, love it. Many who are Guides in their own right, leading you to places you should be, helping you see things you should know. Many who have left pieces behind."

"So they're ghosts," Lucy said.

"That is probably the word most people would use," Mr. Keikiki said, hitching the heavy pack over his shoulders. "Although it is a fairly primitive term."

"Souls?" Lucy tried again.

"They are pieces," Mr. Keikiki said. "Tied together through ancient fragments of Earth. An Earth that wants to live. And so, when it senses the Determiner, it sends portions of itself forward.

"That doesn't make any sense," Henry said. "It's not like the earth is sentient."

Mr. Keikiki pinched his lips together. "All things are sentient on some level, Henry. That is why they respond."

"Respond?" Henry asked.

"To the language," he said, "when it commands."

Lucy turned. "You give commands, and matter responds. The Beast, the trees, the stones—you told them what to do."

"The air, the elements, the everything," Mr. Keikiki continued. "That is what the language does. It speaks. On a level most objects are unaccustomed to. And they obey."

"All things?" Henry asked.

"No," Mr. Keikiki replied. "Only those things that do not possess will. I could not command a human being to do what I wanted. Or a squirrel, for that matter."

"And Earth?" Lucy asked.

"Is a complicated system of organisms at a variety of levels. I could never control it as a whole through the language. But when it senses a danger to itself, it responds. And at certain times a Convincer comes forth."

"So you're saying Earth sent a ghost to talk me into determining in its favor."

"I'm saying Earth is a complex system of organisms, both living and dead, both ancient and new, both viable and not. And that it has an interest in preserving itself." Mr. Keikiki paused. "So, yes."

The sun was a thin line, broken by the trees that crested the mountains. Keikiki began to walk toward it.

Henry shook his head. "Quintuple awesome."

"Oh, come on, Henry," Lucy said, almost smiling and following Keikiki. "It makes as much sense as everything else."

Henry nodded. "Can't argue with that. So where are we going?" he asked.

"First," Mr. Keikiki said, "we'll be staying in places where you can practice your gift. After that, we'll begin looking for the Guide."

"One small stone somewhere on Earth," Henry said, trudging along the barely visible path. "Sure. Sounds easy."

"Guide to where?" Lucy asked.

"To the Four Corners of the Earth," Mr. Keikiki responded.

"Which is?"

Mr. Keikiki raised an eyebrow and smiled, his scar a dagger as always. "You know, I always thought the name would make it obvious. Interestingly, that's never actually been true."

Lucy stopped at a sign on their path. Cole Mountain Trail. "You're taking us on the Appalachian Trail. Won't people find us here?"

Mr. Keikiki looked to the trail that wound in switchbacks up the mountain. "No. And I don't think it's people you need to be worried about on a mountain as ancient as this one."

Around them the birds began to sing their morning songs. Butter yellow sunlight dappled through the leaves, crisscrossing at their feet in exchange with the shadows.

"The Patawani call this *Wapun*," Lucy said. "A time of awakening."

Mr. Keikiki nodded. "As indeed it will be."

"I call it the time every day when I have to pee," Henry mumbled.

Lucy smiled. "That's the thing about *wapun*. You don't always get to choose what awakens."

In front of them, the trees bent low and thick, pressing the sun against the sky, hoisting it into day.

Epilogue

Marxma got the news while on the plane. Henry was dead—killed in a terrorist attack.

She held her phone, staring at the article. It wasn't true. It couldn't be true. But if it was...

Chet's phone rang through. She stopped calling after the third try. He would return her call when he felt ready. The question was, would she be ready to take his call? The country where she was heading barely had a postal service with spotty internet and phone connection.

High above the Atlantic, she clicked over to images on her phone.

A statement from the president, red-faced and ruffled even in the black suit. Mrs. Miller to the side, her own face in shadow.

Marxma swiped, looking for more. Still only the parents. And then, there. A grainy, haphazard shot of the remaining members of the first family being led through a crowd of flashing cameras, microphones pointed in their direction.

Chet's back was bowed, nearly in half, the black-clad Secret Service covering most of his body, a hand on him as though to guide him. His head was tilted just slightly, so that she could see the sharp profile of a face she'd almost always known as laughing, joking, bright. It wasn't now.

"Oh, Chet," she said, placing the phone, face down, on her lap. "I'm so so sorry."

She leaned her head against the seat back, closed her eyes, tried to feel the universe without that vital piece that was Henry.

Somehow, it just didn't feel like he could be gone.

Author's Note: I know we kind of left you on a bit of a cliff hanger. If you want to keep reading, without waiting until the next book comes out, click on THIS LINK to Kindle Vella where you'll find the second book, *Z'astra*, being told episode by episode! The episodes do cost money, but if you're new to Kindle Vella, you'll get the first 200-500 tokens for FREE!

And if you're reading the paperback and can't click anywhere, just go to Kindle, look up The Determiner, find the Kindle Vella version (circular cover instead of square cover) and begin reading on episode 73 (Season 2: Z'astra).

A Guide To Fact And Fiction

In this book, Jean and Jacob had a lot of fun blending facts with fiction. Below is the tell-all guide about what's true and what's not.

David Burnes. Burnes was one of the first historical figures to take shape in *The Determiner*. Yes, he did exist. He owned 650 acres of land in what would become part of Washington D.C.

George Washington really wanted this land to build up the city, and at first Burnes would not sell it. The two gentlemen even had a falling out over it with the usually calm Washington storming out, referring to him as 'obstinate Mr. Burnes.' Later, however, Washington offered Burnes a much more generous amount of money and Burnes sold his property—the area that would house the "President's Mansion" or White House.

Burnes' wife and son did die of waterborne diseases.

And his daughter, Marcia or Marcy (depending on the account), lived as one of the wealthiest women in Washington, later marrying John Peter Van Ness, who served as mayor of Washington D.C. and a U.S. Representative from New York.

And, yes, Burnes' voice has been heard in the White House several times—by FDR's valet, a White House guard, and a reporter during the Truman administration. Each time, his voice was heard near the Oval Office, and each time all the voice said was, "I'm Mr. Burnes."

However, as far as we know, Burnes was never in possession of a magical stone that brought him luck and prosperity in exchange for a portion of suffering and loss. He never talked to an old palm reader or had a strange symbol burned into the floor of his house. Bummer.

The Beast. This is a real nickname for one of the presidential cars. The name was bestowed on the car during the Bush administration and continued through the Obama administration. The cars were created by Cadillac and have been for nine other presidents. And, yes, the car really is as butt-kicking as it is described. Six-inch thick windows. Bomb and bullet proof, doors that can absorb projectile assault. The interior seals off in the event of a chemical attack and it's equipped with oxygen tanks to provide breathable air for two days. It contains weapons in and around the vehicle, including rocket launchers. It can produce a thick cloud of smoke to obscure it for five city blocks. The tires are bulletproof and can travel at high speeds even when deflated. And it can produce an electric current on the outside of the vehicle. It travels with several other cars that look just like it, acting as decoys so no one knows where the president is riding. And there are emergency vehicles in the entourage as well, carrying blood of the president's type in case he should need an emergency transfusion.

The White House. All of the information about the White House and its grounds is as accurate as we could get it without actually living there. Well, except the secret passage in the Queen's bedroom. As far as we know, that doesn't exist (though rumors of tunnels under the White House abound). The White House was originally called the President's Mansion, the President's House, the President's Palace, the Executive Mansion, the People's House. It was officially named the White House by Teddy Roosevelt in 1901.

The White House Staff. The positions of chief usher and curator are real positions in the White House, which are very important. In addition to these positions, there are over one hundred full-time members of the White House staff. The staff care for six stories, 132 rooms, thirty-five bathrooms, three elevators, and eight staircases, a pool, bowling alley, basketball court, game rooms, a movie theater. All of that on the eighteen-acre plot of land. Often they serve at the White House for their entire lives, and in many instances their families have been serving in the White House for generations.

Marine One. Marine One refers to the helicopters used to transport the president. The fleet has been in use since the 1970s. It's been continuously updated with new technologies and well maintained. Efforts to replace the fleet of helicopters, however, have always been stalled due to the extremely high cost of replacement. In our story, replacement was imminent. In real life, 2020 was the next projected date for replacing the aircraft (and we all know how 2020 went). Marine One is still not updated.

The Lincoln Bedroom. Generally this room is used for dignitaries and special guests. People such as Winston Churchill and Princess Wilhemina of the Netherlands have stayed in it while visiting the White House. It is also a common place to see ghosts—Lincoln of course, as well as others. The items in the Lincoln Bedroom are described accurately (and it does contain a signed copy of the Gettysburg Address), although the first family can always change the décor of any room they wish to. It was never actually Lincoln's bedroom. Lincoln used it as an office.

Sidwell Friends School. This is a Quaker school in Washington, D.C. that accepts only seven percent of its applicants. Sidwell Friends has educated the children of many politicians and presidents over the years. Some of its notable presidential students have been Sasha and Malia Obama, Chelsea Clinton, Albert Gore III, Tricia Nixon, and Archibald Roosevelt. At this time, however, the principal is *not* a psychotic alien who wants to use Earth as an energy source for other planets.

Demon Cat. This apparition is most often seen at the Capitol Building, generally in the basement, late at night. It has, however, been seen at the White House before. This ghost behaves just like it does in this book. It grows bigger and bigger, and is often seen with glowing red eyes. When someone tries to attack or swing at it, it vanishes. Several times, it has been seen before disasters, such as the stock market crash of 1929 and the assassinations of Abraham Lincoln and John F. Kennedy.

Willie Lincoln (Will). Did you figure out his true identity? William Wallace Lincoln was born on December 21, 1850 and died on February 20, 1862 at 5:00 pm. He was eleven years old and likely died of typhoid fever from contaminated water (not unusual for the White House at that time). He is a frequent ghost seen at the White House and has been seen by both Abraham and Mary Todd Lincoln, as well as staff of the Grant administration and Lynda Bird Johnson Robb (Lyndon B. Johnson's daughter).

You'll notice that in our story, Henry met Will on February 20th (Willie's death date) as the clock unexpectedly turns to 5:00 (time of death). We did that on purpose and it took some care, so thanks for appreciating that detail. In the first scene with Will, you'll also notice some mignonette flowers. These were often used for burials at that time in history. We don't know if they were the type used for Will or not, BUT he was laid to rest holding a small bouquet, which was later given to his mother as a keepsake.

Alien Sightings. Washington, D.C. (especially in the summer) is indeed a hotspot for alien sightings, a fact that Hollywood has often used to its advantage. It's a fact that during the '50s, these sightings happened frequently and were taken much more seriously. After the '70s, as technology improved and digital filters were used, UFO sightings on radar dropped off significantly. Most could be explained as bends or catches of light, or warps in the atmosphere. For example, under the right atmospheric conditions, a bird flying high could reflect light in a certain way and look like an orb of light in the night sky. However, sightings in D.C. have never died away completely and people continue to speculate on alien activities in the U.S. capital.

Also by Jean Knight Pace and Jacob Kennedy

Grey Stone

Grey Lore

Grey Stories

Get the novella *Grey Fall* FREE by signing up for my newsletter!

jeanknightpace.com

Acknowledgments

We always appreciate this little page where we get to thank those who made this huge undertaking possible.

Thanks to our editor, Carrie, as well as our cover artist, 100 Covers.

A HUGE thank you to our younger beta readers: Brooklyn, Lily, Lucy, Lily, Audrey, Sabrina, Elizabeth, and Savannah. And to those tweens/teens who gave input on the cover. Thank you for your opinions and for keeping us old folks from being too out of touch.

Last and never least, we would like to thank our spouses and children, as well as countless beta readers and friends who helped form this manuscript into a story where the turns and twists twisted and turned instead of belly flopping or breaking their necks.

And to all of you who will buy and recommend this book. Your support, love, and appreciation mean the world to us. Thank you for helping to breathe Henry and Lucy into life in this world. And perhaps a thousand other worlds as well.

About the Author

Jean Knight Pace is the co-author of *Grey Stone*, *Grey Lore,* and *Grey Stories*. She lives in Indiana with her husband, four children, eight ducks, four chickens, and a cat. In addition to fantasy, she writes non-fiction and sweet women's fiction. You can find more about her at jeanknightpace.com.

Jacob Kennedy is an ER doctor who dreams aliens and plot twists in his free time. He is also the co-author of *Grey Stone* and *Grey Lore*. Find him on Facebook @jacobkennedybooks.

www.ingramcontent.com/pod-product-compliance
Lightning Source LLC
Chambersburg PA
CBHW061617210726

48287CB00001B/173